LOVE AND DEATH IN
SAVING EUROPE

LOVE AND DEATH IN SAVING EUROPE

A novel

Rita Dulci Rahman & Jose Miguel Andreu

LM Essential Publishers

To our grandchildren: Kaj, Leonardo, Fae, and Federico.

With all our love and hope for their good future.

Colophon
2012©   Rita Dulci Rahman & Jose Miguel Andreu
Publisher   LM Essential Publishers
Cover Design Raul Behr, Professional IT Services, Paramaribo
ISBN   978-94-91480-01-0

Contact: info@leonon.nl

Book can be purchased as a printed book, eBook and streaming book in all (Web)Bookshops, Amazon.com, Bol.com, Yindo and KOBO

Authors Note

This novel was born out of our concern over the future of Europe. It is a fictitious and humorous love-and-life story with a perspective of solving the current European crisis.

Needless to say that none of the characters, or the circumstances or events in the book have anything to do with reality or with current politicians and governing functionaries in Europe.

Any conceived resemblance by readers is based on coincidence. The book is meant to entertain while it may contribute to fresh thinking on long-term success for the European project, creating a better future for current youngsters and generations to come.

Contents

One

The call that changed the life of the president

"I have told you a thousand times that when someone calls and I'm in the bathroom, you have to say that I'm in a top meeting and cannot be disturbed."
Jacques Perrier, President of France, upset for the disturbance and nervous from having to rush out of the bathroom, was hardly in control of the telephone through which he screamed at his middle-aged secretary on the other end of the line. Meanwhile his eyes caught the digital clock at his desk showing 11.06 hours.
It happened on a chilly morning in October, and none of the involved could have then imagined that this telephone call would be the beginning of the end of the career of the President, and of his, in those days, rather frequent happiness.
"But sir, the Chancellor of Germany is on the line and it is very urgent. She needs to speak to you now. Please, may I put you through?"
"Ok, go ahead, but from now on, be attentive."

So, to put things in the right order, before the call from Berlin came in turning Jacques Perrier's life upside down, the man had first been observing from the windows of his office, that in only minutes, everything around the Palace L'Elysee was disappearing under a white blanket while he could hear frosty drops falling softly from the roofs. What struck him most about the scenery was the deep silence of the normally bustling streets, as if Paris itself had stopped breathing. With the image of his city wrapped in silence, he had gone to the bathroom for even more mindful reflections, when suddenly the phone rang.

He sharply remembered his first encounter with Marlein Ditch, the German Chancellor. Although the persistent rumours about her moodiness and sudden, angry outbursts facing aides and colleagues alike, had reached him long before his election as President de la Republique, at their first meeting her look-lips pressed together, no lipstick, grey suit, no jewellery other than a tiny golden cross on a fine chain, and a somewhat manly handshake-had confirmed his provisional reference to her: a German spinster coming in from the cold.

"Dear friend, my dearest Jacques, sorry for disturbing you, but I had to, it is urgent. Things are really running out of control. You will not believe what I am going to tell you now. I have just been informed by my Ambassador in Rome that the PIGS[1] have initiated a move to create a political federation of four countries inside the Euro zone. It is our friend from Spain, who, unable to run his own ransacked federated country, has convinced our Italian colleague, another dud, to jointly create a new state of 120-million people, just transforming themselves and the other two neighbouring losers into the biggest country of the EU. Unbelievable! I am furious with this Mafiosi way to put pressure on us. We need to stop this immediately."

"Holy Christ, Marlein, first the EU generously helped the Spaniards to develop their country over the past twenty years, and now, out of thanks, our foolish colleague is taking advantage by pulling failing powers to his side. It is a bitter joke that those with today's weakest economies, those who perhaps should not have been admitted to enter in the Euro zone, want to steal us the show and put us in minority. Frankly speaking, I am fed up with this Machiavelli believing he could force us to either abandon the Euro or to fall in his presumed

---

[1] PIGS here stand for Portugal, Italy, Greece and Spain. Note that Ireland has been left out.

leading strings. What a group of crippled countries! We should have ignored them from the very beginning. You can never trust beggars."

By now also Jacques Perrier was furious and, without in any way wishing to be diplomatic, both leaders used strong language to clear their minds bogs, but to be fair to the reader one has to know that the thinking of Perrier in the bathroom, just before the phone rang, although similarly upsetting, had little to do with the Euro crisis and attempted economic shortcuts.

No, until the call from Berlin came in, the thoughts of Perrier in the intimacy of the small room with its colourful tiles and the unmistaken scent of bitter almonds had been of a totally different nature. Lingering on a breathless, quiet Paris, Perrier moved his reflections to the death of his father four months ago and the deep sorrow and emptiness it had left inside him.

As Jacques Perrier had always been a very nervous man, these were feelings he was unable to cope with, but slowly he was learning to control them during the day, sometimes even in the bathroom.

Gone was the man whom he had been meeting so discreetly when both knew that the end was near. In those days, the palliative treatment for lung cancer had made his father serene in facing his last curtain. It was of no use to challenge old Perrier with anything other than fate since he used to refer to almost all subjects as "for God to decide". This caused Jacques to become overwhelmed by the burden of disillusion, as he could no longer demonstrate his extended knowledge of modern political life or on the economic future of Europe in the wake of emerging Asia, issues that for years had been the flavour in routine, catch-up meetings between Jacques Perrier and his father, the late Perrier Sr. from Bayonne.

After the funeral Jacques deeply suffered from sombre moods and many nights he left his tears run freely in his pillow while feeling regretful, also for the fact that not even his extraordinary electoral

9

victory for the presidency of France made it possible to prolong the passing away of his father.

Jacques Perrier Jr. admired his father most for having worked his entire life to maintain and upgrade his family despite his little education. So much so, that by the time Jacques Jr. was a teenager, the family no longer suffered from the stigma of refugee carried by Perrier Sr. from the moment he had fled the Franco regime in Spain at the age of twenty. Thereafter, Perrier Sr. had managed, with little more than the clothes he was wearing, to illegally cross the border and in few weeks to start a Brazilian coffee grinding and retail company in Bayonne.

No wonder, that Jacques Perrier Jr. expected far more compassion from above the skies for his simple-minded but more spiritual father instead of him ending with an incurable disease.

Even more annoying were the persistent telephone calls the President had been receiving in the past weeks, including this morning at 10:00 hours from a mysterious Martha. The woman presented herself as originating from Cahors, but for the last twelve years living in La Defence, and when speaking about her parents, both alive and well, her voice would become remarkably affectionate and clearly driven by love. When this Martha for the first time managed to get hold of the French President directly on the phone (she presented herself as his sister living in Lyon to get through) Jacques Perrier was hard hit by the intimacy of her information over the behaviour of his mother.

Mysterious Martha requested the president to keep his mother away from dating her old father, since this was hurting Martha's mother.

Picture it: his seventy-nine-year-old mother in her full, black, traditional widow's dress, travelling six or more hours from Bayonne down to Paris to meet a eighty-two-year-old married man in a luxury hotel room in the heart of the capital, simply to have a passionate night before travelling back all alone to Bayonne and probably at peace that no Sunday paper journalist had been alerted by a gossiping bellman over the hosting of the President's mother, dressed in full mourning, for a love night with an unknown, old guy.

The image of his wrinkled and slightly overweight mother passionately making love in a hotel bed near L'Elysee with an old, rickety man-whose growling, wasted wife was crying herself to sleep that night-was outrageous. The image had blown his mind as misfortune piled on misfortune, and the echo of Martha's explanations repeated in his ears.

According to Martha, the two paramours had officially been engaged in 1951, just before Martha's father left for Algiers to re-embody the French Legionary army. But when her fiancée returned six years later, Jacques" mother was already married for three years with coffee broker Perrier from Bayonne and had to present herself as the proud mother of two, half-Catalan, half-French children, a boy of two and a girl of ten months. In those days of course she could not dream of the possibility that her little son would once become the first half-immigrant President of the Republic.

Perhaps because of not being able to dream this unthinkable dream, his then twenty-seven-year-old mother had soon after, stubbornly left father Perrier and his two, small children in their factory cum house in Bayonne, and started a new life in Cahors with her uniformed hero. Certainly, it must have broken her poor little heart when few months later-based on a seldom-used article in the Civil Code-the Gendarmerie took her out of the house in Cahors, and straight back to the factory of her immigrant husband in Bayonne.

In all the following decades, Jacques Perrier Jr. never got any information, if true, about this part of the personal life history of his parents, neither from them nor from his Spanish grandmother who had always been living in the room next to his father's office in the constantly-expanding factory cum house in Bayonne.

Only when the mysterious Martha got hold of him three months after the dead of his father, Jacques was forced to wonder if he had ever observed any warm romance between his parents, or better, if he had ever caught them in any intimacy in the twenty-two years that he passed in the house in Bayonne.

However, knowing his mother, Perrier Jr. was almost sure that if it had not been for the bills, neither Martha, nor her mother would have found out that the two old-aged paramours were dating in Paris. In fact, according to Martha, the old man, suffering acute disorientation, once got lost on his way home from the hotel near Place Clichy. When questioned at the police station in the early hours of a rainy Sunday morning, he took a hotel bill from his pocket and explained that his fiancé was waiting there for him.

The detailed and frank communications of mysterious Martha hit Jacques like a bullet straight through his stomach. How long had this love affair gone on? Had his father been blind all these years? Or did his father just hide his heart-breaking secret in the man-to-man conversations the two had over the past thirty-three years? Was he really to speak now to his mother on her detached marriage, dreaming and longing for decades for her Romeo from Cahors, or should he simply decide to send her a spy to catch her in the act and thereafter confront her?

* * *

The alarming telephone call from the German Chancellor, within an hour from the last call of mysterious Martha, plus the communications on the move of the Machiavelli were the last things Jacques wanted on this chilly morning. Consequently, his anger was out of control and his answers were firm, but Chancellor Ditch was also in full power in her reaction.

12

"Mais mon ami, Jacques, keep calm! Do you really believe that these two Latin conspirators-forgive me to say, but I do not consider you Latino-can do more than spend the money of the others, I mean of ours? I suggest us to have an urgent meeting with the president of the European Commission to shorten the legs of these Latino PIGS-mies. Far from things being lost, I actually see great opportunities for Germany and France. This is the right moment to once and for all reintroduce rationality in the political structure of the Union. I am sure that if we play well, we may have a fluke and get rid of the deadwood of the European Union, including the mistake of the acceptance of most of the twelve new comers. I still cannot digest that we have swallowed the monstrous enlargement sold to us by the Brits and their transatlantic nephew. Let's meet in Brussels tomorrow. I am calling the PresCom[2] now."

"Marlein, I see your point. I fully agree to seek the opportunity. Let us meet tomorrow at ten."

After hanging the phone, a now bewildered *President de la France* continued staring at the white, softened Paris landscape. He had a good face, handsome in a bony sort of way, and eyes wide and bright, often with little sparks of excitement dancing in the centers of them. But he had condemned himself to maniacal pursuits, running from one event to another from the first day of his inauguration. However, today"s phone calls certainly had put his eyes in lower spirits. With his nose almost touching the glass of the window, he had to confess to himself that first his mother had gone out of her mind and now the Spanish Machiavelli. Frankly, no one seemed to care about the fact that he had far more important things to worry about!

He remembered his early days after being elected President of the Republic. With what foresight he went to work those days. What great

---

[2] The President of the European Commission is often referred to as PresCom.

expectations-expressed by so many Frenchmen-faced him. But then, his first exchanges with populist press, who in the name of the man in the street had even dared to address him as The Great Conqueror of Europe, were all courtesy and humility. He was aware of the risks and actually considered himself like an amateurish marathon runner, all knees and elbows prepared to sooner or later hit the grit, but still keeping the iodine and plasters as much as possible out of sight for a public with great prospects.

Perrier Jr., still over thinking the uncongenial communications of the past hours, left the window and moved to his gigantic, mahogany desk, flopped into his oversized chair and started reshuffling some papers piled in the left corner. He was an easily overwhelmed person and while his memory was ordering the events of the morning, before and after the call from Berlin, things became rather clear to him.
How often had he repeated to himself in the early days of his presidency: *Man, oh, man, I do not, with any army, need to conquer and sophisticate the separate countries of Europe; they have already started their own unification process! This is a circumstance, which should have made Bonaparte envy me.*
At the beginning, it seemed to him that he could easily push forward in the European Union with merely smart diplomacy and some logrolling. In his understanding in those days, his only and real challenge was to control his impatience and strategically maneuver to reach the Olympus. The more annoying was the content of the Berlin call just now. So much so, that Perrier Jr. started swinging in his oversized chair and fledging his hands while admitting to himself that within a year of his presidency, things had become far more difficult. To start with, the Euro system with its ill architecture and currency fluctuations proved less solid than proclaimed by his predecessors. Secondly, his projected strong French leadership of a Union of twenty-seven, veto-owning countries soon became a nightmare. Recently more experienced, the image playing

14

in his mind whenever thinking of the European Union, or of what had come out of Delors' project, was one of a slow march of a crippled, blind elephant.

At several moments he had almost bemused observed the majority of middle-ranged intelligent member-state leaders who behaved as self-appointed captains on the EU boat. Remarkable, since none of these pretended captains had either navigation maps or skills, while they all seemed to have different, final harbors in mind. Even more, no one wanted to pay for the trip although pretending to do so, thus preferring free riding over allegedly being misused by the others, as they systematically complained.

What caca! These were the things that irritated him most in his European Union affair. In particular, the British position of not wanting to pay; not entering in the Euro but continuing to influence the system; and finally pushing for a mega-enlargement with mainly poor, less-developed nations, promising them full financial support, once again to be paid by others and not by London.

Moving his fingers through his voluminous and still rather dark hair, Perrier tried once more to put his thoughts straight. Come to think of it, in this context of headwinds, even Bonaparte would not have made much progress. Personally disappointing was the fact that no French-German initiative suggested by France in the past years for deepening the Union had progressed. Nothing was possible with the current Chancellor of Germany. Although perhaps the absurd move of the Spanish Machiavelli could create a new opportunity to seduce the spinster to establish a selective European Federation constructed by him, Jacques Perrier.

Put at ease by the new perspective, Perrier finally could relax so he glided out of his chair and walked over to the bookshelves next to the window. Yes, there it was, the little, blue book left behind by his predecessor. While walking closer to the bookshelves and pulling out *Overcoming the EU Crisis*, he remembered the repeated conversations he had with his minister of European Affairs, a leftist intellectual he included in his government just to marginalize the socialist opposition. In those days, both men, although coming from different political backgrounds, considered the proposal of the blue book to establish a voluntary federation of main Euro zone countries on a French-German initiative as something worthwhile, but any attempt to speak on the matter with the German counterpart was set aside by her with the explanation that she was not ready to exorcise federation ghosts in Germany.

* * *

Minutes later, with a cold wind snapping at the old windows of L'Elysee, Jacques Perrier, returned to his desk. Decisively placing the blue book on his desk and passing his eyes over the things he liked most- his photo in silver frame with the American President together inspecting troops in Afghanistan; framed in wood, him in New Delhi at the Presidential Palace with the dark skin, Indian President discussing the nuclear arms race while offering him French mirages; and finally on the ground in front of his desk, the Persian carpet his wife Alexandra recently bought him in Istanbul. He concluded that the Spanish-Italian maneuver gave him the best pretext to demolish the current political architecture of the Union and once and for all to get rid of the abundance of traitors, free-riders, and beggar states accumulated over the last four decades in the hulk of the EU vessel.

Two

Lost love illusions but moving forward in Berlin

One day later, with some delay due to heavy rains in greater Berlin, a chartered jetliner took off for Brussels with on board Chancellor Marlein Ditch and her advisors.

Perhaps her entering the plane at the military airport of Berlin could be the best place to describe her appearance. Marlein Ditch was a small, pretty, skinny, dark blond creature with the kind of skin that quickly tans so that she always looked quite healthy. Light, green-grey eyes under full, dark eyebrows were constantly scrutinizing counterparts to detect uncertainty, hesitance, or half-truths.

Plausibly, she would be far more attractive if she would take better care of her make-up and permit herself more feminine dresses, as currently her facade was nothing more than the manifestation of a plain Jane – the reason why French colleague Perrier could only think of her as the German spinster, while her staff in office had long lost their appetite to examine her extra casual presentation.

* * *

As soon as the fasten-seatbelt-signs in the jetliner went off, the dark-suited senior advisor on EU matters of Fraulein Ditch pulled out of his seat and, standing as straight as possible in the low roofed plane, politely presented the files he prepared for the extra Brussels meeting of the two state-leaders with the PressCom on the issue of the federation of the Southerners.

Lamentably, the bundle of papers in the grey file had no lucky landing on the table in front of the Chancellor, as she, in one, rushed movement threw them into the air while screaming with a high-pitched voice to her dark suited aide.

"Do you really think that I should now review all these documents? How many times have I repeated that I want a minimal twenty-four hours to prepare myself? And presented in bullet points. I am not a bionic woman!"

Racing down on his knees to catch the papers flying around and quickly stuffing them in the copy file in his hands, the aide contained his slight anger.

"Madam Chancellor, excuse me please, but you have called me only twelve hours ago to arrange for the meeting. I am sorry. Were it not for our colleagues in Brussels and Paris like me always willing to overwork ourselves, there would have been little news to report. I apologize, but as I also have been forced to study their inputs, would you mind me instead verbally briefing you now?"

The Chancellor in a new outcry: "No, you cannot! Although I am grateful for your considerate suggestions, to my knowledge you have not presented me with one, single, original idea in the past, three years. Believe me things are too important now for cutting and pasting. I can hardly trust my French colleague, let alone the rest of the bunch."

The civil servant in Hans Schmidt was in obeisance as he neglected her mood and, with his bowed head almost touching the ceiling of the curving plane, remarked with playful gentleness.

"But Mrs. Chancellor, what is it of great importance that you want to pose in Brussels?"

"Mr. Schmidt, tell me. Is there much choice left for me with the mess I have inherited from my predecessors? Please, sit down. I will explain it to you. I am not telling you anything new if I say that this European Union is not a Union. But on the other hand, to speak the truth, I am not at all interested in a Union with this bunch, many of them dreaming of Germany as a Treasury Island, ready to be looted. Believe me, some of them would not even mind the Euro zone returning to inflation rates near those we suffered in times of the Weimar Republic. But as long as I am here, the European Central Bank will have to behave as the Bundesbank in the days before the Euro system. We are no longer feeding beggars."

Moving with greater confidence since the Chancellor was closing in on a subject on which Hans Schmidt had his views and projections clear cut, he sat down opposite Frau Ditch convinced that his one-liner had touched the right string and that even her lavish answer would be easy to ward off. He only was to listen careful and then answer strategically.

"Listen Schmidt, my French colleague has offered me insistently to create a federation formed only by stable countries of the Euro zone. Of course these countries should be pre-selected by him and me before involving anyone else. And frankly, due to the circumstances, I consider his approach at this time in history the right one. Yesterday night I was thinking and rethinking what would be my own pre-selection and believe me, this was far from easy. Let's see. Apart from France and Germany, we have the Dutch, Austria, and Luxembourg. More?
Counting on Belgium in its current political stalemate is absurd. So is Ireland. And of course I have strong doubts on Italy, although pulling them out of the PIGS would fortunately blow the plans of Spain. But then, the Italians are not trustable at all since they love both the underground economy and spending money without paying taxes.
What complications!"

From take-off, thick, dark clouds surrounded the plane and probably the chosen altitude to fly into Brussels would mean continued turbulence. Certainly not Herr Schmidt's favorite flying weather, but as he could observe from the nervous moves of the German Chancellor opposite him, neither hers. He was now bowing slightly in her direction to create a more relaxed atmosphere and started speaking at lower voice.

"So, Mrs. Chancellor, if I hear you well, you are suggesting that France is going to be our only trustworthy counterpart for solving the current financial and political crisis in the EU."

"My dear Schmidt, I would like your deduction to be correct, but the naked truth is that not even the French can be my betting horse. You know, to me all French political parties, except of course the extreme right are tilted to the left, and you know what that means in the current circumstances: increased public expenditure financed by fresh, printed money".

The plane bumped more aggressively and Frau Ditch flung forward to him while her hands anxiously grabbed the arms of her chair. So much so that Herr Schmidt could suddenly smell her perfume or maybe it was just her body lotion. Unmistakably spicy, although he would not have thought her ever using more than the scent of ice, he reflected with a hidden smile while Frau Ditch continued expressing her views on the future of the EU.

"Herr Schmidt, you will agree with me that the current intentions of EU policy makers could take us, if we are not very cautious, to an inflationary process that we Germans strongly detest."

He was aware that he should immediately take a distance from his too personal reflections on the Chancellor and replied. "Madame, if you allow me, and with all my respect, it is my humble view, although shared by some European governments, our Trans-Atlantic friends, Britain, China, India, and others alike, that having public deficits in times of recessions or slow growth will not necessarily be inflationary.

Perhaps, what differentiates the Euro zone situation for the worst is that we have only one Central Bank shared by seventeen nations, which does not enable decision making in relation with printing money since this was forbidden at the construction of the Euro zone. To my understanding, there is only one way out: to change the statutes and make possible that the European Central Bank finances the recovery of the economic activity in the Euro zone without exaggerated, inflationary concerns."

At his last words, the plane entered an even heavier zone of turbulence, seemingly passing an airbag and falling down quite some meters. This time, Schmidt could not avoid crossing eyes with Frau Ditch. Green-grey, they became filled with a dog's fear. During the bump her face came close to his and he could see a pale, satin flush creeping up from her neck and covering her cheeks. In great contrast was her strong reaction on his frank remarks.

"But my dear advisor, you should first and foremost read books of German economic history and you should know that we, the Germans, produced an economic miracle also in the times of Chancellors Adenhauer and Erhard at all times correctly balancing our public budgets. Even now we have only small deficits and we are growing much faster than the French and others."

Schmidt, with his eyes following the line of her cheeks and small shoulders, was now amiably calm. "But madam, if I may say so, note that in times of the former German miracle, we received a strong impulse from the Marshall Plan and that now in reality we are merely living from the budget deficits of the Americans, Chinese, and other EU members. I think that economists like Stieglitz and Krugman, both Nobel Laureates, are right in defending public deficits in times of unemployment. Probably, if the Americans, Chinese, and Europeans would have acted like us, even Germany would now be in cero growth or even worst."

By now the turbulence was so bad that Frau Ditch had to lean backwards and with her eyes in her frozen face staring at the table between them, she signaled with her hand that the conversation was over. Marlein Ditch had been saved by the bell and in order not to be overwhelmed by fear she closed her eyes, leaned backwards, and set herself to pass the rest of the bumpy flight in silence. But first there was a quick glimpse on her watch, which made her figuring out that they would have at minimum another twenty minutes before landing.

Anxious, she decided that instead of restlessly having to count the seconds and minutes till touchdown, she would rather reflect on the arguments of advisor Schmidt.

First of all, she had to admit that Schmidt's opinions were far away from those regularly expressed in her Council of Ministers meetings. But the difference was quite understandable since the latter were mostly defending the traditional way of doing politics in Germany. On the other hand, Schmidt's arguments were, as one could expect, not at all original.

Really, in the past three months, she had been reading the same arguments in most mainstream international weeklies, of course outside of Germany. Could it be just a matter of envy of these internationals with the "German miracle"? Or could it be that they would prove to be right and that her Council of Ministers was mistaken?

If the outsiders were right, the Euro zone would need a Central Bank with statutes similar to those of Central banks in the big, independent, or federal nations. Although, the Euro zone was not one nation so Schmidt and Jacques might be right that the only way to solve the problem of creating jobs without significant inflation would be to establish a Federal European State of several, Euro zone countries.

Nice thought, but not easy for the spirit of Germans, completely averse to systematically having to feed the beggars of the South. Logically, Jacques Perrier repeated several times, "*By just merging interested countries with more or less the same per-capita income, that is to say, homogeneous countries in the Euro zone, thus sidelining free-riders and beggars.*"

He could be right. Federating five, relevant, Euro-zone countries could create a 175-million-people state to start with. But for her, it would probably be more difficult to actively promote this idea. If Germany would promote a super EU state this could also wake up some ugly ghosts of the recent past in the continent.

* * *

Thinking of ghosts, jittery Marlein Ditch in cloudy skies was being knotted slowly by the remembrance of far more unpleasant experiences in her past. Although she had long learned to push matters far to the back of her memory, once in a while, mainly in situations of stress or tension, the nasty events came back to her. And they were coming back to her now.

The story is difficult to tell, for to tell it from the point of view of Marlein would almost certainly end up downgrading it. One has to understand that today, for most people, in modern, united Berlin, Marlein Ditch is a philologist and feminist-never married, no children-who after a hardly visible, unfruitful career as policy staff in a small institution in East Berlin, turned her boring, invisible life upside-down by entering into politics. And then she surprisingly managed to reach the highest level by becoming the second female Chancellor of a United Germany.

Frau Ditch became the chief of the largest country in the EU but hardly anyone around her in modern Berlin or in Brussels would know anything or seemed interested in her past in Leipzig and Dresden, or to be more precise, in the story of her dramatic experience as one of the happy few selected talents for the elite athletic program of the German Democratic Republic.

For the interested reader, one could reflect on Marlein's life story by highlighting the three episodes she was firmly keeping secret. One could state that she had symbolically buried any unwelcome content of her life under the many stones of the Berlin Wall when it collapsed in 1989. At that very moment in time, she effectively seized the opportunity to cross from East into West without her past.

First: the Leipzig period: 1968-1972

In 1968, the 13-year-old Marlein, coming from a small village twenty-four kilometers east of Weimar was admitted to a Training School for Olympic Athletes at the outskirts of Leipzig.

Marlein Ditch was one of the happy few who successfully passed the selection at the annual nationwide competition to enter into the elite athletic program of the German Democratic Republic. The training school itself, beside preparing students to keep up the extremely high level of golden medals GDR athletes used to take home from worldwide competitions, was also the greenhouse for coaches in training at the prestigious Deutsche Hochshule fur Korper Kultur und Sport (currently the University of Leipzig) in the center of the city.

What a glorious day it was, the morning Marlein entered the office of the Rector with her parents and her aunt Frieda. In those days, the latter was a member of the city counsel of Weimar, and consequently a middle cadre of the Socialist Unity Party in the country.

Only two hours later, on the same serene morning, Marlein was able to empty her suitcase, filled mainly with training dresses, in the closet of her new room. It was an artic room on the top floor of the three-story building with a dormer window spreading some daylight on the two, small beds, one for Marlein and the other for another "coming" athlete, who had also been placed in the same class room of the Sport Lyceum.

All the buildings of the Institute (the hostel, the sport-halls, the classrooms, canteen, first-aid, and library) were located in a spacious and hilly, green park with the statue of Karl Marx at the entrance.

Aunt Frieda, a person with a visionary mind, not only supported the admittance of Marlein to the prestigious school, but she also, with an eye on the future, designed elegant nametags and name cards for her soon-to-be-famous niece, ready for use immediately after Marlein would win her first golden medal for excellence, be it on the asymmetric bars, the vault horse or the balance beam.

As it later would appear, the ideas of Aunt Frieda were very premature since Marlein would leave the Sport Lyceum in Leipzig at the age of seventeen and short of any gold medal as she had to skip the Games of 1972 with a chronic fracture and continuing pains in her slightly deformed left knee. All this caused by a serious fall from the balance beam in the second year of arriving at the school and compounded by continued exercising.

In the months after the accident, the fracture in her knee could not cure since from the moment of the fall-Marlein tumbled from the beam during a regional championship in Minsk-until her departure from the school, she continued competing, forced by Coach Friedrich, although endlessly being put on the pain rack. Subsequently her life became a real nightmare in the following twenty months as she could not share her misfortune with anyone.

Condemned to silence by Friedrich with a body stuffed with painkillers, she continued training and competing in at least two more championships for young athletes in Dachau and Moscow.

As she later reflected on these dark days of her youth, it had not only been a matter of performing while passing all torture landmarks, but also the experience of being trapped in a pitch-black tunnel filled with the many false expectations of Aunt Frieda and her parents on the one side, and the lethal pressure of Friedrich on the other.

So when she left the institution at the age of seventeen, not only had her body aged too fast, but also her illusions had swiftly crumbled and, deathly tired, she settled for a gloomy life as a housewife with Friedrich. He was an irresponsible man more than twice her age who offered his small apartment for her to come to terms with her innocence lost and her dreams evaporated.

Second: the Dresden period: 1973-1978

To survive the disappointment of only marginal recovery from the-at her age exceptional-osteoporosis, Marlein completely lost herself in her philology studies at the University of Dresden. There she was, a shy, eighteen-year-old youngster, too small and perhaps too skinny for her age, already married and on rainy days often walking with a slight hobble.

Yet, she surprised professors and deans of the faculty by following classes of two years in one and finalizing her master studies one year ahead of the normal scheduled time. And although it was understandable that she rarely found time to participate in the vibrant student life of the beautiful city with its abundant, historic buildings along the Elbe, it was remarkable that she strongly held back to any mingling in her private life or in her life story, while the opposite would have been something quite natural in a faculty of philology.

As the reader may understand by now, it must have been a deliberate choice of Marlein, who instead of trying to come to terms with her past was probably more occupied, be it in silence, with the preparations of a huge turnaround in the next stage of her life.

No one will definitely know, but fact is that her quiet behavior at the faculty in Dresden secured that nobody would be able to remember anything special of the young, hard-working, loner student by the time she was inaugurated as German Chancellor.

At most, some neighbors in the apartment building in the Garten Strasse in the center of Dresden would be able to recall that, in April, a week before Good Friday in 1978, the husband of Marlein, a forty-year-old

26

sports coach suddenly died during a trip to Moscow, thus leaving his young widow in disarray.

Perhaps these neighbors would also remember that Marlein, who herself informed them of the death of her husband by sticking a note on the information board in the entrance hall of the building block, did not open her door in the days after for anyone ringing in an attempt to show compassion and offer support to the far-too-young widow.

Those who approached Marlein around Good Friday had to settle for her firm refusal, followed by the announcement of a well-balanced, young widow that she was busy packing to leave for East Berlin. As she explained monotonously through the intercom, she had applied for a job as policy staff at the Hendrik Kreamer House in the Linden-Strasse in East Berlin, the only community center of the Dutch Protestant Church in the GDR. The vacancy was brought to her attention already in February by the Vicar of the Kreuzkirche and she was thankful for his support. It had resulted in her appointment to this somewhat exclusive institute in East Berlin. With her voice slightly cracking, she would add that her misfortune with the loss of her husband had thus become more bearable.

Nevertheless, the reader should be informed that neither Marlein's parents or her Aunt Frieda, let alone the neighbors and her colleagues at the faculty in Dresden were aware of the truth that the man who Marlein proclaimed dead, was alive and well in Potsdam, some 150 kilometers from Dresden, preparing to leave on a scholarship to Moscow.

In the wa-wa hours of the night of the Monday before Good Friday, with the knowledge and stimulation of Marlein, Friedrich had unnoticeably moved out. He was lucky that he could temporary settle in a small apartment in the compound of the athletic training institute of Potsdam. Even more, the next day, he was happy to start living in his scarcely furnished studio with a young, well-proportioned, Cuban woman he actually picked from the streets two weeks before in Dresden. It is also objective to state here that things worked out far less-fortunate for Friedrich since only days after settling for his new love life with the Latino and her jiggling buttocks and artificially-oversized breasts; he found out that his new partner was living on a daily dose of lithium to balance her bi-polar moods. The situation was unbearable in the confinement of the small studio in Potsdam but it was already far too late for him to solicit a welcome back in Dresden.

Little did he know that the announcement of his alleged dead was already made, including the information that his funeral was taking place in Warsaw, which not only was half-way from Moscow to Dresden, but also, according to his presumed widow, his hometown.

All that takes us back to reflect a little on the marriage life of the couple over the past five years.

Marlein started being disappointed after the first three years as she expected far more interest for her academic endeavors from the coach and, if not, at least some more sophistication in his behavior.

Certainly Marlein had not imagined that she would find Friedrich at the sofa in their living room with the Vietnamese cleaning maid of the faculty, or that he would repeat his extra-marital affairs with other cleaning maids, which as far as she knew happened repeatedly, and which she cynically categorized as his favorite group to hunt.

Coach Friedrich was in his way also disappointed with his wife. Perhaps he expected far cozier homecomings, but instead his young spouse buried herself in her study and preferred reading books till the early morning hours. In these circumstances, he fell asleep alone in the double bed, dreaming of making love with Marlein before a post-orgasmic daze would wake him up. Yet, Marlein from her side was determined not to compromise to the needs and wants of what she considered routine of primitive man. So while one could explain Friedrich's disappointment and misbehavior as the result of his slowly but steadily exclusion by his academically advancing wife, one could also consider that Marlein from her side was convinced that Friedrich was regularly seducing young, female athletes at the institute in Dresden, or if not, exotic, cleaning maids from overseas, socialist countries and she would not want to expose herself to the risk of any sexually transmitted diseases.

By the time the fourth youngster made her appearance, this time from Cuba, Marlein coldly asked Friedrich to step out of her life, preferably as soon and invisibly as possible! Subsequently, the sports trainer walked out of Marlein's life just before dawn with only a few of his clothes and shoes.

In the same week, Marlein calmly announced his dead at the faculty and asked for two weeks off for attending his funeral in Warsaw. As she explained, having been prescribed good tranquilizers, there would be no problems with her traveling alone.

Just one week before the announcement of Friedrich's passing; the Vicar of the Kreutz Kirche had brought her the positive news on her application for the vacancy at the Hendrik Kreamer House. Showing only restrained delight with being accepted, Marlein timidly asked the Vicar if she could donate some of her things to the church when leaving for Berlin.

The first week of her leave to attend the faked funeral in Warsaw was quietly passed by Marlein in a small hotel up in the north of Rostock; and in the second week, dressed in dark colors for the occasion, she stayed at her family home in the outskirts of Weimar.

Yet, the tears she shed with Aunt Frieda and her mom, both in no doubt over the fact that Marlein had just returned from entombing poor Friedrich, were real as was her somber mood. Together back home in Weimar, the three women grieved over Marlein's misfortunes over the past seven years, starting with the failure of becoming a gold medal athlete. And afterwards, the three prayed together in the St Peter and

Paul Church for seven, better years to come for the young Marlein. It is fair to say that also these prayers were for real.

Third: the East Berlin period 1978-1989

Time left a hole in her memory concerning the East Berlin period, except for the fact that the years went by quiet and the people in the Kreamer House were very trustworthy. In 1982, Marlein, for the first time in her life, spent two months in the West. The Ecumenical Community of Berlin negotiated and paid for her knee operation in the academic hospital of Leiden, the oldest university city of the Netherlands. After a successful, ultra-modern implantation, she passed another month for her revalidation in the Hendrik Kreamer House in Oegstgeest, the sister house of the institution she was working for in East Berlin. In Oegstgeest, Marlein was surprised by the existence of hundreds of Christians preparing for trips to Eastern Europe in their campers and mobile homes stuffed with bibles, all destined for forbidden Christian gatherings in Romania and Hungary. How things had changed!

* * *

At the announcement of preparing for landing in Brussels, a slightly emotional Marlein Ditch abandoned her reflections, opened her bag, and pulled out her lipstick she might have bought years ago but hardly used since it was against her convictions as a feminist. Perhaps it could be of some help today. One never knows, but sometimes a colorful smile could suddenly move the will of translators, aides, advisors, or even the PresCom in a good direction for the preparation of a voluntary federation of Euro zone countries.

Three

A French-German initiative is overcoming turmoil

Brussels was cold with some porous sunlight in a distance when Chancellor Ditch arrived at Berlaymont, the EU Commission premises in the Rue de la Loi. Approaching the monstrous building in steel and glass panels, Marlein knew for sure that one of her predecessors would have agreed with the construction of this-to her taste-ugly building, and then again right in the capital of the most politically dysfunctional member of the European Union, but it would probably not have been her choice.

Entering the building-in her view also furnished with bad taste-the ambiance converted even cooler when the Chancellor surprisingly ran into the British Prime Minister. He certainly was the last person on earth she would want to meet this morning.

"Madam Chancellor, what a pleasant surprise. How are you doing? Looking good as usual."

"Do not flatter me. I am fine, but what on earth are you doing here my friend? Meetings?"

"No, no, nothing formal, I just met some of my parliamentarians and I have to admit that I have used the opportunity to meet the PresCom over breakfast. And as you may understand, I have of course insisted on cutting the British contribution to the EU budget".

"Dear friend, so you continue with the same demarche of your predecessors who tried to pull the legs of the European Council. And this even after the blow Britain received on this issue with twenty-four votes against."

"Madam Chancellor, dearest Marlein, this is simply what the British people want. Do I have another choice as a democratically elected Prime Minister than to honor the view of the people?"

"Dear Prime Minister, would you agree with me that even the British people, as by the way also the German people, could change their view provided that they were well-informed on their long-term interests?"

While taking off his glasses and hooking them in the top pocket of his jacket, the Brit produced one of his well-known, diplomatic non-answers.

"Changing the subject, what is the cause of your sudden visit from Berlin? Is it to the PresCom?"

"Yes. I just wanted to have a first-hand account of the move of the Southerners. You may be aware."

"Madam Chancellor, I have to confess that I have been informed a week ago by my four ambassadors *in situ* about the Spanish initiative, but actually, I do not see any matter for concern. One should expect many wild ideas, given the current problems in the Euro zone. Fortunately Britain is not part of it. As you know, we over and over again warned about the instability of the monetary union created in Maastricht."

"But dear colleague, perhaps things would have developed far better if Britain and some others had not opted out. To say the truth, you have not entered the Euro zone, but in exchange you have presented us the gift of the omnibus enlargement of 2004. I am still mad about the trick, but I have no time now to go into discussion. So, let us agree to disagree, I have to rush".

As Marlein abandoned the company of the British Prime Minister, she concluded that the Brits, irrespective of their political color, were behaving the same in relation to the EU: they probably joined to kill the project as, years ago, de Gaulle suspected.

At arrival at the door of the PresCom office, Frau Ditch still felt disturbed over her unexpected encounter and the prickly open-ended conversation over the political crisis in the EU. And all that, in his mother tongue, an asymmetric situation Marlein more and more detested.

Subsequently, the man in the marine blue and yellow outfit, full of golden tassels and stripes, waiting for her to clear the way to the President of the Commission, was at first almost overlooked by Marlein. Only when the bogus lackey announced that both the President of France and the PresCom would join them with some minutes delay, Marlein granted him a look to immediately turn her eyes off while remarking in clear disturbance-and this time, in German-to Hans Schmidt.

"Thank God, with our Federation, this whole theater of phony monarchy lackeys will be something of the past".

After the Chancellor and her aide took a seat in the *ante-chambre*, they started hearing the loud, incomprehensible, and agitated speaking of the President of France in the room next door. Jacques Perrier was apparently on the phone and in bad temper.

* * *

"Alexandra, listen. You cannot do this to me, and certainly not in this way. I married you, just before my inauguration as President of the Republic. I expect you to fulfil your duties and to let me terminate my first mandate before any act of divorce. Really, this is a blow under the belt. Something I have never received from the opposition in the National Assembly, or from any of the unfriendly friends in my party." On the other side of the line, his wife Alexandra pretended to apologize while explaining in a serene voice.

"It is not me leaving you, Jacques; it is you who has systematically left me from the first days of our marriage. Yes, I could understand that you did not sleep with me when you tripped to the US or China and I had to remain home. But what is not acceptable to me is that you did not stay with me and left for Le Havre to confront some unimportant, striking port workers, or because you had left for Val d"Isere to inaugurate a petty snow canon in the ski-station of one of your friends. Your hyper-activity and lack of priority is simply absurd for a man with so many ministers at his disposal. Ah, and do not think that I have invented this argument; all Frenchmen say the same.

Anyway, to make sure that you are not unpleasantly surprised by information coming from your ambassadors, or that you have to read rumours in glossy magazines, I prefer to inform you that I am currently in Istanbul, accompanied by a man of my age, perhaps a little younger, of Turkish nationality."

"*Merde*, you call me in Brussels to say that you are cheating me with a Turkish lover-boy?

What the hell is going on?"

"Calm down please. Do you remember the guide who the Turkish president offered us to show us around in Istanbul when we were visiting Ankara and you suddenly preferred to remain in the hotel to make a thousand calls to Paris to satisfy your micro-management?

I felt very alone then, but paradoxically these two days turned into very nice after the guide cheered me up. In reward, I invited him to Paris for a visit, which totally unplanned ended up in us developing a relationship. I know it may be very painful for you. I am very sorry.

And although at this moment, I would prefer living with him, I can promise you that I will remain with you till the finish of your term."

"Enough, Xandra, I cannot hear this. I will not talk to you any longer. I am in a meeting."

An angry and humiliated President of France, at the brink of a nervous breakdown but simultaneously also aware that he had some time to react before any divorce, caught himself thinking about possible solutions for getting rid of the Turkish guide while walking slowly towards the *ante-chambre.*

Come to think of it, he recognised that he might have committed mistakes the first years of his presidency, in particular his endless rushing from here to there to wave his flag. But this in no way justified the behaviour of Alexandra. Would he ever understand women? Thank God she had given him some breathing space till the end of his first term.

Perhaps he would be able to recover his skills to charm the young writer he married shortly before his electoral success. Nevertheless, provoking the disappearance of the Turkish guide from her side was a very urgent issue. At all costs, he should elude that the media would in one way or another become aware of any affair of Alexandra, which would certainly affect his career. Not to mention the fact that, of all existing possibilities, she had chosen a Turk.

* * *

Having waited for more than five minutes, an impatient German Chancellor started stretching, when at that very moment her irritated glance hit a worried French President who was hasting towards her. As Perrier was trying to camouflage his furious screaming of some minutes before, he drew up an artificial smile on his bony face and discreetly tried to wipe off the sweating on his forehead. Yet, Frau Ditch was boiling with curiosity to know what his emotional conversation had been about.

"I hope it was not bad news you got, Jacques. Be assured that we could only hear you speaking without understanding a word".

Jacques Perrier was quick with his response, "My wife has called me, first to say she loves me and secondly to complain about her relation with my eldest son who's becoming more and more difficult. And I have understood that if things do not change, I will have to make a choice between him and her. I am sure the last observation was pure bluff of Alexandra. Anyway, it was a debate of minor importance but, nonetheless, frequent among couples. Luckily for you, Marlein, you have none of these problems. You see, even becoming president of France does not guarantee a happy family. Perhaps you did well not to marry."

Marlein decided to drop the conversation by answering, "Absolutely my friend, for me, the grass was never greener on the other side. Alas, few people understand the constraints of combining state leadership with family life, but as far as I know, our combination is far more difficult than the family life of movie stars, as we are also supposed to show high morals and set the example."

In the following minutes, the two top politicians used the waiting time to exchange views on the morning news, in particular on the headlines concerning the bluffs of the Iranian president in relation to Israel, fresh political protests in Tunis and Cairo, and the euro-dollar fluctuations, when suddenly another lackey, again in full EU colours, yellow stars and cavalry head, opened the double doors to the PresCom office and announced, "The President of the European Commission".

While Carlos Bopoulos, the PresCom was approaching in a completely hassle-free way, he started talking.

"Dear friends, sorry for the delay, but as you may imagine my meeting with the Budget Commissioner has lasted far longer than expected. Ach, you all know how the Union finances are faring. I have explained a thousand times in several forums that with our squalid EU budget we cannot reach much progress. I would have liked to see the two of you in my place, suffering with available funds of only one-percent of the EU GDP, when at the same time everybody travels to Brussels for showing me his or her hand palm as did the medieval monks of Mendicant Orders. Yet, conversely to the latter, the current begging hand is accompanied by extreme urgency and arrogance as if the money they demand was their indisputable right."

Contrary to the French President, PresCom Bopoulos was 1.90 meters high and extremely wrinkled in forehead and around the eyes and ears. His curly hair had notoriously been rejuvenated with an overdose of shiny, black dye that should match his dark eyes behind fashionable framed glasses, but under his severe overhanging eyelids his eyes were almost fully invisible. To complete the picture, his sky blue tie could have been a gift from Aznar, while his deep blue shirt, undoubtedly Italian, could have been a gift from Prodi. However, the origin of his buttons was clear: marine blue flags with the usual ring of yellow stars in the middle in great harmony with the uniforms of his lackeys. One should note that these buttons were typically part of the small presents that his secretary kept for third-world country visitors or journalists. The last odd detail of the PresCom in full ornate were his shoes; almost cherry red, they were in stark contrast with his cream suit.

Certainly the multicolour appearance of Bopoulos well reflected his political past. Before becoming European PresCom, the man had shifted several times and even from one extreme of the political spectrum to the other in the various political parties of Greece. An experience which probably made him rather acceptable to the diverse EU member states who crowned him as President of the Commission only after four years of being EU Commissioner of Sport and Culture.

On the other hand, one should not neglect either the fact that his fluency in more than eight languages, including Flemish and Serbian, might have contributed to his popularity in the European Parliament and even so in the European Council, but perhaps the mere fact that he had no enemies was most outstanding. He had a fame of being completely relaxed, someone who never splashed a single drop outside the pot. Immediately after Marlein and Jacques-with their respective aides at back benches-had seated themselves, the French President expressed his agreement with the budget remarks of the PresCom at entrance.

"You are right, Carlos. I have also said in many forums that if the EU wants to be a serious institution with full political capacities, it should count at least on six to eight-percent of its joint GDP. In reality this is not a big figure in comparison to the federal budget of the US government or even the national budgets of our member states.

Actually, I felt disgusted when some minutes ago the German Chancellor reported to me the content of her conversation with our friend, the Prime Minister of Britain, who openly revealed to her that he had been pleading once again for the check rebound. Let us not forget that Britain shamelessly started demanding the rebound already some few months after entering in the Union in 1973. This is exactly as some pinchpenny grooms do, claiming back the rings and jewelleries from their wives one day after the marriage to deliver them to the pawnbroker under the threat of immediate divorce."

This time the German Chancellor reacted itched. "Six to eight-percent of EU GDP, what are you saying, Jacques? Let us be frank. Do you really believe that after Germany is contributing almost two-percent of its GDP while others prefer free-riding, any German would agree to increase our EU burden with a single Euro cent? Should I remind you that we Germans have paid double for our own unification: first from our own national budget and secondly by our extra contribution to the EU? And all this while member-states complained in those days about our increased power, and others started their economic miracle by diverting our capitals to their territories, by means of lowering the rate of their corporate tax. As you may understand, I am referring here to the Irish miracle which finally turned into a nightmare."

At Marlein's last words, President Perrier, erecting from his armchair as a tiger and requesting his aide to retrieve the blue book on solving the EU crisis, quickly responded, "My dear Marlein, you have not fully understood my remark. With my proposed budget I was referring to that of the federation. This budget would be equivalent to six to eight-percent of the joint GDP of the federating countries, which would be a magnificent business for Germany, France and all who join us. Note that the participating countries, by joining their services, could save huge sums on their defence and security budget, on foreign representation, as well as on public finance, and on other costly sectors such as infrastructure development. The value of these joint services would be well over the six to eight-percent. Believe me, serious studies have figured out a total saving of two-percent on the collective GDP."

As his aide placed the blue book in front of him, Jacques started waving it in the air, adding, "But listen, we are speaking about a serious study and not about a figure of half-a-percent that the architects of the Euro promised us when they delivered the current mess we have nowadays."

By now, Carlos Bopoulos, who kept silent but clearly showed disagreement by moving his head like an Indian Sadhu, decided to intervene and change the subject.

"Colleagues, I had understood that you were here to be informed first-hand on the situation of the attempted federation of our dear member states of the south. Let me assure you that there is no reason to worry whatsoever. I think that the attempt of the Spaniards and Italians is nothing more than a *fuite-a-l'avance*. Although their merger could alter the power play within the EU, thus provoking strong reactions, I have already dealt with the matter. No one less than the Russian Prime Minister, hinting at a possible, future agreement on a free-trade zone with the EU, has informed me that he has rebalanced the problem. As he explained to me, in a recent Russia-Italy bilateral top, Russia expressed great concern over the negative impact on Russian gas exports to the EU following the federation of the

Southerners. If I understood well, some Eastern diplomacy is on its way to blow up the operation."

"Monsieur, speaking from the view of France," said Perrier, "I may agree that this so-called threat of the PIGS is no more than a bluff, which will melt faster than two pieces of ice in a whiskey on the rocks". But the reaction of German Chancellor Ditch was far more reserved.

"Really, I do not want to offend anyone, but I feel that what is hidden under this manoeuvre is a pressure on the rest of the EU member states to lend them the money they cannot borrow on the open, international markets. So, I think that if we guarantee them the money they need, this projected federation of Southerners, who have only in common their tendency to parasite us, would vanish as a soap bubble. But my dear friends, I cannot risk my government falling. As you all know, there is not a single German willing to put more money in any of the bankrupted countries of the Euro zone. Really, in these days of Facebook and Twitter, I will not move in that direction. Indeed, what has become clear with this absurd business of the PIGS is the kind of people we are dealing with. We cannot continue cooperating with leaders who are constantly bargaining with principles, cheating on their deficit figures, and dividing instead of adding. We can no longer accept that Mister PresCom, I think that the moment of putting our house in order has finally arrived. You will have to agree with Jacques and me that with all these purported drivers, the EU project is practically arrested and in need of a radical restatement in its architecture. Although I initially hesitated about the proposal of Jacques, every minute I am more convinced that he is right. The bunch of twenty-seven is unmanageable as most of them have different economic and political interest than the core countries like us. Even more, you must remember that the Germans established clear criteria in the Maastricht Treaty for countries to be part of the monetary union. But at least three countries that did not fulfil the rules were still admitted to enter, and you see how they are now. Others have not only overcome the deficit figures of the Stability Pact, but have reached levels three or four times on top of it, which is the case of Spain and Portugal. And here we have it, the full picture of the PIGS. Prescom, you will agree with me that we cannot continue in such an unstable situation in which every two months another weak brother may fall if we don't advance money. Consequently, Jacques and I believe that the strongest and most courageous countries of the Euro zone should turn the page of the current stalemate and make a rapid move towards a political union of a selected group of member states, thus fulfilling the dreams of Monet, Schuman, and others."

Carlos Bopoulos, who during the intervention of Marlein became visibly restless with his face growing congested, was cracking his fingers and slowly weighing his words in his answer.

"Dear friends, I have listened attentively to both of you and I do understand your concerns and some anger. Yet, you may understand that as PresCom for twenty-seven member states, I will have to look at things from a broader perspective. First of all, one should never oversee the fact that Europe has experienced its longest, peaceful period in its turbulent and frequently violent history. This is the most important achievement of the Union, not to mention the fact that our diversity has anchored the average political behaviour of member states in a more centred and lukewarm position, far away from the dangers of fascism, communism, and extreme capitalism. The things you both have described to me are certainly worrisome, but are not more than stones on the way. On the other hand, I think that one of the most important values of the Union is solidarity and I think that at this historical moment in time, it would be wrong to abandon to their own survival those who are less affluent than the core countries, or those who have committed some serious economic mistakes. I am certainly convinced that in the near future the current, economic slowdown will be overcome, and that in two decades all of us will be citizens of a Mega Union of more than 600-million people, just doubling the population of the USA. Madam et Monsieur, I see no reason whatsoever why Germany and France should not cooperate for the consolidation of this Mega Union, in which Germany and France will always play a leading role while overtly profiting from a huge market."

The last words of the PresCom were the sign for the President of France to leave. He felt outraged over what he considered the continuous, hollow mantra of Bopoulos cum suits. Jacques pondered that he had heard the same arguments many times in different forums since the commemoration of the fiftieth anniversary of the Treaty of Rome. Clearly, this PresCom, like so many other second-rate EU politicians, lacked a theory on the future of Europe. It was a waste of time to continue listening to things that would only convince those working in Brussels, fearing to lose their jobs.

Thus, Jacques aggressively gathered his belongings, looked at his Rolex, and announced, "I will no longer jeopardize the future of France and its great citizens for village politics of small, backwards countries that are hardly interested in a common destiny. I am off, but I will immediately start initiating the promotion of a voluntary, self-selected federation of five to six, economically-homogeneous countries who are already in our monetary union. Bonjour a tous."

At his last words he was at the door followed by the German Chancellor who was quickly apologising to the PresCom for having to leave as well, but thanked him politely for his views concerning the feasibility of the PIGS project.

On their way out and no longer in hearing distance of the PresCom or his proxy lackeys, the German Chancellor at low voice invited the French President to meet at the German Ambassador's Residence in Brussels for a *tête a tête*.

The German Ambassador-pink tie, dark suit-was standing at the gate of the residence with his partner and all the servants in white jackets forming a straight line. Nothing unusual except perhaps for the male partner of the Ambassador; a Caribbean, muscle-bound ex-boxer with curly, dark hair and a bright smile in his ebony face, who on top of all counted visibly some twenty years younger than his spouse, the Head of Mission.

At the stop of the two diplomatic cars in front of the Residence, the German Ambassador subtly signaled to the German Chamber Orchestra, on tour in Brussels, to start playing the Marseillaise.

However, Jacques Perrier, trying to quickly move out of the car, lost his equilibrium and unexpectedly landed in the strong arms of the ex-boxer, who with his extremely, high-pitched voice, started screaming

"Oh what an honor to receive the president of France in my arms!"
The German Ambassador swiftly turned to the scene and was gazing severely annoyed at his partner before he ordered him to immediately put the French president down and join the ranks of the servants for listening to the anthems.

"But Dieter, darling, I have only instinctively helped him not to fall", jested the ex-boxer. Correcting his suit and tie, and picking off a curly hair from his hand, the French president produced a smile on his face as he exclaimed to the German Chancellor, "My dear colleague, have not you just understood from the PresCom that our two countries are in peace since 1945? So why would you provoke a political raw, by playing the French anthem even before I could stand in position?"

Meanwhile, the German Chancellor was throwing an angry eye on her ambassador before hastily bending over in the direction of the president of France and apologizing to him. At low voice so her ambassador who stood at attention for the German anthem could not hear, she reflected on the more and more overt exhibition of same-sex relations in diplomacy, military army, and parliament. In these days of ultra-liberty, ethical relativism, and political correctness, being sexually opposite was almost provocatively promoted while, at the same time, even the most humble, religious symbols were being forbidden.

* * *

The library of the Residence was a room with dark oak woodwork and bookshelves on all but one wall, leaving only space for one large window; and a very modern fireplace in an iron box which was hanging from the ceiling. On the comfortable sofas on one side of the library the tête a tête would take place.

After the coffee had been served and both political leaders were able to glance around, commenting politely on some book titles while enjoying their aromatic cups, the conversation started. The German Chancellor was the first to speak.

With secret undertones and looking straight in the eyes of Jacques Perrier, she remarked, "Believe me, I had not expected a different reaction from the PresCom. In my view, although he may experience the EU"s top-level inefficiency and non-governability on a daily basis, he will cling to his position cost what cost."

"You are right, Marlein. My experience with him is one of merely a puppet of Downing Street. Perhaps we should no longer lose our time with him and others alike. I feel that Europe has lost precious time in the last two decades while China and India are economically churning out. Even the US with respectively a second-rank actor, two Texans and a saxophone player, not to mention the current, legal modernist has economically grown faster than us. All this wasting time has to stop, which is why we should start the EU federating process right now. What about a secret bilateral of the two of us *en marge* of the inauguration of the new plant for French Mirage 29? We have to move firm and fast with our federation."

Four

Love and foul-play in Dubai

Although it was 06.30 hours in the morning, the international airport of Dubai was full of pilgrims trying to board planes to go to Mecca when Ibrahim arrived from Istanbul.

In contrast to the fasting horde, his first activity back on the ground was the gobbling of two cakes and two croissants before he entered the public bathroom at the airport to drink some cool water. All activities were meant to refill his empty stomach and to recover from dehydration caused by the low-budget flight in which nothing was offered for free, not even water, after a four-hour delay at Istanbul airport. Not to mention the fact that taking a seat at the airport had also been impossible. The extreme hardship of the trip had raised his appetite to boiling levels. He was eager to finally embrace Alexandra with whom he would meet at the Sheraton Creek Hotel in central Dubai at midday.

After trailing his luggage up to the taxi stand, he boarded a yellow taxi alike to those rushing in New York. It was his first time in Dubai, but if things with Alexandra developed positively, visits to Dubai could become a regular part of his existence.

* * *

On the way from the airport to the hotel, Ibrahim started a conversation with the driver who appeared to be from Pakistan. The driver, a young man in his twenties, was eager to know more about the life in Istanbul. In particular, he mentioned his desire to visit the

Sofia Mosque. However, such a visit might be no more than a dream since, as the driver explained, he had to send all his earnings to Karachi and consequently he had to live in a room of forty square-meters with just one bathroom, together with around twenty roommates. Changing the subject, the conversation moved to the objective of Ibrahim's visit to Dubai.

The driver asked, "Business or holiday, sir?"

"Let us say, holiday. Four days touring with my fiancée."

"Oh sir, so lucky you are. These Dubai women, much money have and father always want Muslim man come from Istanbul, for husband. Too much nice."

"No, no, my fiancée is neither Arab nor Muslim, she is French."

"Ha-an, sir, even better. Never mind sir, I say, too much sexy have these French ladies. No problem virginity losing before marriage. Pak family much more difficult. My father-in law too much me control no sex before marriage, but me much clever. This girl, my wife now, me take to other village. Hi-hi. You also other village take now Sir, hi-hi?"

"Ok, I see it is taking time for you to take me to the hotel. My information is that this trip should not cost more than eighty Dirham and your meter is already showing seventy-four. So are we near?"

"But sir, no problem, everybody knows crisis have in America and Europe, and also in Dubai, inflation coming everywhere. Now Arab also democracy want oil price more up. But you my brother, sir, you pay eighty Dirham and my tip as per your own convenience."

* * *

In his hotel suite, rented by Alexandra, Ibrahim took a long warm bath with Mediterranean salts, ordered a full American breakfast at room service, and waited for the food in his white gown and slippers while sitting in front of the window facing the creek.

Letting his eyes pass over the water and the small boats with cargo and tourists crossing, Ibrahim reflected on the complications of his relation with Alexandra. First of all, he was sincerely in love with her, and he was convinced that she had similar feelings for him. However, they were living in worlds apart. She was the wife of no one less than the President of France and Ibrahim was no one more than a young and clever economist employed by the Turkish president as a personal advisor. In this position, he was regularly asked to accompany state leaders and their wives to visit the monuments of Ankara and Istanbul, while explaining the splendid future of Turkey and the added value it would offer when entering into the EU.

Although he was excitedly waiting for Alexandra, he was also overrun by a certain discontent. Picture it, his greatest love of all would be landing in some hours at the Dubai airport, but he could not be there to close her in his loving arms. It was a sad and miserable situation ever since, as a cover up, she would be accompanied by two old classmates with whom she would be visiting a fashion show in the famous seven-star hotel Bourg Al Arab. Given that she would be staying in that hotel, he would have to settle for seeing her only when it would fit in her program and she would be ready to take a cab to visit him in the Sheraton Creek Hotel. The mere fact that he would have to wait passively, not knowing if and when she would be coming to meet him, made his humiliation more intense.

* * *

A telephone ring woke him up. He probably had fallen asleep while waiting for Xandra. A quick look at his Omega, a present from his

47

father, confirmed that it was midday and that he had been sleeping more than four hours.

"My love, how are you? Alexandra sounded cheerful. "I am now in a cab on my way to you. My mates are having their lunch in Bourg Al Arab."

"Darling, you caught me in the middle of a pleasant dream. Of course, my dream was with you in the center, lighting up my life.
Oh, how I have missed you. Upon arrival, please come up directly to my room, 421. I will impatiently be waiting for you. I am hungry for your touch and full of energy."

"Oh, I feel the same but cannot speak freely now. Notice my low voice. I have a Pak driver in the cab who, after me asking for the Sheraton Creek Hotel and detecting that I am French, has remarked that he delivered a man to the same hotel in the morning, a brother Muslim from Istanbul who confessed to him having a French fiancée. I trust you have not entered in more details about us."

"No darling, nothing, although believe me, I would like nothing more than to scream across the streets that I am in love with you."

"Keep quiet. Your time will come. The cab driver himself is going to help you. Ha ha. You know that this man is now praying to Allah because he considers that the coincidence of first driving you, and then driving me, is a sign of good luck. Darling, I have to hang because our Pak friend has big ears, also literally, hi-hi."

At arrival at the Sheraton Creek Hotel, a good-tempered Alexandra offered a splendid tip to the still praying Pak driver and rushed to the lift. Minutes later at the fourth floor, she softly knocked on 421.
An elated Ibrahim flung the door open. "Be welcome my beautiful and smart queen. Oh, you look better than ever, darling; come, let me hold you. I have a fantastic wine waiting for us and all my loving."

A passionate deep kiss averted her from answering him. "How I have longed for your lips," she murmured while being fervidly carried by him into the suite. As they took refuge in each other's warmth, long kisses followed, only to be suspended for breathing.

Minutes later, as the first heat was receding, Alexandra recovered some rationality.

"Lovely Ibrahim, being with you is paradise to me, but we should take care not spoiling it. I mean, you should not talk with strangers about your feelings, let alone our love."

"Believe me, darling, I have neither mentioned your name nor have I shared any other information with that cab driver. Besides, his English was not easy to understand and I guess mine for him was as well difficult."

"It was probably enough for this creepy man to keep on trying to touch my hand when I was leaving the cab as if we were sharing a secret. In no part of the world you should trust taxi drivers and certainly not in the Middle East. According to Jacques, some of them are confidents of anyone for little money, be it Taliban or FBI."

"I am sorry, darling, but my mind was so full of you that I could not keep my lips sealed. By the way, do me the favor from your side not to mention your husband's name when we are together. I often pray for our relation to have a happy ending. Try to understand, I am tired of this secrecy. I beg you, leave him, please! Oh, I plea, come with me to Istanbul. I love you!"

"Don't break my heart, Ibrahim, I cannot leave him now. He married me shortly before his inauguration and I will not leave him before his turn is over. And now I am with you, okay?"

At her last words she started nervously looking into her Gucci bag for a cigarette, but was stopped in the act by Ibrahim who, whilst unbuttoning her blouse, started kissing her breast and consequently the two bodies moved compellingly to the bed.

Two hours later, they both had had their showers after the passionate encounter, Alexandra was again looking for a cigarette and this time discovered that she had forgotten the package in Bourg Al Arab. A gratified Ibrahim now offered to go down to the lobby to get her a new package.

***

Ibrahim was not the only man waiting for the lift to take him down to the lobby. Two men, apparently Europeans, left the room next door and joined the waiting in the corridor. According to their clothes, they were on their way to the fitness center in the basement of the hotel.

After an almost involuntary greeting, there was a silence among them till the lift arrived, but when the two men and Ibrahim entered the lift, the taller and thinner indifferently asked if Ibrahim was going to the lobby, before presumably pressing the buttons of the lobby and the fitness. Seconds later-the lift had surprisingly not stopped at the lobby-Ibrahim found himself standing in front of the open lift in the basement, overseeing the entrance to the fitness on the left and the garage to the right. As he had planned to go to the lobby, he moved backwards to let the two gentlemen pass, but suddenly he felt the cold metal of a pistol in his neck while he was being pushed softly by the longer man who murmured, "Do not resist, keep calm, keep silent and nothing will happen."

He was pushed in the direction of a white, four-wheel-drive Toyota, waiting for them in the middle of the garage with the engine on.

When all three men were inside, the car started driving away slowly and Ibrahim was forced to smile to the guard at the entrance, the gun pushing hard and cold in his back.

* * *

The clock in the lobby showed 15.32 hours when a nervous-looking Alexandra made her entrance. She had been waiting for more than fifty minutes for Ibrahim to return with cigarettes and had become very concerned. Rushing from one shop to another in the shopping corridor of the hotel and not finding any sign of Ibrahim made her a prey of fear, even more so as she could not ask for him without leaving traces of their secret affair.

Finally she decided to start looking for Ibrahim outside the hotel, and as the reader may imagine, suddenly the Pak taxi driver walked over to her and, with his smile from ear to ear, jovially remarked, "Ha-an madam, little problem, I see. Never mind me saying madam, love with Arab man always difficult. Just me sleep in parking garage in cab when I see this, your almost husband, quickly leaving with Arab friends. This one problem, me know. Always Arab mansab every evening go coffee shop with friends and madam home stay alone."

"Please, I have no time for jokes. Who were these men that left with Ibrahim? Arabs? What did you see, please tell me! When did you see it happen? Please, where have they gone?" The questions were rolling out of her mouth while she feared the worst.

"Madam, these Arab men, much European looking; no white *kurta pajamas* wear, but European suit. First me see men parking in garage with motor running, little bit strange. Also me see no number plate, car all cover with black plastic. Much clever, these men, no camera see plate."

"Okay, tell me, what direction did they take? Tell me please."

"This one me not know, madam. Garage left, all me see."

Alexandra took a deep breath, moved her hands over her eyes, and waited three seconds in silence before she requested the taxi driver to take her back to Bourg Al Arab.

* * *

On the way back, her mind was full of conflicting thoughts. Had Ibrahim been kidnapped? My God, could Jacques be involved in this? Should she call him to find out? But, if Jacques was not involved, by calling him, she would reveal the reason of her trip to Dubai.
A puzzled Alexandra left the cab and included a twenty-dollar tip to the driver with a friendly smile and a wink.

"Thank you for the service and do not forget, this was nothing but business."
The taxi driver, looking somewhat confused, shrouded his shoulders and repeated: "Yes madam, just business."

While Alexandra walked intently towards the coffee shop at the beach of Bourg Al Arab, where she planned to have a whiskey to calm down before meeting her friends, a noisy helicopter flying above the sea caught her attention. Little could she know at that time that this helicopter was carrying Ibrahim, handcuffed and blindfolded. Nor that he was on his way to a private plane at a nearby small airport, which would take him to a secret destination for thorough investigation. And although Ibrahim could not see the faces of his captors, he unmistakably recognized their accent as American.

Five

Sharing cooks but missing soups brings love back

Three weeks after the meeting in Brussels with the PressCom, German Chancellor Ditch received a report from her advisors concerning the voluntary federation, as proposed by the president of France.

The most remarkable conclusions in the German report were: 1) that the number of countries that had provisionally been considered in the meeting of Marlein and Jacques at the German Ambassador's Residence in Brussels was too small and should include a minimum of one, large country south of the Euro zone to make a round territory, climatically diverse with a total population well over 200-million people and, 2) that the countries joining the federation should be economically homogeneous, which would not exclude Spain, Italy, Slovenia, and Finland. But after reading the report, Marlein considered that she would only accept that Spain and Italy entered in the Federation, if these two countries would correct their high imbalances in a reasonable period of time. And of course, on the condition also that these countries would not continue with their outlandish idea of establishing the Southerners" Federation.

In Marlein's view, the Italians were having a long history of lacking solidarity with the rest of the European Union and within their own society. She could remember the two or three times in the past when they had left the cooperation process, in particular in the case of the serpent and the European monetary system. And then, again, she remembered the short duration of many governments in Italy as a consequence of the various breakaway fractions and strategic games by which they used to make politics.

The Spaniards, although far more sympathetic, Marlein considered little more than a group of *bon vivants* and fun-makers. Nice chaps to go out for drinks and tapas, but not much inclined for hard working and fulfillment of commitments or contracts, particularly with women. Not to mention that they continuously had problems with breakaway Basques and Catalans, something that could produce severe headaches in the Federation.

Reflecting on the cases of Finland and Slovenia, both also members of the Euro zone and with good behavior records in their young membership, she would not mind including them, but they should be invited to join, similar to Spain and Italy, only after the five core members would have agreed on the main lines of the Federation.

The eight, resting countries[3] of the Euro zone, plus ten more EU member states[4], she judged as being far from mature for this initiative. Indeed, they either misbehaved or they hadn't reached the desired economic homogeneity, so for now they should be sidelined.

* * *

At a thousand kilometers distance, but more or less at the same time, French president Perrier received his own advisory report. In this report, the candidacy of the Italians was straightforward rejected by his aides while Spain was not even mentioned. In line with his initial proposal, the report focused entirely on the five countries, suggesting three layers of excluded Euro zone member countries. First, there was

---

[3] The eight excluded Euro-zone countries would be Belgium, Ireland, Portugal, Greece, Malta, Cyprus, Slovakia, and Estonia

[4] The remaining ten non-Euro-zone member states would be Britain, Denmark, Sweden, Poland, Hungary, Czech Republic, Romania, Bulgaria, Lithuania and Latvia.

the layer of the bad performing countries such as Ireland, Greece, and Portugal. Second layer was formed by the states with doubtful behavior, Belgium, Spain, and Italy. And third, the little populated states of the periphery as Slovenia and Finland. In the French report, all the excluded countries could have an opportunity to enter the Federation after a ten-year period, provided they behaved economically well. The report suggested also that none of the initially excluded Euro zone countries should receive bad treatment from the Federating core members. Even more, it was underlined that the excluded countries could remain in the Euro zone provided that they renounced to form part of the board of the European Central Bank, hence of the monetary policy and decision-making.

Having finished reading the one-page summary of the report with satisfaction and in full agreement, Jacques Perrier started cleaning up his desk to rush to the helicopter that was to take him to Gap in order to chair a local event. He was to give the winning trophies for
    "Snowboarding for juniors" in the French championship.

However, at the moment he was closing the door of his office, his private Blackberry rang, disquieting him. This could only be a close contact, so he answered, be it impatiently: "Yes, Perrier ", but then again, before being able to ask who was on the other side of the line, some overlapped, Arab and English words caught his ears. Puzzled he requested, "Who is calling?" The silence on the other side was only interrupted by heavy breathing. Jacques repeated at louder voice
    "Who are you?"
Silence again, but then he was capable to hear at a distance someone, probably chewing bubblegum with grinding jaws, confirming to another person that Jacques Perrier was on the phone.
This was the signal for whoever was calling to start speaking to Jacques. Few words… before hanging, and with a grave voice:

"Monsieur le President, we have served your cause" and the line went cold.

In the silence that followed, Jacques tried to find the logic of what he just heard. Unquestionably, his Blackberry was accessible only for a very close circle of people. Besides, although the number of the caller was blocked, the call had unmistakably come from long distance.
Moreover, he felt that he had been connected to the Arab world.
Albeit, his connections with the Arab world were restrained to Lebanon, Iraq, and the Maghreb, the caller had been someone or an institution unrestrained in the possession of his secret number.
Besides, his closer network was all French-speaking, while those calling him just now were clearly Anglophone, not to forget that he could catch the chewing of bubblegum.
Making memories, he started returning to his desk to look for a business card while remembering a confidential meeting he had in Cairo with the president of Egypt and his Chief of Intelligence. At that meeting, a US Senator and an Afro-American lady in her forties-who appeared to be the Vice Councilor for Security of the American president-were attending. At the end of the informative conversations, Jacques spontaneously invited the two Americans for dinner at the French residence in Cairo.

* * *

During the aperitif they toasted to French-American cooperation with a breathtaking view on the Nile and the Vice Councilor for Security explained that she had just arrived from Afghanistan and was worried that the NATO partners were not progressing fast enough, thus losing public support in the US. And all this while victory seemed to move further and further away. During her speaking,

Jacques had problems not being distracted by the fact that she, from time to time, showed a piece of pink gum that she was chewing.

Thereafter, as she had been placed opposite him at the dinner table, he could observe during the entire, copious meal that she did not get rid of her chewing gum. At first, it intrigued him more than annoying him that she managed to eat a second course of prawns in a sauce of garlic butter and cognac while occasionally and totally comfortable moving the chewing gum from one cheek to another, but finally it made him nervous and he lost the thread of her story about the difference in approach between the US and the EU in combating terrorism.

Come to think of it, he suddenly feared that someone working in the security cloaks of the US or an allied Arab country might have called him just now. But why behaving so secretly and what was he to do with the remark, "We have served your cause"?

Back behind his desk, he decided to attempt a reality check and impatiently opened his computer to send a confidential e-mail to his own Security Advisor. Typing fast, he ordered the latter to contact the Afro-American vice Councilor, currently in office in Washington. He also requested his Security Advisor to use his best diplomatic skills to find out cautiously if the Afro-American Security Deputy knew anything about the whereabouts of a certain Ibrahim Orzgol, a Turkish, top-level civil servant, who according to Downing Street, disappeared during a visit to Dubai one week ago.

"Please keep it all between these walls to preserve good-neighborhood policies with Ankara," was Jacques written instruction to his Security Advisor, before he rushed out from his office and to the patio of L'Elysee, where his helicopter was already geared up for departure.

57

But long after entering the helicopter and putting his helmet on to soften the noise of the engines, the last words of the clandestine call kept on hammering in his mind and during the trip Jacques Perrier repeated to himself that there had not been any Arab connection involved in anything he had arranged to separate the worlds of his wife and her Turkish lover. So he had to keep calm.

* * *

Two hour-and-a-half later and looking back at what he used to call a successful performance as *President de la Republique* at one of his many "meet the people" functions, Jacques Perrier decided to forget about the Ibrahim case and instead to share his good mood with his wife Alexandra.

As far as he had observed in the past week, Alexandra had not shown any sign of uneasiness with him; she had never strayed her eyes away as they spoke, and although Jacques was curious to find out if she knew anything about the kidnapping of her presumed boyfriend, he avoided even the slightest hint in that direction.

Thus Jacques decided to call her at the spot and to propose to have a nice dinner together, considering that if Alexandra knew something about the kidnapping, her overall mood of the past week had been more like wanting to forget about it and reshape her life with her husband, instead of blaming him. However, the possibility that she did not know about the disappearance of Ibrahim could mean that the whole affair was already over when the man vanished. The best would be for Jacques to keep all the real subjects off limits tonight.

"Salute, Jacques, where are you?" she answered.

"I am entering the helicopter, sweetheart. I am on my way back from Gap. I will be home in about seventy minutes. Miss you disproportionably."

58

As Alexandra did not immediately react to his flirt, he continued, "I am looking back at a very good performance this evening. Polls show my strong recovery so a good reason to celebrate my comeback. Wonder if we could have a cozy diner together. I feel a second term much nearer than two weeks ago."

"Nice for you, but I may remember you that I do not consider myself bond to you for a second term," was her blunt answer.

Ignoring her mood, he insisted amicably, "My darling, we have had a thousand cozy diners together during which we had good times commenting on all the idiots we met along the day. Why change a winning horse? I promise you not only an amusing diner but also a sparkling desert. And, surprise, I have in my pocket a box of third-generation blue pills. Wow!"

A slowly defrosting Alexandra answered, "Jacques, frankly speaking, I am not interested in your third-generation pills, but I will wait for you. Do your best to make me comfortable. See you."

At the last words, Alexandra put off her Blackberry and walked over to the window of her bedroom. She actually had been lying in bed when the phone rang. Come to think of it, she was not in any mood for dinner with Jacques. She was almost sure that Jacques was the instigator of the disappearance of Ibrahim, but she decided not to say anything to him till she had hard facts, for which she had undertaken her own secret research. And although Ibrahim had at times expressed some doubts about the future of the relation, she was convinced that the probability that he had opted for a French farewell was almost nil.

* * *

Jacques private Secretary made the last-minute arrangements for the meal between the President and the First Lady with the kitchen staff of L'Elysee; something less and less common in the Palace since, as a consequence of the hectic life of the couple, joint dining was almost entirely reserved for representative banquets with official guests. The instruction to the kitchen staff and attendants were to create an intimate atmosphere in the small, blue dining room near the President's bedroom and to prepare a light, but haute cuisine, three-course meal with champagne.

So, when Alexandra arrived, the dimmers of the blue room were all on low and a dozen candles in the antique silver candleholders created an intimate atmosphere. Yet she was still not in the mood and more concerned with not seeing much in the darkness, in particular not seeing Jacques.

Without looking around she walked straight to the table and requested the attendant, "Any idea if the President is going to be on time?"

"Yes, the President will be in time" was the joking answer of Jacques jumping from the little Victorian sofa in the corner.

"Sorry, I could not see you in this complete darkness. Why have you turned off all lights? Is this your new energy policy in the residence to please the green party"?

"Sweetheart, don't be so arrant. Things are far less complicated than you think. Let's say that I simply wanted to have a comfortable dinner with my beloved wife. I have selected your favorite music."

At Jacques" last words, Andrea Botticelli's caressing voice started warming the room and Jacques called for the champagne and some exclusive canapés before inviting her to sit next to him.

Cheering up, he raised his flute for a toast, "That our good luck continues."

A sarcastic answer from Alexandra followed; "I really do not know what good luck you are referring to. Certainly not mine in the last week."

"But Xandra, look at you, look around you. You are a young woman in your early-forties. The best time of your life and you are the First Lady of France, one of the most important republics in the world."

With a skeptical look at him, she shared another prod.

"Yes, fine. That is why I have to share you with 65-million French people, who by the way are more and more critical of you. I have to see them voting you in again."

"Ah darling, stop complaining. You are not black, you are not poor, and you are not a Muslim. This means that you not only belong to the Western society as a select collective of sixteen-percent of the global population, but also to the small, exclusive peak, one-tenth of a percent of that sixteen who by the way still rule the world. Being in this position and then complaining is like defying destiny. A destiny that, Let's be honest, has treated us exceptionally well. So if I may suggest, just enjoy the evening with me, let us bring back the good, old days."

Alexandra turned off her face, took a slow sip from the flute, and started staring at the candlelight in front of her. She was upset with the fact that he had prepared this show as if nothing had happened since she informed him of her relation with Ibrahim. Even more, no doubt that Jacques played a central role in the abduction of Ibrahim. Against this background, it was annoying to sit by him with his candles and champagne.

"So, you Jacques, you are toasting on our good luck. Probably, for you and the exclusive peak of the happy few to which we belong, good or bad luck can be arranged. This sounds to me as if you all have been granted the role as the left hand of God."

"You are flattering me, Xandra. Believe me…, you are giving me far more power than I actually have. Take it from me; I am far more limited. Not only by the opposition in the National Assembly, or by some fools in Brussels, or by the whims of the Americans, but also by all the national and international rules that we have to fulfill. You know quite well that people like me are scrutinized around the clock, and darling, I hope that you keep in mind that this scrutinizing also happens with the First Lady."

Meanwhile the soup, as a first course, was served and without speaking further they both moved from the sofa to the table.
Immediately after being seated, Jacques placed his spoon in the soup and bowed it softly forward, but he pulled back surprised when the spoon appeared to be capable of standing upright alone in the viscose substance. In the next second he signed to the attendant to approach him and mildly raising his voice remarked that the soup was not a consommé. The butler was quick in his answer.

"But Mr. President, as far as I know, this is a Chinese noodle soup prepared by your new Chinese team in the kitchen. May I remind you that you recently have agreed with your Chinese colleague on an exchange of presidential cooks for three weeks?"

"So, call my guest cook. I will have to explain him something. What is his name? I guess at least he speaks English."

Within two minutes, a nervously bowing, white dressed, and pale-to-almost-yellow Chinese cook made his audience in front of the president, sure to suffer a reprimand.

"Excuse me, Lee. Your name is Lee, is not it? May I say, I have been served several-thousand of soups in my life, of course French soups mostly, but I cannot understand what you have served me today as a soup? This is neither a soup nor a cream." The president skimmed the edge of the soup's surface repeatedly with his spoon.

With a trembling voice, the Chinese cook, who hardly spoke any other language than Mandarin, answered the President.

"But Sir, this not French soup, sir. This Chinese noodle soup."

"Please, do not use the word soup for this dish. Do you know the definition of a soup? As my Catalan grandmother used to say when serving the soup at Christmas, a soup has to be minimally sixty-percent liquid, irrespective of the ingredients you put in it. Consequently, if my spoon can stay upright like now, this is not a soup. Understand?"

"But this famous Chinese noodle soup, sir! President Hu always likes this Chinese soup!

Perrier, increasingly agitated, continued pointing at the spoon standing upright in the soup as he repeated, "Per definition, a soup is minimal sixty-percent liquid. This is not a soup, and if you do not understand that, you are not much of a cook."

This was the moment for a slightly irritated Alexandra to intervene.

"Jacques, please stop it. You cannot lecture him about Chinese soups. On top of that, you speak Franglais and he speaks Chinglish so you two will never understand each other while you are discussing an irrelevant matter as Byzantium priests used to do when they were discussing on the gender of angels."

At her last words, Alexandra herself burst out in laughing, but Jacques did not seize the opportunity.

"Fine, then I will have a French soup. Please bring me a French consommé. Otherwise, bring me some caviar," he ordered the cook.

Alexandra had now laid her hand in a comforting gesture on the hand of Perrier while saying, "My dearest Jacques, there are moments like now that I really do not understand you. Are you aware that sometimes you behave to anything but the President? Extraordinary! Just like some days ago. Please, may I refresh your memory? Listen, remember your "meet the people" discussion with that rightist barkeeper in Clichy-Sur-Blois? The man was complaining that the neighborhood was being poured by brown shit of sparrows, which according to the barkeeper was the result of the sparrows being fed by the immigrants from the Maghreb with Arab baguettes. His complain was utterly nonsense and full of prejudice. But my God, Jacques, I will never forget how you seriously tried to gain political support out of such idiocy and in such an absurd way. It was a perfect piece for a theater play. Nothing more! And how I suffered a lot in those moments because I wanted to cry out laughing, but I could not."

"So, darling what did I do? I cannot remember."

"Let me revive the event for you Jacques. I will do it like a script of the play it was:

The barkeeper: "Mister President, we are confronted with a new phenomenon in this neighborhood: sparrows shitting dark in huge quantities. This is because these birds are now being fed by Muslims from Maghreb countries and with Arab baguettes."

You: "Really? Tell me more. This is another serious problem of non-Western immigrants in France. It is too bad that these people who refuse to speak good French and who dress with headscarves and burkas are now even changing the flora and fauna of our neighborhoods. But what is it about the sparrows? It's the first time I'm hearing about this detail."

The barkeeper: "Mister President, these poor birds are now forced to eat multicultural bread. That bread makes them shit brown. Before, they would have been fed with our French baguettes and they would shit white. Do we also force our sparrows to adjust to these intruders? It is really horrible. Every restaurant I enter and ask for a tea, they will ask me first if I want Moroccan or mint-tea, and even if I ask for coffee. I am first offered Turkish coffee."

You: "I fully understand your complaint. What do you suggest: no more non-French bakeries in Clichy-Sur-Blois, no more Turkish bread, no more Arab baguette, no more pitta and whatever they call it? I agree. I fully agree. From now on, bakeries in Clichy-Sur-Blois should sell only French baguettes for the people and for the sparrows alike. You have my support."

<u>Another attendant at the meeting</u>: "But, Mister President, a Moroccan baguette costs forty Euro cents and a French baguette eighty. So, I shall buy the Moroccan as long as I am unemployed, right? And believe me, Excellency; these cheaper baguettes taste fine, while at the same time, I personally did not observe any change in the color of my shit."

<u>You</u> (as you always claimed the last word, instead of laughing aloud): "The Moroccan baguette does not comply, I mean in weight and compact, with a real, French baguette. So, a Moroccan baguette is not a baguette."

"My God, Jacques, I could not keep my laughing, but I had to keep up appearances. Jacques, I have to say it, you are often just an idiot, but you certainly are my idiot!" She was now leaning towards him, closer and closer, and started caressing his arm. "In the end I could only hope that I could walk away and laugh as I am doing now."

Jacques was surprised. Unbelievable, but Alexandra's mood had totally changed and he believed she was-figuratively speaking-ready to eat out of his hands. Some pleasant though savage instinct took hold of him.

This time, Jacques" observation was correct. After Alexandra had spontaneously reflected on the Byzantium habits and the idiocies of Jacques, and she was to admit to herself that, truth be told, the life as First Lady might not always be romantic but it could be rather funny while in his own clownish way, her husband was willing to put her on a pedestal. She also knew that contrary to what she had said to Jacques, she had never been sure about leaving him. Let's say he was the boss of

65

all the civil servants in France, why would she leave him for a middle-rank civil servant in a hybrid East-West country where women were still fighting to be put on a pedestal?

The candles lit Alexandra's attractive, oval face; her artistic, modern haircut partly overhanging one eye; the rather small but well-shaped nose and her beautiful upper lip under a pearl pink lipstick matching with the bronze eye-shadow which further accentuated her big and sparkling, brown eyes. Hence, Jacques was slowly moving in the direction of her lips but he was also half-expecting her to fear up while reminding him of the presence of the serving staff in the room when the little beep of his phone broke the glamour with the honking information that he received a new message in his inbox. In putting the phone off to avoid further disturbance, his eyes caught the first line of the message originating from his security advisor: *the suspect you informed about, is already one week in an overseas Information Treatment Centre in Africa, according to trustable source.*

It was a simple but scary line which Jacques immediately was trying to move as fast as possible to the back of his memory in order to let life leap over oblivion, since almost at the same instant Alexandra surprisingly took the initiative to cover his lips with hers. The mixture of scents of sweet honey, cinnamon, and anisette overwhelmed Jacques. Her tender lips warmed his heart up and melted his mind.

Six

Voluntary federating the best and angering the rest

The Press Conference had been scheduled for Friday at 11:30 am in the ballroom of Hotel Negresco in Nice, Cote D'Azur. Actually, since the days of the Treaty of Nice in 2000, it was the first time that this elegant city in the south of France was once again hosting several, top European politicians and advisors. They all arrived sometime on Wednesday afternoon and immediately on the first evening started their negotiation on a selective and voluntary European Federation.

By now, the reader may wonder who "they" were, but this was certainly not a question for the many journalists who had already awaited the participants of the selected EU integration meeting at the airport of Nice on that rainy Wednesday. Even more, the rumors of the event had previously spread in all the twenty-seven capitals of the European Union and even far beyond.

Hence it was no surprise for the journalists at Nice-Cote D'Azur airport, be it Terminal One or Two, to register over the day the arrival of the German Chancellor and the Prime Ministers of The Netherlands, Austria and Luxemburg.

Most guests came by chartered planes and one could observe slightly stressed expressions on the faces over the complicated landing in the pouring rain: landing-gear almost touching the sea water before touching down on the tarmac amidst a strong, eastern wind.

Nevertheless, as soon as they were safe and sound in the VIP arrival lounge, all would agree that even with the sun hiding behind clouds, the grey overshadowed bay of the main city of the blue cost remained beautiful as ever. The last to arrive was the President of France, Jacques Perrier, who at a blunt question of a British journalist, "Mr.

Perrier, why have you not invited your British colleague?" resolutely answered, "Regrettably, we have not invited those who opted out from the Monetary Union."

Another journalist, challenged by the answer of the French President, remarked, "But what about the remaining twelve countries of the Monetary Union who are also absent?"
Again Jacques Perrier, walking stiff to the car waiting for him, was firm in his reply. "We will inform you on Friday why we are five and what we have agreed, if any."
Yet, his answer was not accepted by the journalists crowding around him and an Italian TV reporter decided to put things more sharply,

"Is it possible to agree on anything in absence of twelve of the partners of the Euro zone? This smells like as a *coup d'Etat*. Are "the five" here for blowing up the Union because you do not want to be in solidarity with member states in financial problems or economic delay?"
The President of France, pretending not to hear the last question, entered his car and left for Hotel Negresco where, except for a few rooms, almost the entire three stories had been reserved for the participants and their accompanying aids.
The moment the French President arrived in front of the lobby of the hotel, the rain stopped but the masses Jacques silently had hoped to see welcoming him were absent. At best there was no need for a slightly disappointed Jacques Perrier to show his IDs to the two bellmen in sixteenth-century uniforms. However, for the press conference on Friday, journalists would have to pass a second filter with probably better screening equipment than the White House.

* * *

Friday morning, the big day of the press conference, was cheered up by a hesitating, morning sun glazing over the bay in contrast to the two past days which yielded mild but persistent raining. At 10:30, the ballroom of Negresco was already fully occupied with excited journalists.

There were newspapers and TV reporters, not only from the twenty-seven member states but also from USA, Russia, China, India, Indonesia, and several countries from the south of the Mediterranean Sea including Egypt. Turkey was also represented. The room started bustling as most journalists were still puzzled about the objective of the Nice-Top-for-Five and they were left sharing rumors from Wednesday evening onwards. To pop up the expectations some journalist started broadcasting interviews with other reporters.

South African TV was asking the editor of *The Economist* to express his view on the exclusion of Italy and Spain from the top, just when the two were near to request bailout support. The answer of the editor was short and clear. Spain went too far with the housing bubble and could become practically a corpse in the coming decade.

Concerning Italy, the editor believed that in the last, two decades Italy lost gas and its electro brain scan had become almost flat.

Consequently, both countries could become an unbearable burden for the Euro zone.

* * *

At exactly 11:25 all eyes in the ballroom turned to the left side door through which the hosts of the press conference made their entrée. As one could have expected, first there was the French President Perrier, followed by the German Chancellor Ditch and, two steps behind, the

69

Prime Ministers of the Netherlands and Luxembourg with Austria closing the parade.

Immediately after the hosts seated themselves behind the table at the podium, the French President started reading the press briefing from the five initiators of the projected European Federation. Contrary to his normal practice, Jacques Perrier was reading calm and skillful, given that the text was also prepared by the five and their aides, weighing word after word.

Ladies and Gentlemen,

In the current, economic crisis and taking into account the industrial shift to Asia combined with the fact that the growth rate of the EU twenty-seven as a whole will remain extremely low and condemned to an almost jobless growth for the coming decade, we, the five countries of the Euro zone here represented have considered it high time to take a drastic initiative to pull the future of our nationals out of the dip.

Having experienced also that the governance of twenty-seven countries on the basis of consensus has become extremely time-consuming and severely indecisive, and considering that the architecture of the Euro zone is hardly operative, we, the five, most stable Euro zone members have taken the initiative to break the stalemate by working out the possibility of moving forward and setting up a political federation among some Euro zone members: those who have a real European vocation and are economically homogeneous. This is no more than our duty towards workers and employers and young and old in our societies, who since the introduction of the monetary union, have observed their living conditions and the future of their children become bleak.

During our deliberations, we have decided to also invite Italy, Spain, Slovenia, and Finland to embody in the future European Federation. So if these four Euro zone members join us, it is our intention to set up at short-term, a federated state of around 300-million people, a figure similar to the population of the United States of America and with a per-capita GDP significantly higher than that of the current EU Twenty-Seven.

In our view, the construction of a political and economic Federation of nine states containing 300-million people will have huge advantages for the participating countries such as:

1. *Economies of Integration of different branches of our public sectors, which, as figured out, would generate a saving up to two-percent of the joint GDP of the federated countries, from which one point of the joint GDP will be saved through the integration and reorganization of the current national armies into one federated army. Mentioned financial savings could be devoted to tax reductions and stimulation of jobs creation inside the European Federation (EF).*

2. *Other dynamic advantages would include a jump in research and technology to improve the productivity per hour of the workers of the European Federation without increasing working time, thus enabling a more human life for the population of the Federation.*

3. *It is our intention that the economy of the Federation moves on the coordinates of the Social Economy of Market, which means that the current social advantages, mainly pensions and insurances of unemployment and health, will converge at a Federal level into unique systems, after a transitory period of twenty-five to thirty years.*

4. *The Federation will finally enable, within its borders, the arrival of a real, unique European market, while at the same time it will provide a federal wide security net for those expelled from this unique market.*

5. *The Federation will also enable the recovery of the effectiveness and sustainability of the economic policy, thus overcoming the defective organization, fragmented policies and lack of control in public finance as practiced in the last ten years in the Monetary Union. It is*

71

well known that the coordination between the European Central Bank and the Finance Ministries of the Euro zone States has been chaotic, particularly since the last crisis started in 2008.

Ladies and gentlemen, after admitting that some serious mistakes were made in the construction of the Europe project in the past twenty years, the five countries here represented have decided to correct the direction and speed of the project. For your information, we are in full agreement that: first, the current deficient architecture of the Euro system is unworkable; second, the admission of twelve newcomers in 2004-2007, most of them lacking maturity in economic and political development although well intended in terms of keeping peace in Europe, was premature; and thirdly, that several attempts for a soft, economic, and political reorganization of Europe have ended up in an unsolvable conundrum.

In front of the deadlock, we, the five, represented member states, have, after careful deliberations, concluded that we had two options: either to continue as we are, or to set up a selective Federation. In our view, the first option would drive us towards further jobless, slow economic growth and progressive, economic divergence in relation to the USA and emerging Asia. Observe that this option and its expected outcome will be inconsistent with the economic aspirations of our nationals and will undermine the desire of our countries to continue playing a global role.

Taking into account that for the five of us the first option was a blind alley, we have decided to put in common some precious parts of our sovereignty in exchange of finally achieving the dreams of the founders of European Project. We are sure whatsoever that with the formation of the Federation, our economy will step up its rhythm of growth as a consequence of a far better governance, which will benefit the EF citizens.

And of course, the Federation will play an international, political role, much more relevant than before, according to the size and power of a big, federal state of 300-million people. Finally, the five member states here represented, declare solemnly that our Federation will be born with a vocation of integration of the Euro zone members. Although some may remain out for the time being, they will always be welcome to join the Federation, provided that they fulfill the required economic homogeneity with the pioneers.

Note also that the selected Federation is certainly not intending to abandon the rest of the EU-Twenty-Seven. Indeed, all the economic treaties signed until now by the federating countries will continue ruling with the remaining EU countries. However, these remaining EU countries will not intervene in any form in agenda-setting and decision-making of the Federation. I thank you for your patience and welcome your questions.

While Jacques Perrier was reading the joint statement, one could observe growing nervousness among the participating journalists as the majority started using their Smartphone and IPods to inform their headquarters.

The more in contrast was the silence after Jacques Perrier's concluding statement. For a few seconds, no one moved, no one spoke, no one reacted, and just when an overwhelmed Marlein Ditch reached for her bag, the audience started applauding endlessly.

At this point, a far more confident Hans Schmidt, the aide of the German Chancellor on EU matters stood up and while walking to the reading desk in the corner of the podium, signaled for silence with his hands waving in the air. Smiling happily, this time he personally claimed some of the victory. Hans Schmidt announced to the participating reporters that under his guidance they now had the opportunity to put questions and seek clarifications.

So the German advisor was fully in charge when he granted the first question to a female journalist from New York Times and the New Yorker played straight with her question.

"So finally, the magic word "federation", feared by many Europeans and worshiped by others, has appeared in a proposal for the future by two of the most powerful members of the EU. Is it your intention to become a global player at the same level as the US and China?"

This time Marlein Ditch, the German Chancellor, could finally daze with a determined answer, "Of course, this is our intention, as part of our ambition to contribute to the creation of a multi-polar, globalizing world. Indeed in the past twenty years, we have lived in a context in which there existed only one hegemonic power and one emerging challenger. We do believe that this has not been good for the social and political stability of the world. You have to accept that the more distributed is the power, the more balanced will be the global, economic progress, the more equitable will be solutions of global problems and less probable will be the abuses coming from the powerful, large countries. Next question please."

A Hungarian journalist from HTV had a question for Jacques Perrier. "Reflecting on your meeting, one may clearly deduce that France and Germany have masterminded this restrictive, federating project. Would you confirm this? And if you confirm, my second question is, do France and Germany consider themselves to be entitled to take an initiative that could exclude the majority of EU-27 countries? And my third question: is the restrictive federation a way for Germany and France to halt the financing of the newcomers of 2004 and 2007?"

Jacques Perrier replied, "Of course, the magnum projects of mankind are always planned by minorities. In relation to Europe, and from the very beginning in 1951, France and Germany have been the main animators of the different steps of the integration process of Europe. And in the current EU crisis we have again decided to take the steering wheel for changing the orientation of the project. As to your second question: for decades the EU project gained in a balanced way both geographical extension and economic and political integration. Regrettably, the EU project got derailed in the 1990s when some member states opted out of the Euro while others entered without fulfilling the conditions or even lying on provided data. On top of that, between 2004 and 2007, many newcomers have entered the EU without economically being mature and at the same time having big, financial needs. All this has transformed the up-to-the-Maastricht Treaty workable governance of former EU-12 into a consensus based unmanageable mess of twenty-seven countries with different economic positions, interests, and political ambitions. Since the financial crisis in the West, which started in 2008, it has become crystal clear that the countries of the Euro zone, for their own economic survival and to complete their aspirations, need to politically integrate into a unitary state. Finally, the mere fact that we have bailed out several Euro zone countries proves our being in solidarity with them. Even more, we do believe that the economies of scale, raised by the Federation, will result in important budget savings which will also enable us to increase the budget for economic cooperation with EU members and non-members."

The next question was again addressed to Perrier. A representative of the Italian Corriere de la Sera submitted, "Sir, what about the sovereignty given up by the member countries entering the Federation? Are you conscious that your federation project, if put into referendums in each of the nine nations at this critical moment in time, could get some majority rejections?" Perrier was visibly relaxed. The Italian reporter had put an expected question to him, one he had discussed over and over again with his advisors.

"My dear friend, in the last twenty years, we have been trying in the EU to make omelets without breaking eggs but this, as anyone knows, is impossible. We cannot be a political union and at the same time be all of us independent. In fact, the citizens of the nine countries of the Euro zone called to form part of the federation, when time arrives, will have to dramatically decide between only two options: either they give up part of the remaining sovereignty or they remain in the current stalemate. But given the fact that the referendum will take place at the same day and time in all the nine countries, a majority "no" vote in one country may mean that this country should stay out of the federation for at least ten years or more, due to the fact that we cannot build a federation with hesitating countries. And note that a period of ten or fifteen years at the current, critical moment of history has a galactic dimension. In fifteen years, our world will have changed dramatically, and if we do not radically change our political organization now, we may lose the train. The balance, you know . . . Jesus Christ!

In few seconds, while Perrier was talking, three, totally naked women, only a rope around their waists suddenly fell from the ceiling of the ballroom. The effect was stunning. Perrier could not but stare at the naked bodies in front of him: nipples affected by the exposure to cold air, flat bellies, bushy triangles, a serious sisal rode. The three women, their blonde hair covered with big boinas, started screaming in chorus, "Gora Euzkadi Azkatuta", "Long live a free Bask Country" and "Vive le Pays Basque livre".

From different corners of the ballroom, hastily German and French guards emerged as photo cameras and Smartphone's started splashing their lights while the ladies entered into the next stage of their protest and ignited small strings of fireworks.

"ETA Attack! ETA Attack!" shouted some journalists who worriedly started rushing out of the ballroom or looking to hide somewhere in case of an explosion. Some guards, now with their revolvers up, were speedily approaching the naked women and if it was not for the cool and decisive reaction of Marlein Ditch, things could have ended far worse.

"Stop, do not shoot. No one is armed" she was screaming, placing herself swiftly between the activist women and the guards. "Are you mad! You want to be killed?" she continued yelling to the Bask activists who started moving to the side door left. And to the journalists, who were busy rushing out of the ballroom, thereby almost provoking a stampede, Marlein ordered, "Please calm down. Nothing serious is going on. How things have radicalized after September 11th. These three women could have been killed for a simple protest like we all used to organize in the 60s and 70s."

These were miraculous words of the German Chancellor since simultaneously a team of four, special agents of the Gendarmerie, fully armed with automatic long guns stormed the ballroom.

"Freeze!"

As it appeared, the first journalists who left the ballroom not only informed outside guards of an ongoing terrorist attack in the ballroom, but someone also spread the rumor that the Dutch and Austrian Prime Ministers had been abducted by ETA terrorists; a rumor that in seconds had reentered the ballroom.

While everyone was freezing somewhat, a heavily sweating and completely distressed Perrier, who had been hiding under the table and lost all control of the situation from the moment the naked women landed in front of him, cautiously reappeared. Looking around somewhat bewildered and speaking to himself, "My God, the three terrorists and the two Prime Ministers are missing! What bad luck I have: two Prime Ministers taken hostage by ETA terrorists in

Nice, during a ceremony organized by me. Horrible; how will this end?"

And then directed to the Special Forces he shouted, "I am the President of the Republic. I order you to use all means you have to rescue my guests from Holland and Austria".

"No, wait, we are sound and safe." A smiling Dutch Prime Minister and his Austrian colleague were returning to the ballroom from backstage, accompanied by the three, female activists who were no longer naked but wrapped in ballroom curtains to cover their bodies. The Dutchman explained, "As you can all see, we have been using our soft diplomacy skills and convinced the ladies that they should go home quietly since the future of some regions in the Federation will be reconsidered by us."

"Thank God my guests are safe, but these three activists will have to face French court" affirmed Jacques Perrier.

Meanwhile Hans Schmidt had exited the ballroom and was trying to gather the journalists for a continuation of the press conference, but as the Spanish and Italian TV teams remarked, "Could we have any more spectacular news? First, an exclusive federation and then a terrorist attack by ETA combined with a sex show. We are going back to cut and paste for the evening news. Bye, bye."

Seven

A rainy night in Brussels

It was a dark, rainy night in Brussels, not unusual for the time of the year, but still the type of weather that would keep many people off the streets. Yet, the radio presenter of a nocturnal music program reminded the occupants of the Volkswagen Polo that it was 1:30 in the morning and that the day had long past.

The two people in the car had defied a rain storm that showed no sign of stopping, persisting for hours and hours pouring monotonously from the clouded skies. No wonder that the roads near the Grand Palace, primarily tiled with stone cobbles, had changed in a slippery, shining dark surface. Nonetheless, the young lady behind the steering wheel of the small car exposed a remarkable imprudent driving style, clearly against the logic of physics, which could only annoy the person sitting next to her. At times... compelling her to drive more careful, "My love, please slow down, you are taking us straight to the emergency if not worse," but then again almost aloof as this man had to divide his attention between the young driver and the piling professional problems he had, no one less than Bopoulos, the PressCom of the European Union, was sitting as the company of the young lady.

However, the more Bopoulos expressed concern about the dangerous driving style of Clara, the more inclined the twenty-five-year-old waitress was to speed up the engine and cut off corners by running over the pavements. Clara was showing her anger with the thirty-five-year-older Bopoulos as all initial promises concerning the future of the relation had slowly dissipated into smoke. The two had met by incidence in a bistro in the center of Brussels. Bopoulos, the president of the EU Commission, exceptionally happened to participate in the birthday party for his secretary, and Clara, a substitute waitress, young, good-looking and forthright, had been charming in a naïve way. So when Clara, while serving coffees, bluntly remarked that she had no clue what the EU was, everyone laughed. Even more, she underlined-with a broad smile showing quality teeth-that this was the first time in her entire life that she had heard the words European Commission.

Listening to her, Carlos Bopoulos was swayed and quickly offered to tell her the whole history, background, and possible future of the European Union whenever she was ready for a cup of coffee.

Much to his surprise Clara did call the next day and a date was fixed. Certainly his normally attentive secretary did not pay much attention to Clara's call as probably no one signaled any sexual undertone in the spontaneous invitation of Bopoulos to educate the young waitress on the European Union.

The truth is that the history of the EU was never explained to Clara, not on their first afternoon encounter and never thereafter. On their first coffee date, they both instinctively bypassed the EU history lesson and immediately started flirting by playful interviewing each other about their private life. Exchanging glances and warmly closing in, they talked to each other, gauging one another's proclivity for commitment. Of course, all this was not arbitrary. They were both, for different reasons, exploring the options for a more intimate encounter.

Carlos Bopoulos was staggered by the intense attraction of her young body, something he had been dreaming of from the moment he started noticing grey hairs growing out of his ears and nose, his arms getting shaggy, and the mirror in his bathroom showing the hairs on his chest becoming grey and brushy, as were his disheveled eyebrows.

For Clara, although not clear what the European Commission stood for, the mere fact that she was having coffee with a president created visions of being cared for as a princess in wealthy surroundings by an old, odd-dressed rich man. Subsequently, the initial, innocent coffee appointment on that first Thursday afternoon ended suddenly in making love ardently in the pied-a-terre of an Italian Parliament member and good friend of Bopoulos who had left some days for Milan.

Thereafter, Clara and Carlos met for more than four months, usually only on Thursday evenings, taking advantage of the fact that Bopoulos" wife, the so-called, "Duchess of Algarve", would generally go see her parents who were living in Algarve Thursday mornings and return the next day in the evening, while on Thursday the Italian Euro-parliamentarian would also travel to his family in Milan.

Yet, as remarked earlier, the intentions of the two in the affair were totally different. For Bopoulos, his double life at the weekly, one-day love encounter, which he more and more tried to limit to the confines of the pied-a-terre of his Italian friend to avoid uninvited eyes, was first and foremost to set hard proof for a man of sixty that he continued being able to seduce and sexually satisfy a beautiful youngster.

Nonetheless, his victory feeling at Thursday evenings was momentary as by Friday evening home with his wife-who was known for her remarkable, social character but uncompromising classiness-he felt increasingly ashamed and well aware of the disastrous consequences things could have if his affair would ever be known by her. The family would certainly fall apart, and with some influence of their mother, his two children could totally turn their back on him. Even more, as almost all the luxury and wealth he enjoyed in his private life originated from his wife, or better said from his father-in-law, breaking up would also have severe financial consequences for him.

Breaking up with Clara, rational the best option, seemed easier when she was not around, as the minute they would meet, he would lose rational and go for the immense satisfaction of his lover boy victory. So

81

his main challenge was to keep both balls in the air but invisible to one another.

For pretty Clara, at first sight, she was like a real life copy of Barbie-the projected scope of the relation was a more lasting one, preferably concluding with her marriage to a well-known man with a good income. So her hopes were that Bopoulos would leave his wife and secure her a more wealthy future.

As the asymmetric interests were becoming more manifest to Clara due to the lack of interest of Bopoulos to even extend their meeting days, but on the contrary opting for more and more secrecy and almost solely locking themselves within the confines of the apartment and the bed of his Italian friend, Clara started becoming less compliant on the Thursday evenings and it happened more often that she would completely lose control and would start shouting in repetition what her expectations were and that he had to leave his wife.

So that rainy night in Brussels, Clara was once again near freaking out as Bopoulos spent almost the entire evening-from the moment she picked him up at the side door of a motel restaurant in Brussels South, on their way to the pied-a-terre to making love in the apartment of the Italian, to now on her way to drop him off again-making endless phone calls over a subject she could not and did not want to understand. She was outrageous over his lack of attention for her company and the words popping up repeatedly in his phone conversations, "federation" and "PIGS", caused her temper to flare. So, when he warned her to slow down on the slippery road, her tone became scolding and her behavior hysteric. "I have given all I have, Carlos, but you are too fucking egoist to even worry about my feelings. If it is not your work, it is your wife. If it is not your wife, it is your Commission. I am only good for Thursday evenings in bed behind close curtains. Go to hell!"

The more she screamed, the harder she hit the pedal. Carlos was trying to calm her down by speaking softly. "Please Clara, slow down, the roads are slippery. You will kill us both".

"You would deserve that. You have taken everything from me. It is time for your wife to know the truth. I am tired of playing cat-and-mouse with your Federation nonsense."

"Please Clara, slow down."

"I will if you leave your wife and marry me. Say it, say it now."

As Clara raised her voice even more, his phone started ringing and the car started slipping. Carlos, with his left hand also on the wheel, was trying hard to keep the car on the right side of the road when there was a loud bang followed by a human body, presumably a man, flying over the front of the car followed by the remains of a bicycle that was crushed under the front left wheel. Clara's screams were blood-curdling, but slowly ebbed away.

In the total silence that followed the crash, Carlos Bopoulos saw his future as in a movie falling apart: first, his wife walking out on him; next, his children hatefully accusing him; next, his office staff making a mockery of him; and finally Clara changing into a hysteric witch. Only this last image was real since the road accident provoked an explosive wrath in Clara.

While no longer accusing her of reckless driving, Bopoulos had to make all efforts to cool her down and drag her from behind the steering wheel. She started blaming him loudly for the accident and her whole, misfortunate life. It was his refusal to commit to her that made her to understand that she had to give up, to move on and run away. She was screaming. Although the streets were rather empty at this time of the night, some people living in the neighborhood heard the bang of the crash and started looking through their windows while calling the police. Considering the short arrival of police and emergency services and perhaps even a delayed journalist, Bopoulos was painfully aware of his possible recognition which could be followed by an exposure to awkward questioning. And of course, the appearing journalists would focus on the fact that he was in the company of a hysterical youngster who easily would be identified as not his wife. This could severely damage his career as well as his family and all that just for not controlling his aging hormones. Thenceforth, he understood that he had no other choice than to quickly disappear from the scene and as far as possible away from the hysteric youngster.

A few cars were already passing by the place of the accident, rolling down windows, and observing the details of a fresh crash with probably one victim. Misfortune over misfortune, one of the cars, having a diplomatic plate, was driven by the British Consul who a couple of minutes before abandoned a disco-bar in the neighborhood. Instantaneously, the Consul identified Bopoulos, the PresCom, in a heated debate with a young woman who certainly was not the so-called "Duchess of Algarve" meters away from the bleeding victim. The police had not yet arrived.

In a bright second, smelling scandal, the British diplomat decided to pass and stop his car around the first corner, got out, and walked back stealthily to observe what was going on.

Meanwhile Bopoulos regained his calm and was trying to overrule Clara to solve the accident business without him.

"Dear Clara, you were driving. So you are responsible for what has happened. Please, you have to explain things to the police when they arrive, in particular that you were alone in the car. It would make things worse, also for you, to say that you were with me. You hear me, you were alone! We will meet tomorrow and I will compensate you abundantly, so please do not spoil my career. Be assured, I will compensate you generously, very generously!"

Although Clara did not fully believe what he was saying-remembering that he often had remarked cynically that, "promises were to be broken", she decided to go along by saying to the police that she had been driving alone. Maybe this would change her position with him for the better. And besides, spoiling the career of the president of the EU Commission, although she was only vaguely aware of what it stood for, could also be inconvenient for her future, not in the least since from now on he would owe her.

"Okay, you can go, but where do we meet tomorrow?" was her quick and calm reaction. Carlos Bopoulos confirmed an appointment at midday at a café in Grand Place, although it was passing his mind that the next day, first thing in the morning, he would have to be in Strasbourg and thereafter in the afternoon and evening he would have to share his time with his wife and children in the residence in the historical Sonian Forest in Brussels. He could not escape any of these arrangements. The meeting in Strasbourg with the European Parliament was about a financial support for Ireland and hence utterly important as was the family dinner with his two daughters, all university students, who as usual would be traveling home from campus in Gent and Paris to share family life for at least one weekend. This was something their father insisted on, supported by his wife even though Carlos was sure that she would have enjoyed passing the weekends with her parents in Algarve.

* * *

Eleven minutes after the accident, an ambulance and a police patrol arrived on the spot to find the nervous, young waitress in tears explaining that she, being aware of the slippery state of the cobles, had been driving very careful and all alone on a dark, rainy night in

Brussels when, all of a sudden and out of nowhere, an unfortunate cyclist crossed her path, probably he himself in a slip with his cycle. Although Clara did all she could to avoid an accident, he ran into her car and severely hurt himself.

"What misfortune for both of us," she ended her story wiping of tears from her innocent, sparkling, blue eyes.

As there were no eyewitnesses and the cyclist was in coma, her story seemed to convince the two policemen. The elder among them even started apologizing for the misfortune that the Greek goddess Ate, daughter of Zeus, installed on poor, little Clara and offered her a glass of water brought in by one of the neighbors while all the bystanders, including the British Consul, attuned in nodding their heads and sighing that such a poor, little girl did not deserve such misfortune.

The ambulance people had already picked up the victim-who as they explained was in very bad condition and one should pray for his life-and left for the nearest hospital. The policemen hereafter invited a much calmer Clara to accompany them to the police station for deposition, but they both repeatedly explicated in full harmony with the bystanders that Clara had nothing to fear and suggested even that she was already acquitted, while the second-hand Polo, an hour earlier recklessly driven by annoyed Clara, was towed away.

* * *

In spite of the smoothness of police handling at the accident spot, for Carlos Bopoulos things worked out less fortunate. First, the British diplomat did not go home when the spot of the accident was cleared, but instead at nearly 2:00 in the morning, he returned to his office to report to his level at the Foreign Office, but with copy to the High Commissioner, over the things he had witnessed past midnight near Grand Place: the involvement of the EU PressCom in the company of a young woman in a car accident, the flight of the PressCom before the police arrived, and probably under instruction of the PressCom, the make-up of the story by the youngster in order to wipe off any involvement of the PressCom. This led to the closing comment in the report of the British Consul that the car accident probably coincided with a case of adultery by the PressCom. This event, according to the written comment of the Consul, would certainly have a tail and one should see his report as wagging the tail in order for the political staff at the embassy to scan for more information, and henceforth the interpretation of possible consequences.

* * *

Bopoulos, from his side, continued his flight from the scene by jumping into a cab and ordering the driver to just drive him around on the ring of Brussels till further instruction, and not as the readers might have thought, to his residence in the Sonian Forest, close to the center of Brussels. Carlos Bopoulos preferred to quietly reflect how to escape the problem of hysteric Clara having him now somehow in her grip.
And of course, he would have to find a way to avoid any damage on his career and on his comfortable family life. How was he to divide himself between the three constraints awaiting him tomorrow? What an idiot a man could be in front of sexual attraction! And then, what was he to do next? First and foremost, he had to get rid of the waitress in good harmony, regardless of the cost. Perhaps a job as some low-ranking assistant in an EU Delegation office in Ouagadougou would help.

* * *

Things got even more complicated when Bopoulos was woken up on Friday morning by his Blackberry ringing. The call came from none other than the British Prime Minister.

"My dear Carlos, sorry for disturbing you so early but knowing you will be flying to Strasbourg, and things being urgent, I took the liberty to intrude on your privacy. To put things straight, I have to ask you to immediately convene a meeting for at latest on Monday with the European Commission. It is on the issue of Nice and the proposed fractioning of the European Union by France and Germany, that is to say, on the issue of the five to nine voluntary federation, clearly aimed at sidelining the UK."

A sleepy Bopoulos walked to the closet with the Blackberry between his shoulder and jaw. On the way, he took his shirt from last night from the dress boy and he routinely started checking his collar on lipstick stains next to smelling the shoulders to disclose female perfume, his routine on Friday morning in order not to alarm anyone.

Meanwhile listening to the Brit, his first reaction was to take away any prominence of the Nice rendezvous of the five EU member states by calmly answering.

"Let me be frank too, if I were you mister PM, I would not give much importance to the issue. Nothing concrete will happen. The whole thing is too complicated! I have to see these countries progress a single step forward in the development of a political federation. The best would be to wait and see. Believe me, it is highly unlikely that the citizens of even the initiating two countries, France and Germany, having been enemies again and again for the last ten centuries, will finally give up a serious part of their sovereignty-remember that they even talked in Nice of integrating their armed forces in exchange for just promises of a more prosperous future."

"I'm not so sure about what you're saying Carlos", was the quick reply of the British PM who continued. "Correct me if I am wrong, but I think that they may be right in their economic appreciations at this very moment of globalization and economic slowdown in Europe. To form a federation of nine countries, as they have expressed in Nice, would give them an immense potential. This would be a community of 300-million people with a very high level in human capital and infrastructure. And it would give them space for weighty positions in international issues, which certainly could also cause fractions in the, till now, unitary positions of the West in international affairs. You will agree with me that in a time in which the economies of China and India are churning out, the West should not become fragmented, neither economically nor politically. Believe me, if this federation proposal would change into a fact, our American friends-and I know this first hand-would feel rather offended as the federation, which perhaps would have been useful in times of the Cold War, now may result very counterproductive."

"Yep, I could not have analyzed things better, but our union of twenty-seven states, which I proudly co-manage as head of the commission-and this is also thanks to past, full-fledged, British support to my candidacy-represents a market far wider and stronger with all Europeans in their distinct, cultural history, united under one, unique project. Indeed, I am so convinced of what I'm saying, that I promise you my full cooperation to abort this plan for the creation of a selective federation of the nine. But as I said before, no need to act now. We should not start shooting our cannons to kill ants."

"Dear Bopoulos, prevention is better than curing. Even more, I suggest you to urgently make all efforts to dissuade Italy and Spain from entering the club of the five core countries. I would not have called you personally if things were not urgent. By the way, dear PressCom, I have received information from my High Commissioner in Brussels of your unfortunate car accident last night. I hope you have resulted unscathed. You were not driving, I understood".

His last remarks struck like a bomb. For seconds Carlos Bopoulos was speechless. Someone probably not only had seen what had happened, but had already leaked it into diplomatic circles. He would give a fortune to know who else was involved, but knowing the rules of the game he reacted with composure.

"I may have overlooked some things, I am sorry. I will have to deeply rethink the issue of the five-to-nine federation, and of course I am most willing to order an urgent meeting of the commission on Monday in order to jointly analyze the different alternatives in front of us".

"My dear Carlos, I will be happy to hear the outcome. In the meantime, convey my warmest regards to your better half".

After ending the conversation with the British PM, which left Bopoulos with an acid taste in his mouth, he had a quick look at his missed calls. He recognized the number of Clara and, before going into the bathroom, he decided to immediately delete all messages in his voicemail without listening to them.

In front of the mirror, while brushing his teeth, he had a closer look at his face with the two, deep-set dark eyes. He had grown older overnight since, even after taking two tranquilizers, he had remained awake, turning from one side into another.

But, there was no time to lean back now that things were closing in on him. Slowly he started weighing the options he had for today and in the near future. Perhaps he could keep things secret for his wife, but this would mean that he would remain feeble in the hands of the British and anyone else they would inform while there was a chance that Clara would try to find a way to inform his wife.

Indeed, a constant pressure from these two sides could seriously affect his health as he was suffering from high blood pressure for already more than a decade. Besides, he had no clue what could happen if he would inform his wife of his affair with Clara. In all the thirty years of their marriage, his wife, or the Duchess, had never hidden her conviction that she would return back to the family castle in Algarve if things did not work out to her satisfaction. And more than once she had explained to Carlos that her bossy father repeatedly hinted that he was in standby to help reorganize the life of his daughter, if her Greek husband was not behaving. Carlos Bopoulos did understand the threat of his father-in-law, repeated also towards him, be it in a more subtle formulation. It would not only have financial consequences, it could also hurt his career.

The reader should know that the father-in-law of Bopoulos, known among friends and family as the "Duke of Portugal" was actually not a duke and his daughter was not a duchess either. In reality, the old man was a retired banker who, after leaving his posting in Swiss at the age of sixty-seven, settled with his shrewdly procured wealth in an impressive castle in Algarve.

And the retired Portuguese could well afford himself the aristocratic nickname, "Duke of Portugal" since he was not only a very wealthy man, but also a person with highly influential friends among entrepreneurs, politicians, and bankers in most countries of Europe. Not surprising since, besides belonging to a historically influential Portuguese family-with Jew ancestors who in times of the rule of the Augsburg in Spain and Portugal had become bankers of the Castile Crown-the Duke of Portugal had in the first years of the Second World War succeeded in becoming vice president of a bank in Swiss. A success directly related to the fact that he had been one of the masterminds of opening the bank to "foreign gold deposits".

Although not proven, Bopoulos was aware of rumours that his father-in-law could have been one of the bankers facilitating that Jews could secretly deposit gold. Most of these Jews had never come back to request their savings as they lost their lives while their inheritors could not be traced or did not possess any proof of the existence of the accounts of their ancestors and consequently some middle men became the final gainers.

False or true, the position of his father-in-law as vice president of the bank had over the years provided him with innumerable contacts with people who after the war had ended, reached important functions and positions in all the governments of Central Europe, particularly in Holland, France, Germany, and Luxembourg.

So after the war, the man was endowed with a network of contacts covering almost all important persons and positions in the war-torn continent. This gave him the opportunity to act as an independent host for the secret meetings in his residence in Zurich between top French and German civil servants, all in preparation for the European Cooperation institutions that preceded the EEC and subsequently the EU.

No wonder that when Bopoulos married the only daughter of the "the Duke of Portugal", his father-in-law instantly helped him to climb up, first in the Greek administration and later in the European Commission in Brussels. All this meant that Carlos Bopoulos had to count even harder with the old man to solve the mess of his affair with Clara.

Finally, there was Clara. She might at first have presented herself as a spontaneous, naïve, and adventurous youngster with no strings attached, but along the four months of their Thursday sex affairs, she slowly changed into a spoiled and angrily pressing beauty who wanted to get good value for her attractive appearance, even by settling with an old, presumed rich guy.

Summing up, he had caged himself and escaping was not going to be easy. Looking at his decadent image in the mirror he started speaking to himself, "Well, well, who could have imagined that such an intelligent, strategic, life-loving, and charming man would end up being sandwiched between three attackers? And that for the petty prize of enjoying a young body?" While shaving, he finally decided not to decide, to leave the things just as they were-although progressively getting rid of Clara-and trusting his own good luck which always favored him during his career.

At his arrival at the office in the Rue de la Loi, PresCom Carlos Bopoulos already devised a strategy to block the embodiment of the two, main, southern countries into the voluntary Federation of nine as initiated by the five in Nice. Best for him would be to visit the top leaders of the two countries at stake beginning with Spain. If he left today for Spain immediately after the meeting in Strasbourg, he would not have to meet or talk to Clara, nor would he have to face his wife and daughters.

* * *

But once again Ate, the goddess of misfortune as Carlos learned in primary school in Athens, had put her desires on him. Little time after arriving in Madrid in the afternoon, actually immediately after shaking hands at the Palacio de la Moncloa in Madrid, the Spanish Prime Minister informed Bopoulos that after the revolutionary gathering in Nice of the five Euro zone countries and their challenging final declaration, things had drastically turned around in Madrid and Rome, and consequently Spain and Italy wholeheartedly decided to form part of the selective Euro zone Federation initiated by the German Chancellor and the President of France.

"Believe me, Bopoulos, having read the project of Marlein and Jacques as presented in Nice, I first became silent though deeply impressed and finally I turned into a fanatic supporter of their very timely project. The world is changing and so should we. I'm convinced that they are right. I'm also grateful, and so is my cabinet, that they have invited Spain to form part of the federation of nine. Certainly to belong to a state of 300-million people with a common army, a common Ministry of Finance, etcetera, is something that the Spaniards will appreciate as you will witness in the corresponding referendum"

"So, you are abandoning the boat of the EU-27 to join the German-French adventure. Have you also considered that if the federating project fails it will blow up the whole EU-27 project in exchange of nothing? It seems to me not a very rational initiative."

"My dear Carlos, I think that at this historical moment, Marlein and Jacques have found the correct roadmap for our continent. I agree with them that the European Project as it was developed in last decades, had already years ago entered in a blind alley. Really, our current organization, although it may make that some member states-those who recently entered in the union, I mean in 2004-07-felt happy with their embodiment, the reality is that today with the issues of unanimities and different speeds of embodiment of newcomers, it is very difficult to almost impossible to take any decision and move forward. Indeed, of late, we have only succeeded in issues of international trade while our international, political capacities have practically not progressed in the fast-changing world we live in. And this means that if nothing is done, we will continue with our current decadence while we lose track of main, global developments and fight among ourselves over marginal things. I feel too responsible to my people to leave things untouched."

Bopoulos felt growing anger as he was listening to the Spanish Premier and he considered with some disgust that some months ago this same man had been defending a federation of the four, just to get more power within the EU-27. Could one think this man to be trustable? Or was he just someone playing to the best bet, irrespective of principles?

As the Spanish Premier observed some concern in the face of Bopoulos, or perhaps repulsion, and taking into account that the PressCom was Greek, and Greece was not in the list of nine, the Spanish leader even dared to make one of his typical summersaults by offering Carlos Bopoulos a bargain.

"You may imagine that when the new federation becomes a fact, there will be a new common nationality and passport for the citizens of the nine federated countries. In my view, up to now you, Carlos, have acted as a European citizen and you therefore would deserve to be among the first to receive a real European passport as a citizen of the Federation. However, being Greek, the only way out for you would be to apply for the Spanish nationality as soon as possible. And I can assure you now that I will personally see to it to happen. Let us not forget your new nationality would also create opportunities for you in reaching once again a top-ranking, civil servant position in Europe, this time in the federation of nine."

He continued, "I say nine since you may have heard dear colleague that the other three invited countries have already informed Spain of their considered positive reaction to the extraordinary opportunity offered by the five of Nice."

A depressed Bopoulus, incapable of grasping why his breaking attempt on instigation of the British PM was bound to fail, had only one last question, "Do you the federating countries really believe that the rest of the current EU members, in particular the more powerful like the UK, will take no action against your group? Do you think that the British will do nothing? Just remember that when finally the CEE was created in 1957, the British reacted by creating EFTA. And why would they not attempt to construct a simple, common market with the rest, or with a selection of the rest, and thereafter renegotiate the common market rules with the federation, excluding f.i. movements of people?

And do you think that the Americans will be happy with your exclusive club? My friend, do not forget, your federation could damage unity in the West!

"Carlos, I suggest you to be realistic. Instead of opposing the formation of the federation of nine, you should try to convince the others that far from losing, they will all profit from the existence of the federation of nine. It will be far more prosperous for them to remain in a position of common market with the federation"

* * *

When Carlos Bopoulos left Moncloa, Madrid enjoyed splendid spring weather and the streets were bustling, full of jolly people, but he felt deeply down in the dumps. He was to board a plane for Rome at 8:30 pm, but instead, accepting his defeat, he took one for Brussels at 9:10 pm, well aware of the fact that he still would have to face his wife-a late sleeper-around midnight.

* * *

Early Saturday morning, a broken Bopoulos finally arrived at the Sonian Forest residence. After a gruff farewell to his driver and a surly hello to the guard, he entered the house. At every step in the corridor underway to the living room, he was fully aware of the fact that he would have to overcome a lot of difficulties to fulfill the will of the British PM to stop the formation of the federation of nine. Not to mention the other problems in his private life.

Carlos Bopoulos found his wife impatiently waiting for him in the living room and with yet another set of unanswerable questions.

Sitting at the edge of the sofa in the spacious living room, the "Duchess" hardly answered his quick greeting kiss, but affectionately started explaining to the still-standing Carlos that from seven o"clock onwards on Friday evening, a certain Clara repeatedly called to the residence and asked for him. The housekeeper first explained to the caller that Mr. Bopoulos was not home and that, for business-related issues, the PressCom preferred calls to his office in the Rue De La Loi, where there would also be a weekend service telephone for urgent matters.

However, at the sixth, stubborn call, once again patiently and also unrelentingly answered by the housekeeper, Madam Clara had become rather hysterical and insisted that she in that case wanted to speak immediately to Mrs. Bopoulos. Of course "the Duchess" refused when asked by the housekeeper, but this did not stop the undisclosed Clara from calling over and over again. Actually, her calls did not stop until the "Duchess" gave permission to the housekeeper to take the phone off the hook at around ten.

As his wife gently explained, it crossed her mind to call for the police to stop the stalker, but something told her that it was better to leave third parties out and to wait first for clarification from Carlos.

At her last words, the Duchess pierced her light brown eyes in the dog-tired eyes of Mr. Bopoulus, at which wacked Carlos, with his shoulders down and sweat running in his back, could do little more than begging his wife to let him clear up the issue by tomorrow, amplifying that it was certainly not what she was thinking but that he was too exhausted now to touch the story of stalking Clara.

Carlos Bopoulos hastily explained that he mistakenly had left his high blood-pressure pills home when traveling to Madrid, and that he should be going to the bedroom to take one immediately, and added that Madrid had also been a disaster.

"Please darling, if you do not want me to drop dead right now and here, I beg you, let me go upstairs for my medicine and give me time to explain things tomorrow. Believe me. It is not what you think and it can wait till tomorrow. I am sorry for the trouble it caused and believe me, I am exhausted."

Without awaiting her confirmation, he stumbled up the stairs to their bedroom.

Eight

From Russia with Love

The banquet and dancing offered by the Russian President in honor of the German Chancellor in the Kremlin's Catherine Hall was about to start when Marlein Ditch got the shock of her life. Of course she highly appreciated the whole glamorous event in the Kremlin and she was well-aware that this gesture of the president to her was somewhat over prescriptions from protocol, but neither she, nor the Russian President would deny a certain warm sympathy in the way both were filling in the Russian-German relations, which taking history into consideration, was almost a paradigm shift.

Although the Chancellor of Germany was on a bilateral working visit to Moscow, the Russian President offered her a state banquet for which he invited G-20 ambassadors and the top representatives from the Russian society: political leaders of three parties, the business community, bankers, the academic world, religious leaders, and even some famous artists: musicians, dancers, film actors, and writers.

Actually, the Russian President invited the same group as he usually invited for the biggest party of the political calendar in Moscow: Kremlin's New Year's banquet in which some 1000 guests would socialize and network while enjoying exclusive food prepared by twenty top cooks from all over the world.

It was Marlein's first visit to the antique and artful, decorated area of the Kremlin Palace, and as she heard rumored, the palace had recently been restored by the current Russian President to its 1906 decoration and design by the last Tsarina, Alexandra Feodorovna, wife of Nicolas II, the last Tsar of Russia.

Although not showing, a rather impressed Marlein agreed that after the toast of the Russian President on her behalf. She would in a short speech explain to the guests the why of the voluntary federation and what would be the positive opportunities for the Russian society once the nine candidate countries would have made the leap forward in their political integration. Of course, Marlein was not planning to say more than trivial statements since the referendum was still pending, but saying no would have been impossible after the fruitful, German-Russian deliberations of the day for which both parties spent their precious time in a remarkable, open atmosphere.

* * *

Looking back, the one-day program was well-invested. After a working breakfast in the Germany Embassy in Moscow following her arrival at 8.45 in the morning at the airport, Marlein Ditch left the Embassy for a first meeting with the Russian Premier accompanied by the German Ambassador; advisor Hans Schmidt; and Peter Baum, a top, German diplomat specialized in Russian issues.

As usual, the first meeting started with looking into the future perspectives of Russian-German trade and investments, in particular gas and other raw materials before touching down on foreign relations and international politics.

Since about eighty-percent of the exports of Russia consisted of raw materials and half-fabrics, particularly petrol, gas, and globally scarce minerals, German interest was to balance the Russian raw materials exported to Germany with exports of luxury cars and other exclusive manufactures to the Russian market.

One should not forget either that the absolute number of billionaires and millionaires living in Moscow and St. Petersburg was one of the largest in the world. Marlein shrewdly informed the Russian Premier that the expectations for Germany were good in relation to investments and budget cuts already done, which together would continue triggering growth in Germany in the midst of the ongoing financial crisis in the West.

In fact, this information of Marlein was against the advice of Hans Schmidt who, during the preparatory breakfast, pointed out that, in the next-quarter, the economic growth rate of Germany could converge to the average low growth rate of Europe.

So all went well in the first meeting, but it is fair to say that for Marlein, the big thing was yet to come: deliberations with the Russian president, something she considered the summit of her working visit.

* * *

No wonder that punctual Marlein felt embarrassed when the delegation arrived almost an hour too late at the Kremlin, but the delay should be attributed utterly to the complete failure of the escorting police. These four, Russian policemen on heavy Chinese motorbikes were outright incapable of smoothly leading the delegation through the horrifying traffic jams near the Red Square. Clearly, no Russian car, bus, or motorbike driver was even slightly impressed by the four policemen in their somewhat over-decorated uniforms nor was any attention paid to their gesturing with arms and hands in order to make way for the two Mercedes Benz with diplomatic sign plates and country flags.

Most cars and busses did not only completely neglect the somewhat conflicting signals of the four policemen, but also aggressively continued looking for any small space in front to quickly move in, thus transforming a four-lane road in six to seven rows of cars, closing in on each other and constantly changing lanes. Thereafter it was simply impossible for anyone to move an inch forward.

"It is absurd, they should all be stripped of their driving license" was the repeated snappily remark of the German Chancellor to aid Hans Schmidt, while looking at her watch to find that they were already forty minutes or more too late on appointment.

Were it not for the Russian President-who broke the ice at their arrival with a lively narrated story of a police escort in Palestine-Marlein would have held consultations with the President tied up to the roof with nerves. The Russ told them that when he was visiting the Occupied Territories last year, the policeman escorting his car, had half-way run out of gasoline and his motorbike suddenly halted in the middle of the road, after which he was literally scooped by the car he was escorting. Luckily, the policemen survived with only some scratches while they all watched his motorbike falling from the cliffs.

So while the whole delegation was in laughter over the ridiculous accident, Chancellor Ditch restored herself and the session took off with some polite exchanges.

As soon as the routine was over, the Russian President cut short by expressing his real interest in the German-Russian consultations.

Surprisingly, this was not related to the Israel-Palestine issue, or with the recent developments in the Arab world, and not even with the financial crisis in the West or the Euro instability, but it dealt almost exclusively with Russian economic interests on the North Pole.

In brief: as the economy of Russia was still mainly driven by the export of raw materials and given the fact that climate change was progressively making possible the exploitation of huge deposits of raw materials in the North Pole, the Russian President was interested in knowing the view of Marlein Ditch concerning the ownership of these deposits.

According to him, Russia with its two-hundred-mile zone along the coast of the North Pole was without any dispute one of the main owners of these deposits, but much to his concern, the Russian President had noticed that countries with less linear coasts such as the US and Canada, seemed to believe that they were in their right to exploit the wealth of the entire Pole, irrespective of the length of their lineal coast on the Pole. Even more, Denmark, using theoretical rights on Greenland was queuing with the claimants. And then Britain and Iceland, having hardly a coast to the Pole, had also appointed themselves as candidates to accede the supposed rich stock of raw materials hidden under the ice cap. Having explained his concerns, the Russian President had put a direct question to the German Chancellor.

"Dear Marlein, soon the discussion over this issue will have to arrive at the UN since this would be the only way out of the conflicting interests. So could you, without going into detail, enlighten me at forehand on what position Germany will take? Would Germany support the Russian position? Would you abstain? Or would you support the doctrines that is basing ownership on the order of arrival of the exploiters to the territory and on their exploitation capabilities? Let us not forget that this doctrine had in the past resulted in many bloody wars in times of colonialism. Something no one should want to repeat."

Marlein was taken by surprise. It was the last thing she would want to discuss during her visit: risking to disturb German-Russian relations on an issue with little direct German interest, but great German concern in terms of protecting the planet.

Putting all her charms in the bascule, she answered, "My dear friend, really you have caught me on an unprepared domain. So let me give you my personal view since this issue has yet to be discussed in my Council of Ministers and the German Parliament. And if the European Federation is alive and well, the issue of strategic raw materials will be high on the agenda of our international policies as will our concern with sustaining the environment of our planet. But for now, frankly speaking, I think that although in the current UN legality the Russians would have a majority ownership right, if we seriously consider the new environmental and social circumstances of the world today, we will be forced to globally reschedule ownership and exploitation of natural resources, irrespective of whether they are in the seas or on land. Not in the least because the exploitation of natural resources of the North Pole will become possible only if we continue with our suicidal global warming and hence the reduction of the iced surface of the Pole. By the time we have reached that state, I fear life on the planet may have changed so much that even exploitation of the deposits at the Pole could become irrelevant.

On the other hand, the parallelism observed in relation with the race for the wealth of the North Pole-consisting of rushing to take advantage over the others without any general agreement or concern on the issue-reminds me of the so-called "Scramble for Africa", in which the Western countries-including Germany-distributed sub-Sahara Africa among themselves in an urgent, imprudent, and irrational way and without any knowledge or concern about the geography and sociology of its inhabitants. It was blatant colonizing euphoria and nothing less."

"Come on Marlein, I do not think that the German concern over global warming will be sufficient to stop the ambitions of the interested countries to start exploitation. On the other hand, I have no doubt that the global warming problem will be rebalanced very soon by using technologies now already well under research in Russia. Do not forget that the quality in research comes from the quantity and the absolute number of Russian academic graduates is currently higher than in any other European country."

"If you don't mind, Mr. President, I could introduce a different argument, the social one. Taking into consideration the fact that the global population has multiplied almost per three in the last sixty-five years, and will continue to grow, production and prices of strategic raw materials cannot be dependent on the will of a single country, or a group of them forming a cartel, let alone from multinationals and speculators.

This is an issue so serious-provoking numerous economic disturbances in the last forty years-that the production and distribution of strategic raw materials will have to be controlled by the United Nations."

"Marlein, should I expect Germany to say so because you are destined to stay out of the Security Council club of permanent members? Anyway, I would be able to agree with you, but only on one condition: real power sharing in the United Nations. Do you really believe that production of the Russian oil reserves should depend on a UN dominated by the West and western interests? Russia could only agree with you, with Germany, on the condition that this UN would be democratic. And you, Marlein, know what this implies: that the West, currently with only sixteen percent of the global population, would lose control of the UN. Do you think that the West would give up its current, oversized, international power and the profits stemming from it in exchange for nothing?"

"Of course," answered Marlein, "I am not talking in terms of the next five to ten years, but current economic trends suggest that in around twenty to twenty-five years, the economic and military dominance of the West could be over without being replaced by another dominating region or nation. As you and me will both be on retreat by then, I can only dream of how things may evolve. But my dear friend, as usual it has been a great pleasure for me talking with you."

And so the bilateral consultations between the two countries were over faster and in greater harmony than expected, and Marlein and her team could sigh released and prepare for a joyful evening in the Catherine Hall of the Kremlin; but it was there that Marlein got the shock of her life.

* * *

As Hans Schmidt, aid for European affairs, explained to the Chancellor on their way to the party, the Banquet Hall had undergone a huge facelift ordered by the current, Russian President, who probably wanted to bring back the glamour and chic of the pre-Soviet days.
Even more, his example had been followed by the Russian society.
Not only the hall with its eighteenth century ceiling paintings and decorated arches; its high roof windows, some with glass in lead and others with heavy brocade curtains; and chairs and sofas in Louis XIV-style, had been recovered and upgraded with a winkle to the days of Nicolas II, but also the dresses of the women, accompanying their husbands this evening in black tie, portrayed that the Russian ladies had seized the opportunity to glitter in Tsarina-style. Consequently, on the evening offered to her as chief guest of honor, Marlein Ditch was sadly condemned to look more plain Jane than ever, although for the first time she had dressed in pink Thai silk with a for her style very remarkable low décolleté and a fancy collier with some small stones.
During the reception in anticipation of the diner, some guests were personally introduced to the German Chancellor by the seemingly rather popular Russian President and Marlein managed to use some socializing words in Russian she still remembered from her days in school in Weimar. Meanwhile the Russian Symphony Orchestra was sweetening the memories of the guests by playing romantic, Russian composers including Modest and Tchaikovsky and the colorful guests, greatly wrapped in rustling chiffon, were sipping on glasses with cocktails based on vodka, while mingling around.
So, love was in the air when the President announced, with a jolly smile all over his face, that he was going to introduce Marlein to someone very dear to him. This person was the most successful Russian businessmen of the post-Jeltsin period, and besides his ancestors originated from Germany.

106

And there he was! Friedrich Greber, Marlein's former husband from Dresden, was standing eye in eye with the German Chancellor. For at least ten seconds, Marlein froze and had to make strong efforts to recover breathing. Friedrich, looking rather well cared with a body shaped by sport and elegantly dressed, introduced himself to her as Friedrich Pechov and his Russian wife, a stylish blond on extremely high heels, as Anastasia.

"How very nice," Marlein said quietly while slowly coming forward. Friedrich took her hand, raised it to his lips and bowed, before humbly waving away the compliments of the Russian President over his success in business and his outstanding support for cultural events in Moscow.

"My support is not more than my duty as a citizen," Friedrich said,

"but meeting the Chancellor in person tonight is for me a real honor". And smiling at Marlein he continued, "Madam, I am overcome by your performance in meetings and press briefings. You really are the most convincing and the most involved of all political leaders of the European Union." "You are flattering me, Mr. Pechov.

But really, I would swear we have met before," a fully recovered Marlein asked sharply as she gave Friedrich an understanding smile.

Friedrich, looking around first at the Russian President and perhaps also at his wife Anastasia was careful in responding, "Yes, come to think of it, must have been some thirty years ago in Minsk. You, Madam Chancellor, if I remember well, were participating in a youth championship of athletes and I was a young freelance trainer who had been contracted contemporary by the team from the German Democratic Republic, as one of the official coaches fell ill." Friedrich was now looking mainly at his wife and the Russian president while he was trying to hide the former intimate relation with Marlein. Crossing eyes with Marlein, he continued, "What days they were. No one could dream in those days in the stadium of Minsk that Germany would years later be united, or that the small *Osi* girl fighting for the trophy would finally become the Bundeskanzler for East and West."

Marlein replied sarcastic as it was clear to her that Friedrich did not want to recount their past. "Equally, who would have thought in Minsk that the young trainer for some days would become a millionaire in oil? I am very impressed."

And then smiling mean, she decided to give him a low blow. "Dear Mr. Pechov, excuse me my blunt question, but have you also been capable of profiting from the fast privatization in Russia during the transition under President Jeltsin?"

It sounded false even in Marlein's own ears and she started looking at the hands of Friedrich and his Russian wife to detect, as unnoticeably as possible, if the couple was wearing marriage rings. Of course they did! The word bigamy crossed her mind as she was looking straight into the eyes of the now rather uncomfortable Friedrich. They had never filed for divorce and they both were aware of that at the very moment of Marlein's mean remark.

"Madam Chancellor, as you may well know, the privatization or dismantling of state firms under president Jeltsin was for the full one-hundred percent policy devised by IMF and WorldBank, the so-called Washington-consensus. These policies, stemming from the so-called international society, were simply imposed on the Russian society. So tell me, Madam Bundeskanzler, who profited most, the Russians or the international speculators financing Russian intermediaries?"

Friedrich was losing control, something also noticed by the Russian President who hastily introduced a new guest to Marlein in order to stop further quarreling between the two.

* * *

As the table setting clearly dated from before their mutual, verbal aggressions, Friedrich had been honored with a seat at the main table and opposite Marlein, be it two places away to the left. But as the overwhelmingly French dishes on the menu were served-*blinis au caviar beluga; fois gras, daube de bœuf a la Beaujolais, tarte au fromage et pommes en Calvados*-they could easily avoid any eye-contact between them.

In her speech, made just before the last course was served, Marlein called upon Russia, its government and its active population to support the European Federation in the making as it would create greater opportunities for stabilizing Russian exports to Europe and perhaps one day the cooperation would result in a common market.

The Chancellor's words were welcomed by the guests with an ovation and a second toast at which Friedrich reached out to touch her flute. A sign of settling for unconditioned peace, which he had decided to repeat by asking her to dance with him at the moment the third Viennese waltz of Joseph Lanner was played by the orchestra some time after the last course.

During dancing they did not speak, but as he appeared to be a well-experienced waltz dancer, she hung elegantly in his arms, and with her eyes fixed to a detail of a ceiling painting she gave herself fully to be led by him and becoming slightly lenient by the mixture of the musk scent of his aftershave and the cognac he was breathing out. For a fraction, it was like the first weeks of their life together in Dresden when she still fully trusted him.

So on the way back to her chair she became entirely willing to listen to his warm voice. He remarked, "Marlein, I think the best for us is to keep me dead. I am now Friedrich Pechov, a naturalized, Russian businessman, married, and with two, adolescent children. Any other format would have negative consequences for both of us."

Marlein was flabbergasted by the cold way in which Friedrich broke the enchantment. He solely seemed to be interested in averting problems with his wife. And of course, she was also surprised by the fact that he seemed to know that she had announced him dead when she forced him to step out of the relation. As to the bigamy business, he was clearly not interested in that. So, she nodded without saying a word, thus giving him the conduct in the conversation.

"Besides Marlein, have I told you that you are looking gorgeous tonight and that you have become a great dancer? I have sincerely enjoyed our dancing." And my dear Friedrich, have I told you that you have become an even greater liar? You must be on cloud nine with your new family wanting to keep the truth out? What about your women hunting addiction?"

"Marlein please, do not be mean for no reason. That is not you. I have become a cheerful, respected, sophisticated businessman and you have become the German Chancellor. What else would we want? Please let us burry the past tonight forever. Would you accept my invitation to be guest of my family in our residence just some meters away from the Red Square before you return to Berlin?"

"No Friedrich, not at all. Are we to sit with your wife and lie? As you have remarked just now, let us forever lay our joint past to rest. And let us both never more say to anyone that we knew each other in our past lives. It is probably for you no problem to live in bigamy, is it?"

"Do not use this ugly word, Marlein. After so many years, it would have no value in any judicial system. After killing me, would you now be resurrecting me? Starting clearance would have more negative consequences for you than for me. I take the deal. I will, from now on, say that we met for the first time in the Kremlin because you should not think that you will never meet me again. I will be in Berlin next week to meet your minister of energy. So a decent solution would be: *It has been a pleasure to meet you, Madam Chancellor and my heartfelt thanks for the opportunity to dance with you*".

As they were now in hearing distance of the guests still sitting at the tables, Marlein softly and restricted murmured, "It is a deal, Friedrich; from Russia with love."

Nine

A birthday party in the Basque Country

By and by, the summer was arriving at L'Elisée and Jacques Perrier had acquired a bronze tan that matched well with the sunny weather in Paris. However, his tan had been picked up overseas, as the couple had made an official trip to Martinique on the occasion of the official memorial service in Fort-de-France for the famous French-Caribbean poet and politician Cheshire. This man was to be the first black French politician and artist to be honored with one placate in the Pantheon.

Alexandra, French First Lady and herself being a writer, had gladly accompanied Jacques, something he highly appreciated since it was well known that he and Cheshire had been on bad terms for more than a decade as politicians who were almost on different ends of the political spectrum. So Alexandra, with her charm and impressive knowledge of colonial and post-colonial history and art had been of great help to Jacques in encountering the friends and relatives of Cheshire under the wicked eyes of French media, and in bridging the lack of sympathy of the black Caribbean community for the President of the Republic. Even more, thanks to the good behavior of Alexandra during their touring in Martinique and Guadeloupe, the press reporting of the trip of the President to the oversea departments was not only mild but unvarying positive.

Accordingly, Jacques Perrier was in an excellent mood when the couple returned and as Alexandra did not show any sign of being upset with him, Jacques felt released to conclude that his problems, one after the other, were already on track for resolution. The fact that the former lover of his wife had vanished without any political cost or personal implication and surprisingly ended up in the strong hands of the transatlantic friends further supported his euphoria. Then there was also the hazard of the Southerners, the PIGS, which had been dissolved almost automatically when Italy and Spain enthusiastically agreed to abandon the PIGS faction and enter into the Federation of Euro zone countries as proposed in Nice. And although there were some adverse reactions to the European Federation, mainly from Britain, almost all editorials of important newspapers, including London-based weeklies, reminded the British that they themselves took a sideline position by rejecting to join the single currency a decade ago. Definitely, the Americans seemed to be too busy with internal budget quarrels between Democrats and Republicans and the growing influence of China, to get involved in political events in Europe.

Only one thing kept worrying the President of France and tempering his good humor: the affair of his mother with a married man in Paris who also appeared to be an old official of the Legion Etrangére. No wonder that Perrier seized the opportunity of the celebration of the eighty-first birthday of his mother to travel to Bayonne, the city of his childhood, in an attempt to set things straight.

Thought and done. Jacques Perrier left Paris in the very morning in his official airplane, under the pretext of inaugurating a "new" five-star hotel directed by an old schoolmate. This hotel had, after minor reconstruction, changed its former name -Hotel Belle Vue, into Hotel de la Federation-immediately following the press release in Nice, thus proving that the owner had a sharp wisdom for business.
Having finished the official act at 12:15 and after checking by cellular that Alexandra was at friends in Paris, he was quickly driven to the birthday party which was to be celebrated with a lunch offered in a picturesque restaurant at the outskirts, some four kilometers from the old centre of Bayonne at the seafront of Anglet. The three-story restaurant was built on cliffs with on one side a wonderful view on the

Atlantic Ocean, and on the other side looking down on the historic city of Bayonne with the Church of Saint André, the Synagogue, the Basque Museum, and the great Gate of Spain all along the meandering Gascon River.

When Jacques Perrier made his entrée, the party had already started and much to his surprise was pepped up with around thirty people standing in groups, bustling and full of laughter with champagne glasses in their hands in a reserved spacious room at the top floor of the restaurant. The room had the best view in both directions and Jacques noticed that because of his participation, the restaurant was duly but discretely examined by the Gendarmerie.

His mother, clearly the *grand madam* of the party was dressed in a lilac, deux piece with light, purple lace and covered her grey hair under a spectacular Elizabeth Taylor hat with an attached artificial bouquet of lavender flowers and yellow daisies.

"I had hoped you would come, mainly as a dream not to disappoint myself, but here you are for real. Welcome my son, I am honored and so are my friends. Dear friends, may we welcome my son, the President of the Republic!"

She spoke loud and clear and had now all the attention of the participants, which forced Jacques to say something, even if his words would be worth little more than twenty-five, potential votes. After expressing his appreciation for the long-lasting friendships his family had enjoyed in Bayonne, he ended up by pointing out that in a few months from now, Bayonne and Anglet would become border cities of the European Federation, the new state of 300-million inhabitants.

After a fresh round of champagne and canapés served with both Basque and Perigord flavors, and after Jacques toasted to the health and wealth of his mother, an impatient Perrier Jr. made a first rushed attempt to take his mother apart for some minutes in order to talk about the Legionnaire affair, but failed as she resolutely refused.

 Slightly annoyed by his insistence to have some minutes alone with her in the middle of her birthday party, she quickly got rid of him by means of introducing him to a couple of Tunisians, who many years ago had become French citizens, and had lived since then as neighbors of the Perrier family. Mr. Suleiman, a sixty-one-year-old man was a medical doctor and his wife Leila of fifty-eight was proud to announce that she was a professor of Contemporary History at the University of Toulouse, faculty of political science.

Suddenly, Jacques, following his political instinct, forgot for some minutes the leitmotiv of his participation in the birthday party and started a conversation with the neighbors of his mother about the so-called Tunisian Jasmine Revolution, a political process which resulted in overthrowing already two, dictators in the Middle East and North Africa. A remarkable revolution since its overthrowing power was formed by popular street protests of mainly unemployed youngsters, mobilized via Facebook and Twitter. These uprisings of youngsters were rapidly spreading throughout the Arab world and, although in essence welcomed as a wave of democracy almost similar to the one in the former Soviet Union and satellite countries, Perrier observed a strong tempering in solidarity among his constituency in France. This happened from the moment that large groups of economic refugees started leaving North Africa for Europe in particular for France and Italy.

In order to update his insights in the problem, Jacques Perrier swiftly decided to invite the French-Tunisians to go out with him to the balcony to enjoy the views and the refreshing breeze from the ocean.

Without any preamble because-as he proclaimed from his first sentence-he was very concerned with the unexpected migration flows after things politically improved and the dictators were thrown out, and so he requested the guest of his mother for some sort of personal advise. It was fully logical-he affirmed-given the historical implication of France in Tunisia, independent from the French only since 1956, that Tunisians were attracted to immigrate to France; but that would have been more understandable before throwing down the dictator then thereafter. Just at the moment when things had become far more promising to join hands to build their own country democratically, people were risking their lives to flee to Europe. Without any pause, he directly requested the doctor and his wife.

"My dear Mediterranean friends... imagine you are me. Tell me, how would you explain to the French society that we should give asylum or safe haven to thousands of young Tunisians who have actually stopped being endangered by authoritarian government? And then just at the very moment in history when unemployment in France is also hitting young educated French. To make things worse, it is a fact that young Maghrebians who have been living for decades in the outskirts of Paris are making life in these areas more and more unsafe and unpleasant for the original French population. I simply have no clue."

The medical doctor was overwhelmed and speechless but his wife, the historian was ready to react.

"Mr. President, the news we receive every day from Tunis are frankly still very worrisome. Demonstrations continue, successive, provisional governments have fallen, political parties make extremists remarks today and deny their remarks tomorrow, single-issue interest groups pop-up daily: pro and contra Sharia, pro and contra scarves, pro and contra privatization of public firms, etc. Clearly, the country will not be stable for the coming five years if not more. We were all happy the first days after the flight of the dictator, but as the French have themselves experienced, in some few days after the euphoria, things appeared to be much more complex. Let us not forget that it took almost one-hundred years in France and many bloody battles among different interest groups, before the French revolution resulted in a sustained democracy in the country. Today in Tunis, I am sure things will not take another one-hundred years, but much will depend also on the outside support. And to be frank, that worries me most. Real interest in developments is very short lived in our days of modern mass media. In some hours, news items could completely disappear not only on TV screen but also on agendas of parliaments and governments with huge negative impacts on aid and solidarity."

While Mrs. Suleiman was talking, Jacques was becoming more and more impatient and as he sensed some accusation towards him at her last words, he interrupted her rapidly but joyful, "But, Madam, all sounds to me like an academic speech; are you lecturing me?"
In reaction the black eyes of his mother's neighbor perforated Jacques friendly smiling brown look, and with a slight rise in her voice she continued, "I would not dare lecturing you Mr. President, but please, let me explain. I remember visiting Tunis some years ago. This was for me to speech at a UN seminar titled, *Roads To Sustainable Democracy in the Arab World, The Roads of Tunisia*. After the seminar in which quite a number of civil servants participated, I had a very interesting lunch with the two women who initiated the seminar.
These two women had written a paper on global experiences with sustaining democracy in developing countries in an evolutionary and not in a revolutionary way. Starting with analyzing necessary and sufficient conditions for democratization processes to sustain, they distanced themselves from, for instance, the Iraq experience of external military interference. Learning also from the French revolution they proposed a step-by-step involvement of international cooperation in countries where some necessary conditions were fulfilled like in Tunisia. More than other countries in the region, in Tunisia some important development goals had been achieved such as the participation of women at the labor market, and reproductive rights.

But as the two ladies explained to me, one could compare the democratization process with a plane taking off. While taking off, all seatbelts have to remain fastened, but when the plane has reached its cruise level, the purser will announce the possibility for passengers to free themselves from their seatbelts. Similarly, as these women explained, at initial take off in a country after independence, some seatbelts could be tightened in terms of liberal politics, for instance forbidding political parties which could cause factions, but if thereafter not released timely, stability would not remain. The two women predicted in their conference document that the protests against the ruling one party was going to increase fast as the redistribution of personal income had too long been limited via patronage to rank and files of the ruling party, while more and more educated youngsters were unemployment, food prices were rising, and access to modern media was denied. Consequently, it was better to loosen the seatbelts step-by-step in the development plane of Tunisia, because if not, a more radical change could also cause throwing the child with the bathwater.

But the two women were shouting in the desert as the opportunity got lost. Mr. President, as things are now, we need far more help from France and fast."

"Madame, please, you have missed some crucial points. First, we French did help and are still helping Tunisia. From the independence onward, yours has been one of the countries receiving the biggest chunk of our development aid budget. And not least than 800,000 Tunisian immigrants live and study in France, of whom almost thirty-percent are unemployed enjoying social services and other benefits to which they originally did not contribute. But enough is enough. When is our historical debt over? Do my children have to compensate wrong doings of their ancestors in the nineteenth century? Absurd! It is time for you, the former colonized, to take on own responsibility for your life and future." Jacques spoke slightly irritated and probably had raised his voice, hence it was Mr Suleiman who, having kept silent till so far, was ready to intervene, "Please Mr. President, my wife and me are full-fledged French citizens and our reaction to your question is a reaction of compatriots, even if we sometimes express ourselves in a way which seems as if we were still immigrants."

Mrs. Suleiman stubbornly claimed the last word by adding, "As the French society still enjoys the fruits of colonialism, they will have to share opportunities with former colonies in order to create win-win situations. If you allow me, Mr. President, I have to stress that most colonial powers for long-took capital (raw materials and lives) and now are hardly willing to pay the interest. Note, Mr. President that refusing to pay interest for capital taken is contrary to the normal practice of capitalism."

Luckily the *grandee dame* arrived at the spot just in time to restore peace at the balcony by explaining with a big smile, "Dear friends, my son is himself an immigrant, so do not worry. He is very much in favor of multicultural France as we all are. Actually, if I would now ask all my guests to tell me where their grandparents or great-grandparents originated from, we would suddenly find out that the whole gathering here is multicultural with grandmothers or great-grandfathers from Sweden or from Germany or from Vietnam or from Italy or from Croatia or from Spain or from Lebanon and so on and so on. So not a big deal, if we add Tunisia or Egypt to the list. Jacques, dear, let my guests enjoy the good food I am offering and let me enjoy your company for the little time left because such is the life of the mother of the President of France. She hardly sees her son other than on the television screen."

Mrs. Suleiman said, "No problem, Mrs. Perrier. I just wanted to establish an interesting dialog with the President of the Republic. For me it has been an honor and an opportunity to talk with your son. And perhaps, I silently hoped, he would agree with my opinions."

Jacques, a little bit puzzled by the indecisive discussion, and remaining with neither a direct answer to his question nor a tête a tête with his mother on her affair with a married man, finished his drink, and was about to see himself out even before the guests joined the table, when suddenly his mother joined him in leaving the balcony.

Softly speaking, he remarked, "As I said before, Mom, I will not stay for the lunch, but could we have a little chat for a minute?"

"Depend on what it is about. Tell me."

"I need to talk about your adventure with that man from Cahors."

His direct answer embarrassed her, so much so that her head first hurriedly turned to left and right to make sure that no one was overhearing any of his words before she somewhat aggressively whispered, "These are things of my privacy and you have no right to enter in it."

"Yes, as long as it does not interfere with my career! As my mother you are also in the spotlight."

"So is your wife. Please stop this nonsense. I will not answer your questioning as I consider it offensive. Truth be told, I will not talk about this but with my confessor, Father Martin."

"Mother, you don't understand how hard people play in politics. Even Father Martin could make and break, perhaps unwillingly, by incidentally placing some generic observations without quoting names and sources-thus preserving the essence of the confession secret-which at the end of the day, and after some investigation, could lead to me and provoke severe cracks on my political career."

"My dear son, you are the President of the Republic, but you have no power over my private life, particularly after all these years without visiting me. I will not forget this. What do you think, that you may force me to do this or that, because it is of convenience to you, when I personally may count with just 1300 days more of average life expectancy?" The two of them had now arrived in the room with the tables set for the thirty guests, which was still empty. In the faraway corner they continued murmuring their unfriendly conversation.

"At least you will have to let me know what Father Martin has advised you in relation with the Paris issue."

"Do I have to tell you that Father Martin has his canonic secret obligations, and my sins are only known by God and I. Father Martin is just a very safe intermediary; I fully trust him. And I will not continue with this issue. Really I cannot understand why you have come to my birthday celebration to spoil it. Why do you seek to make me feel nasty at my eighty-first birthday with all this questioning on something belonging to my private life? Business finished.., no more words. If you ask me, your career seems to be more in danger with the problems you have with your wife. Some weeks ago, Alexandra called me to say-something that I could not understand well-that you were doing terrible things and that you were possibly involved in the elimination of a Turkish politician. True or not-I have never trusted writers since they often confuse reality with fiction-you had better give your attention to her instead of on my presumed, committed mistakes. This is my thing and you should keep your distance. Perhaps time for you to confess my son."

The last remarks of his mother were a shot in the rose. He was unpleasantly touched by the fact that Alexandra had called his mother and suggested that he was eliminating love competitors. Who was imagining things, his wife or his mother? Best would be to let bygones be bygones. "Mom, do enjoy your party and forget all I have said just now. A kiss, please! " With a warm embrace and passing his hand palm softly over her cheek, he said farewell and felt sorry for the fact that he had somewhat misbehaved by first being impatient with the Tunisians and thereafter putting pressure on his mother to discuss something she perhaps herself felt ashamed over. Mission impossible! Oh, how would he have loved to just have a dive in the beautiful sea and swim away as far as possible!

Ten

Blunt Truths in the Spanish Parliament

If anyone had told Hans Schmidt that he would one day hold Chancellor Ditch in his arms and lightly kiss her ear, he would have laughed over so much fantasy and so little sense. One should know that, with the exception of his mother, Hans Schmidt had kept the other gender at great distance all along his thirty-nine years. So the closing in did happen, be it by incidence, and consequently thereafter he felt somewhat bruised by the sharp corners of reality.

All started with the fact that his boss, Marlein Ditch, agreed to personally address the Spanish Parliament two hours before the latter would have to vote on the draft constitution of the European Federation. Parliamentary agreement with the Federal constitution in all nine candidate countries, with voting occurring simultaneously at the same time and day in all nine parliaments, was the first step.

Thereafter an all member-states-wide referendum would give the societies at large the chance to participate more directly, paving the way for the takeoff of the Federation with a caretaker government. Ten months later the first, federal elections would follow, creating the opportunity for the federated societies to democratically elect a federal parliament and to form a first government of the European Federation.

Learning from history, the Spanish Prime Minister had accepted the suggestion of the German Chancellor to organize an information-exchange parliamentary session in Madrid before the voting and with herself as guest-speaker. Indeed all the leaders involved in preparing the Federation were well aware of the risks of a rejection vote in

Spain due to the highly complicated Spanish governing system and the weak financial situation in the country, not to speak of the ongoing protests of outside parliament opposition of young unemployed.

"A bad result in Italy and Spain could send us down the boulevard of the broken dreams, so to speak," Marlein repeatedly expressed in different conversations to Jacques Perrier as well as to her aid Hans Schmidt. She had clarified that the dream of constructing a state with around 300-million people under one federal government, who would be in control of the federal finances, socio-economic, foreign policy, and security needs and expectations of the collective would vanish like a soap bubble in the hands of a child if large candidate countries like Spain or Italy would go their own way, merely as a consequence of internal, political turmoil or misunderstandings."

"I am not so worried by the Italians-Frau Ditch would continue explaining-because, frankly speaking, though most of them are overtly inclined to superficiality, the Italians have a sixth sense-a sense of survival-that has guided them ever since the times of the Roman Empire. In my experience, they are generally more interested in maximizing pleasure over the rest of civilization aims, particularly in comparison with for instance Dutch and Germans so I consider that if they in any moment have entered in negotiations with the Spaniards over a Southerner's Union, it was just because it would have given them the opportunity to exercise leadership in that group. But today, having given warranties and offering them the selective federation project, their participation in the European Federation will actually save them from their own inclinations to superficiality and liberate them from their unstable internal policies with all its negative outcomes up to the recent past."

"Voila, Marlein, so what you consider worrisome is the case of Spain, is not it?" Jacques replied, giving the German Chancellor the opportunity to restate her slightly-biased opinion on Spanish governance. But Frau Ditch remained very steadfast in her strong opinions.

"Gentlemen, Spain is a country sociologically inclined to the left and to the siesta, even at sunrise. We have experienced this even these days when our team had to call to the Spanish Ministry of Foreign Affairs for feedback on the classified draft-constitution. Until ten in the morning, no one responsible answered any phone at the ministry. And then again, let us not forget that Spain is a country partially divided between the so-called historical communities and the rest.
Perhaps one should be Spaniard to understand the commotion among communities. As far as I know, many historical communities are self-proclaimed candidates to be future mini-states, though with no feasibility at all. This is in particular true for the Basque autonomous community. Let's not forget that although there are many regional ethnic groups in Europe who proclaim their uniqueness, the Basques in Spain are among the few who have taken up arms and use terrorist attacks to fight for their independence."

"Marlein, you are right," Jacques answered. "By the way, you remember how shocked I was with the sudden appearance of these three naked Basque ladies in Nice. We do have to contain Spain's participation in the Federation in a right way. Really, you should go and speak to them in parliament in your own outspoken and intelligent way."

Aid Hans Schmidt, letting aside his slight embarrassment over the blunt and somewhat stereotyping remarks of his boss, had taken the liberty to add, "According to our ambassador in Madrid, some of them, those from Bilbao, the main, Basque city, use to say-half-yoking-that they are the only ones in the world that have been born where they wanted. Also according to our German ambassador, the legal Basques political parties have been utterly intelligent in using the ETA threat in their negotiations with national parties in the post-Franco times when establishing Spanish democracy. I have also understood-although we will seriously have to check it when the European Federation is established-that the Basques do not pay taxes in net terms to the central government. So the Spanish army, foreign representation, and other national, public goods are for free for them and paid by others."

"Jacques, wish me luck. Hans help me! I will have to find the right words to clarify in Spanish Parliament that neither the Catalans nor the Basque, nor any other regional ethnic group in any of the candidate federating member-states, be it the Friezes in Holland, the Sorbs in Germany, the Corsicans in France or the Laps in Finland, should dream of becoming an independent member-state in the context of the European Federation. And of course we will continue and improve the protection of the cultures and the languages of all ethnic communities in the Federation, but it would be totally against the spirit of the Federation to give independence to breakaway factions. We are building a Federation to improve and simplify the administration, thereby creating economies of scale."

Was it not for another volcanic outburst in Iceland with ash clouds causing hundreds of flights from Berlin to be cancelled, the German Chancellor and her team, consisting of aide Hans Schmidt and two, tall, and bold security guards would have left for Madrid in a jetliner and the whole story of Schmidt accidently kissing her ear would never have happened.
But with the ash clouds throwing their dark shadows over the European sky, the Chancellor insisted on taking a high-speed train from Berlin to Madrid. According to the Secretary of Frau Ditch, the alternative of a long drive in car would be a bad signal to the public,

so short after the German Cabinet banned nuclear power stations and was calling for less cars and more public transport. And although it was on his lips to inquire about the airplanes, Hans Schmidt meekly prepared for early departure from the Hauptbahnhof of Berlin.

* * *

Probably, Hans Schmidt was the most humble, civil servant of the German Ministry of Foreign Affairs. Being a career diplomat going into forty, he was extraordinary content with the fact that he had been appointed to assist the German Chancellor in all issues concerning the European Union for a period of four years. Son of a German ambassador, it was his mother who had insisted that he should join the ranks of the Foreign Service, but probably not with the intention that her only son would become a well-dressed, super-intelligent recluse, building his private life entirely and obsessively around papers, books, theaters and wines, and apathetically avoiding contact with the other gender.

By the time he was nineteen, Hans had left for campus in Bonn while his parents were enjoying their new posting in Kuala Lumpur, including the residence with the luscious garden full of mango trees and various types of palms.
But by the time he was twenty-two, his visits to home in Kuala Lumpur were overshadowed by complaints and self-pity of his mother, the ambassadress, who was fighting against the fact that her husband prematurely entered the age of decline.
As she repeatedly explained to Hans, "Your father is going off.
Though both his cholesterol and his blood pressure have been diagnosed too high, for which he was overwhelmingly medicated, he refuses to moderate his gin and tonics in receptions, and

consequently we regularly have to depart shortly after arrival, with him being soaked in his head and at times also in his pants. And then there is the problem of his acute memory failures. I am partly doing his job together with his secretary, poor woman, but I do not know how long we can hide his fall out for headquarters in Bonn.

Nonetheless, the more legless he is, the more he hangs out the young provocateur he once was, making statements and expressing opinions fully anti-system or becoming a playboy by underhand pinching the Muslim waitress.

I really do not know where this will end. It is highly excruciating. I fear the worst for his career as he still has another seven years ahead. Really, I am afraid he will have to pass these seven years as a wreck in the basement of the Ministry, ordered to make reports no one will ever read, if even he can make them.

This is not what your father deserves, after all the hardship we suffered. Remember us moving from hot to here every four years, including hostile places like Dhaka, Mogadishu, and Karachi. Too much stress, too much uncertainty, and too much adjustments under very unstable circumstances, not to mention the heroic involvement of your father in humanitarian assistance when Dhaka was flooding and his attempted peace negotiations in Mogadishu with bullets flying all around him. Few people back home are aware of this. That is the tragedy of diplomatic life. For most people back home or at least for many journalists, who, when having to fill their columns, nastily and recklessly will portray ambassadors as nothing more than well paid party-goers reporting gossips in classified messages, your fathers job is useless and too costly. This is very unfair."

So it was odd that just in those days of severe complaints of his mother, she also started pressing him to apply for the Foreign Service, which he did, be it with the adjustment that he had decided not to complicate his life with forcing any partner to have to observe the monsoon from behind second quality windows, while the overpopulated, dirty city was experiencing its next electricity power-cut.

* * *

With satisfaction Hans Schmidt noted at the Central Station in Berlin, that everybody arrived well in time to board the wagon, the first of the train, reserved only for the four of them on their journey to Madrid. The Chancellor-dressed in a marine blue coat, skirt, and with a pearl necklace-arrived at the platform in the company of her driver who carried her small suitcase into the wagon, while she came over to Schmidt and gave him a friendly touch on his upper arm.

"All set for the big challenge ahead, Mr. Schmidt?"

"Yes Madame Chancellor, including as you may have seen from my reporting, a summary of the parliamentary history and the built up of the 1978 Spanish Constitution."

"Ach, ach, how serious you are, Hans Schmidt? I did not mean content, I meant personally: packing, saying farewell to your family, enjoying a good breakfast. We have a lot of hours to travel, more than enough time to prepare."

Luckily the last call for boarding released him from answering her unusual friendliness, and they rushed over to the steps to enter the train, she in front of him.

It is there that it happened. She was waving at her driver and talking to Schmidt with one foot on the first step and the other at the platform when the train suddenly moved and she fell backwards, right in the arms of Hans Schmidt. While screaming anxiously and wrestling with her hands in order to hold on to something to not fall, Hans, who also had lost balance, tried to put her back on her feet. As she tried again to restore her equilibrium, her head and shoulders changed directions and his lips softly touched her ear, not once but twice. It was his closest experience ever with a female stranger and pretty weird as she was his boss. He was aware of his blushing when he managed to put the Chancellor down, save and almost sound in the entrance of the wagon.

The first, two hours of the high-speed train trip were passed in silence. Marlein Ditch had placed her slightly swollen ankle on a cushion at the seat opposite, and had closed her eyes. Was she in pain?
The security guards had taken position near the entrances of the wagon, and were mainly looking outside at the landscape, which at times was passing by so fast, that one could hardly distinguish a thing. And aide Hans Schmidt, still feeling uncomfortable, had positioned opposite the Chancellor, but on the other side of the corridor, reading a document but from time to time stealing a look at his boss, wondering what she would be thinking.

"Hans, have I read well in your report that the majority of Spaniards, up to eighty-five-percent, vote for the two main national parties in general elections. Is this also the case in provincial elections?"
He had instantly veered up to show his attention as the Chancellor continued, "This would mean that the so-called autonomist parties-some of them even rallying for independence of their regions-are simply political opportunists. I was surprised to read that in the last decades, these parties have sometimes supported the Spanish central government, enabling the formation of parliamentary majorities when the winning national party did not gain a comfortable majority in parliament. This gave these small, autonomist parties the opportunity to act as balance of power." Losing his last bid of shyness over the boarding accident, Hans replied, "Yes Madam Chancellor,

even to the absurdity of "contra nature" coalitions in terms of the left-right political contrasts or centralist-decentralist clashes. For example, the opposite interests of coalition parties in government are served in such a way that for agreeing with a law, completely contra the orientation of the regional party, the local community may have received some absurd tax reduction or central financing on a totally unnecessary infrastructure project. In simple words, bribes are paid for support. As I understood, things would have been far better if in 1978 the representation of regional parties in the Lower Chamber in Madrid were excluded and if instead these regional parties accommodation were organized by creating a political Chamber for Autonomic Regions, be it with limited competencies. It would have spared the society continuous shameful logrolling in parliament and it could have made governance more effective; perhaps, resulting in even less unemployed and less wandering immigrants."

"Herr Schmidt, as the course of history cannot be changed-she had her eyes remarkably twinkling-we will have to use all that is useful with imagination and ignore the rest. Perhaps the Spaniards will understand from my frank presentation tomorrow that the European Federation could offer a new opportunity for them, a second chance to reform their defective governing system towards a more sustainable democracy."

"Madam Chancellor, I suggest you also to pay attention to the M-15, the outside parliament opposition, I mean the movement of the many unemployed youngsters."

"Hans, we are all having this problem in Europe. I am afraid it might even drift towards Germany. What am I to say?"

"You could advise the Spanish politicians to look around. Note for instance that the employment situation in the Netherlands is far less extreme. In the past decades, The Hague introduced some creative and flexible labor policies; Spain could perhaps learn from that. And besides, the mere fact of Spain joining the Federation will give some respite as job opportunities will be up-scaled in some ways."

"Of course Hans, but provided, that Spain does not enter into the Federation with its dirty clothes still on. We will have to challenge their willingness to change the current, Spanish political style of maximal self-interests, long before the referendum and the following simultaneous voting to elect a Federal parliament and government in the nine countries."

* * *

When the German Chancellor entered the Spanish Parliament building the next morning, her ankle was bandaged and she was staggering a tad. Aide Hans Schmidt was walking one step behind carrying her briefcase. However, her grey-green eyes were sparkling and once again she had intentionally painted her lips. All-in-all, she was ready for the chase.

At first, the Spanish Prime Minister and the President of the Parliament received her and immediately took her to a room annexing the Hemicycle. As usual, the Hemicycle was the location for voting laws and hosting other inspirational parliamentary events including extraordinary plenary sessions with chief guests of honor.
The Spanish Prime Minister decided to first introduce the German Chancellor to the chairpersons of the parties in parliament, before all would be moving into the Hemicycle with the rest of the 350 representatives. The Cabinet and the media would also be present.
Hence, in the small room with its walls partly decorated with dark, wooden panels and partly with seventeen century painting in gold-plated frames, the German Chancellor was being welcomed by the party leader for each of the twelve parties in Spanish Parliament.

These twelve politicians, mainly man, were sitting at a large round table with coffee served in elegant porcelain, and all were observing Frau Ditch with interest as she hobbled in. First they politely stood up to await her seating before sitting down again, but remarkably no one rushed in towards her for a more familiar welcome such as shaking hands or embracing.

To break the ice, Marlein started talking even before taking seat,

"Ladies and gentlemen, thank you for inviting me to your deliberations before voting on the federal constitution. What a surprise for me to count just now that Spain has twelve political parties in parliament. Remarkable, as you count with only half of the population of Germany. This seems to me very challenging, but at the same time extremely complicated. Imagine, the Bundestag having twenty-four parties for my government to deal with. I would go mad."

Aide Hans Schmidt had got a little worried with Marlein's no-nonsense start, but was shortly after released when-with some delay due to awaiting the translation-all twelve started laughing and the Prime Minister, chairman of the Labor Party, rebounded.

"Madame Chancellor, we cannot deny that having twelve parties in Spanish Parliament is complicated, but what would you think of the ten parties in the Dutch Parliament with 16-million people. The Dutch example extrapolated to Germany would mean that the Bundestag would count with sixty parties, not to forget that in Holland one can find in Parliament even single issue parties such as a party only for defending animal rights."

The new round of laughter sounded much louder and aide Schmidt, remembering that he had advised the Chancellor to bring in the Netherlands as a good example, be it on tackling unemployment, started bothering over the further developments, when the

Chancellor, showing full recovery, replied, "You may be right about Holland, and we are learning from that in order to design the terms for admissibility of parties in the forthcoming, federal elections.

Believe me, if our projected federation at nine progresses-and I have come here to promote it-I think that in parallel with slimming of our national administrations, with responsibilities transferred to the federal level, we will also have to slim down across countries on national, provincial, and local representations, halving at minimum the number of representatives; and if I may say so, in your case, the representation of regional or so-called autonomist parties in National Parliament. As I will explain later, only federal parties will be admitted to participate in the federal parliament, no national, regional, or single-issue (based on ethnicity, gender, age or whatever) party will be entitled to run for election."

"But Madam Chancellor I have to remind you that the high number of parties in Spanish Parliament has to do with the fact that our country is a decentralized country", answered the Prime Minister.

"Yes, too decentralized," Marlein ironically replied. "I have heard, you may correct me if I am wrong, that you have seventeen autonomous communities, served by councilors who often, in numbers, far overtake the number of ministers of the central government, and even may earn salaries and bonuses well over the salaries of your ministers in Madrid. I have also been informed that at the time of Spain"s democratic transition in 1975, the country counted with a maximum of one-million civil servants, and today one is confronted with a figure of three million. Or to make it clearer, between 2007, at the start of the financial crisis in the West, and today not less than 300.000 more civil servants joined ranks at the different levels."

During the reaction of Marlein Ditch on the remark of the Prime Minister, a growingly nervous Hans Schmidt, sitting behind the Chancellor, was flexing his fingers. He had expected outspoken critics from his boss, but not raids, and he had no clue what the outcome at voting would be in reaction to her verbal aggression. Actually, he had already tried to warn her last night to be more diplomatic when, at the dinner table in the hotel, she compared the Spanish Prime Minister with Don Quixote. According to her, the man had, in the middle of the financial crisis in the West, proclaimed that no such thing existed in Spain.

To prevent further damage Hans therefore quickly wrote a small note to the Chancellor in German, something like, *Chancellor please, careful with offending the Prime Minister, we will need his party's votes;* but to his further uneasiness she gave his note less than a half eye, and instantly shred it in pieces, before closing with the statement, "Dear party leaders, this really cannot go on. The Spanish population simply cannot pay your reckless political game, nor will Germany."

After the unexpected outburst of the German Chancellor with the Prime Minister flushing red and the smiles frozen on the faces of some of the party bosses: those having dreamed of the possibility that the Chancellor could have arrived with some funds for the Central Government to solve the problem of the urgent consolidation of the banks before things would really run out of hands-there was a short but deep, cold silence. Initial positions had to be reshuffled since nodding for the federation in exchange of financial support from Germany was no longer an option.

Others, the more leftist party leaders had come with little expectations, believing that the German Chancellor came to screw the Spanish workers, proposing probably to take away a huge part of the social advantages the trade unions had conquered in the last thirty-five years.

Only the conservative party boss, a man totally neutral even with himself, but fan of the rightist parties in the US, Britain, and

Germany alike-and also in Saudi Arabia and China if they would have existed-dared to applaud Marlein and welcomed her once more for her visit while thanking her for her frank outburst. It was a gesture the man could afford since he knew that, without unveiling any specific problem-solving policy in the last three years, his party could easily count on a landslide victory in next national elections and he would gain the leadership in Spain without having to shoot a single bullet, so to speak. The so-called incumbent factor would work for one-hundred-percent for his party, as it had always worked in times of crisis, in Spain as well as in other countries in Europe.

As Hans Schmidt knew that Marlein Ditch asked the Spanish Prime Minister to not only have her to shake hands with the political leaders of the twelve parties in the small, annexed room, but also to give her the opportunity to present her thoughts in a brief speech *en petit committee* before all of them would be going to the Hemicycle, he even now could not calm his nerves as the Chancellor continued.

"Ladies and gentlemen, friends, I have asked the Prime Minister to give me some minutes before we move into the big audience including journalists, TV cameras, and the whole circus. You will understand that in that setting, I will not be able to be specific. Since I consider it more relevant for my trip that you, the bosses of political parties in Spanish Parliament are well informed and have clear insight of the future of the federation, I will actually address you now. But I beg you to please be discrete on what I will say now. Our projected selective federation has far more enemies than thinkable."

With now having full attention of the twelve, Marlein Ditch started speaking from her heart, on the one hand almost building a secret coalition with them, and on the other hand, putting the same politicians with their backs against the wall.

"I have come to Madrid to promote a European Federation of nine member states. As you know, Spain has become a candidate but not in the first round, not before Nice. This is because the debt markets are all the time putting to our attention that Spain is far from a paradise today. Having said that, you will have to agree with me that with your governing system, in particular in dealing with autonomic communities, you have exceedingly politicized your economy. This has resulted, as I said before, in many unnecessary, public budget spending, lack of control on housing and bankers, not to mention the rapid growth of far too much civil servants.

My friends, you were welcomed in the European Union in 1986, but you will have to agree with me that things have changed; in the World and in Europe, and we cannot continue any longer in the same way, as if only politics counts and economics do not exist.
To make it clear, why would you build an airport in La Mancha, the fatherland of Don Quixote, if hardly ever a plane will land there?
Such a ridiculous investment should be paid personally by the promoters and not with public money. I have heard that some of your autonomous communities and some big cities simply do not want to adjust to the current times of capital, revenues, or funding scarcity. Really, you may have surmised from recent stands towards Ireland, Greece, and Portugal that the happy days are over. The leading countries in the Euro zone will leave to fall all those who do not adjust to the new financial restrictions and continue wasting time while expect miracles from us.

In Germany, Holland, Austria, France, Luxemburg, and Finland neither the populations nor the leadership are inclined to continue paying the debts of other members of the club. There is a generalized fatigue to pay to the others just because they are members of the club, in exchange of almost nothing. And please do not say to me now that

135

Germany has exceedingly been profiting from the EU membership of Spain!

In brief, if you do not correct substantially and adjust your speed, you will exclude yourself, but not only from the Federation but also from the Euro system which, in around one year, will be the monetary system of the Federation and not of the countries not embodied into federation.

In two hours, you may vote and decide for self-exclusion from the federation, which would in the current situation automatically send you to a devaluation of your "new pesetas" by forty to fifty-percent to solve you external disequilibrium. This would mean that the euro of the new federation would cost the Spaniards around 320 pesetas, which means that your flats and assets would be bought by the citizens of the Federation for the half of their current *apparent* value.

This would be a horrifying waking up for Spain. You will balance of course your external accounts but suddenly you will become half rich. And mainly you-emphasized the Chancellor looking at the bosses of parties, particularly to the Spanish Prime Minister who was logically there-will be the responsible of this catastrophe for your compatriots.

Dear friends, all in life has a limit. You have stretched too much the string and it is near to break. You will have to make a choice; and not even in the short term, but just in some minutes after my speech in the Hemicycle. Dear friends, take your full responsibility when you vote. Spain needs the Federation; the Federation needs Spain."

At her last words, the German Chancellor stood up from her chair and looking at the president of Parliament she remarked, "All set and done, I am ready to go to the Hemicycle."

Although the twelve politicians also stood up, they were clearly speechless after the blunt words of the German Chancellor. No applause, no approval followed her sharp wake-up call.

* * *

However, at her entrée in the Hemicycle, Marlein Ditch was encouraged by a spontaneous welcoming applaud, which only ended when the president of the parliament demanded attention and clarified the agenda: first, the German Chancellor would present her discourse, then parliamentarians could put questions for clarification and after a short coffee break the electronic voting would take place at exactly one in the afternoon. And of course the German Chancellor and her aide were most welcome to observe the election.

As agreed with Jacques Perrier, the content of the presentation of the Chancellor in the Hemicycle would be copy conform the speech of the French President in Nice. Starting with new developments in the world in the 21st Century-the shift of the global, economic gravity center towards Asia, the loss of competitiveness in Europe, the economic catching up of developing countries, in particular China and India, plus Russia, Brazil, and South Africa -the Chancellor had followed with a brief description of the stagnation in the European Union and the overwhelming problems mainly caused by the deficient architecture of the Euro System. She then briefly spoke of the past choice for enlargements with economically far weaker countries instead of further political integration of the stronger member states, which all together had transformed the European Union at twenty-seven in an almost ungovernable monster.

Hereafter the German Chancellor explored the advantages of a federation of nine countries with 300-million people to which Spain was invited to participate.

"There is so much to gain from federating, that we should not waste a single minute more. If we federate, we may save around two-percent of our joint GDP as we will be merging our armies, our foreign representations, etc. Also our nine ministries of finance will

137

merge in a single one, which would enable us to recover our full capabilities in fiscal and monetary policy."

Concluding she added, "If we are capable of building up our federation we will form a country called to fly in some few years at the height of the US and China. And I dare to say that if we do not federate, we will be condemned to irrelevance. Note that in the current globalized world all European countries are considered small in size and population, including Germany."

After twenty-five minutes of speech, loud and clearly, perhaps a little monotonous, Marlein remembered the Spanish parliamentarians that she was always speaking within her time, because time was too precious to be wasted. She closed her file with papers and looked around smiling. And then, totally unexpected, there was no applause, but a sea of boos. It started in the corner of the Left (former Communist and others), with the chairman of the United left party screaming in Spanish.

"We do not need Germany lecturing us!"

From all sides of the Hemicycle representatives started boos-ing, and talking and gesturing anxiously, and as it was done in the Spanish language, the only thing Marlein Ditch and Hans Schmidt could understand were the words of the two translators who were explaining from their booths that they could not follow the speakers as they were not using the microphone. "Sorry, I cannot follow the speakers. Sorry, no translation, I do not understand what is being said."

"Order, Order, please sit down!" exclaimed the president of the parliament, repeatedly hammering on the desk in front of him. "We have enough time for you to put your questions. Who can I give the floor?" But his attempts failed and Marlein and Hans were both looking cloudy. "Madam, while you were speaking I noticed someone distributing a leaflet. I have tried to get one. Of course it is in Spanish", remarked aide Schmidt as he handed a piece of paper over to his boss.

The Spanish Prime Minister, his face again blushing, now bowed in the direction of the German Chancellor and her aide and whispered,

"The paper is an almost literally transcript of your speech during the meeting with the twelve chairs of political parties. Probably your words have not fallen well with everyone. And Madame Chancellor, as you can see, the Spanish temperament is different from the German. We simply have to wait."

"I am giving the floor for questioning" was the repeated loud remark of the president of parliament and it took him another seven minutes before the unrest was over and silence returned.

"The floor is open for questions," he repeated again but after the tumults no one seemed to be willing to cooperate, after which the president hammered out the session and announced the start of the coffee break. And once again the 350 parliamentarians were all adrift on their way out.

* * *

Marlein Ditch and Hans Schmidt left the Hemicycle in the company of the Prime Minister, who tried to explain to an astounded Marlein that all was not lost. Perhaps her words had not fallen well to everyone, but she had been so clear that he was convinced that almost all parliamentarians would vote with their mind and not with their heart. Marlein gave him a bitter look and no word. Hans Schmidt suggested that they should no longer consume the precious time of the Prime Minster, who had better be with his party men. This was the sign for the Prime Minister to apologize and to hurry back to another side of the building.

Voting at one pm would take at maximum three minutes as all was electronic and from behind the desks. "Yes" implied nodding to the new federation and accepting the draft constitution and "No" would imply that Spain would remain out of the federation.

The President of the Parliament announced, "Voting starts now; you have sixty seconds to press the button," and seconds later the voting was actually done.

Shortly after the large screens at four points in the Hemicycle projected the outcome: 348 voters were present of which 345 voted Yes, and 3 had voted No.

First there was applause and whistling and the Hemicycle hastily changed into a jubilee with parliamentarians embracing each other, including a highly relieved German Chancellor.

In the middle of the celebration, Hans Schmidt approached his boss with more good news. In all other eight candidate countries Yes votes had also triumphed.

Marlein Ditch spontaneously embraced Hans Schmidt and commanded, "Up to our high speed train, I prefer to celebrate things in my own *heimat*."

As the ash clouds propelled northwards to Siberia, flying from Madrid to Berlin once again became the least time consuming way for the German Chancellor and her aide to return home.

Now then, exactly the one thing Hans Schmidt had feared since their departure from Berlin Hauptbahnhof two days earlier-a remark from his boss over the unfortunate episode when entering the train and his distressed reaction-happened soon after the take-off of the jetliner from Barajas Airport in Madrid.

Leaning backward in her seat opposite him and with her eyes half-closed the German Chancellor first stated, "It has been a good and creative decision of us to go and motivate the Spanish Parliamentarians to accept the draft constitution of the Federation. I really feel enchanted. We have made history today. It's a pity that both of us, when arriving home tonight, will have no one waiting for us to share our delightedness."

As Schmidt did not react she continued, "These are the moments one is painfully reminded of the fact that one is a lonely number. Tell me Schmidt, any specific reason why no nice young woman managed to persuade you that she may look after you and your offspring?"

Perhaps it was the rare formulation of the Chancellor regarding marriage that created a rather wobbly feeling in his chest, forcing Schmidt to cough as the Chancellor sustained, "Sorry, it was not to embarrass you. More and more, I am thinking that perhaps after my career as German Chancellor I should at least adopt one or two children to break the cycle. What about you?"

At her last words, Hans Schmidt moved upwards in his chair and was trying to hide that he had been taken completely by the leap of his boss into his private life. While looking at his fingers that he kept twisting perpetually around each other he spelled out softly, "Perhaps living single in dignity is better than living in couple in discomfiture as my poor mother and father did for almost forty years. Right now, when arriving home, I may speak to my books and plants. And if you allow me to say truth, I have never received a humiliating answer of none of them."

"My dear advisor, one should at least have tried. As my ex used to say-it is better to have loved and lost than not to have loved at all-and I think he was right".

Marlein Ditch was now looking directly into the eyes of advisor Hans Schmidt as she calmly prolonged, "Mind you, Hans, you are from now on one of the happy few who know that I have been married once, be it long time ago. No regrets, I have no regrets as tears subside, except for not having had children. Listen, this is probably my best kept secret. My career became my baby. Should I be happy with that?"

"Madam, few people can become German Chancellor."

"Hans Schmidt, as you are a sympathetic listener, I can admit that my decision not to have children has left me today with mixed feelings. Mixed feelings since political leadership these days is fast losing its glory. Today in Europe all political leaders, regardless of our party background are standing accused of missing direction. But the truth is that the world is changing and in my experience our options for a good direction are mainly decided somewhere else. I may soon become an ex-Chancellor, whom no one will remember. Promise, you will keep my revelations for you."

"Madam Chancellor, if I may say, you have sacrificed a lot for the construction of Europe. I am sure that hundreds years from now you will still be remembered and honored just for that. No one will ever be able to despise your memory since in some decades the European Federation will have become one of the leading five states in the world and the new Euro one of the three, leading currencies. Please Madam, be assured of my loyalty and, may I say, certainly there will be a happy life for you after politics."

The Chancellor had closed her eyes and her face wore the inattentive look of a person who, precisely one minute before, fell into a deep sleep.

Eleven

Ibrahim is set free but the triumph is for Perrier

At 11:30 in the morning, a Japanese Sedan with a Turkish flag entered L'Elisée. It was the car of the Turkish Ambassador to Paris.

Just two hours ago, the ambassador had managed to speak to the President of the Republic by phone in order to request a most immediate meeting over a very serious issue concerning a "family problem" in relation to a Turkish citizen. On listening to the words of the Turkish diplomat, all alarms bells started ringing in the head of Jacques Perrier, and he ordered his secretary and his Chef de Protocol to immediately arrange for the meeting, even if it would mean postponing important issues on the agenda including a possible delay in participating in the extraordinary Council of Ministers meeting in Paris, related to the NATO-Libya intervention.

Those who saw the Turkish Ambassador entering L'Elisée, would have been struck by the look in his face: grave as if he was to transmit condolences or something worse. He was a man of experience, already in his sixties, and he had learned to avoid strong waves both in his career and in his personal life. Accordingly he felt heavily burdened to get involved in the personal life of others, the more so as it involved the President of France.

"Please come in, I am impatiently waiting for you. My time is limited, but this is extremely important. Have a seat", were the friendly words of Jacques Perrier standing up from behind his desk and walking towards the Turkish diplomat when the latter entered.

"Really, this is not something that ambassadors have to do" replied the Turkish Ambassador after sitting. "I am very grateful for your willingness to receive me on so short notice, and really it is very

143

difficult for me to start. However I have to inform you that, according to our Secret Service in Dubai, a Turkish citizen, named Ibrahim Orzgol, was abducted in Dubai, some weeks ago. Till here nothing of particular in this world in which security is deteriorating fast, but the difficulty is that the kidnapped person, an attaché to the President of the Turkish Republic was abducted, probably by an American connection, just when he left a room rented by your wife at Sheraton Creek Hotel" At his last words the Turkish diplomat avoided looking at the French President and instead was facing his hands and fingernails, folded on his legs.

"Sorry Ambassador, this is impossible, and cannot be true". Perrier was waggling with his head, something between yes and no, as he explained, "My wife, what I remember, went to Dubai with some friends, old school mates, and they all stayed in Hotel Burg Al Arab."

"Mr. President, I cannot enter in the assessment of the information you have, but factual information I have received from my headquarters put the truth closer to me. And then there is a Pakistani cab driver who is also on our payroll, who reported, without names but with photos taken in his car by a hidden camera behind the central mirror, that he transferred both your wife and the Turkish attaché the same day to the Sheraton Creek hotel, while both had repeatedly suggested to him that they were going to the hotel for a love encounter. Although this was nothing rare and certainly not the type of reporting he normally provides, he started paying attention to the case when he took your wife back to the Bourg el Arab Hotel, and she was in panic over the sudden disappearance of the Turkish man. At which the Pak cabdriver had confirmed to her that he had seen her boyfriend leaving in a white four-wheel-drive with two men."

The Turkish Ambassador continued, "As far as we had his photo, it was just a matter of days to discover that the disappeared man was one of the advisors of our President. The identification of the other person involved, was even simpler. Your wife, sir, is almost weekly in many glossy magazines, so she is known all over the world; some would say even more than you. Nevertheless we have waited two months before taking any initiative in this nasty affair, hoping perhaps that things would resolve themselves. However, the family of Ibrahim Orzgol started increasing pressure on our government, reason why I am here."

A pale President of France ended by mumbling, "I'm really embarrassed. Believe me, I had a vague idea that my wife was not fully happy, but all this you have described is really unexpected. Give me some time to react. I have to cool down and re-order my mind before doing anything. I can assure you that I will come back to you, but I need some time to sort things out. And as you know, we are all occupied with developments in North Africa today, not to mention the problems of Europe with the financial crisis, and my involvement in the construction of the federation at nine. And now this complication, it is certainly too much."

"Excellency, I fully understand your constraints. The best would be for us to find a diplomatic solution, taking in consideration that a scandal would not be in the interest of the Turkish government either. Reason why the Turkish Information Service has classified everything related to the issue, including the printed material, but as outsiders have been involved, including staff of the Creek Hotel, we cannot guarantee secrecy for an indefinite period."

"Ambassador, take my words for it, I will try to resolve things as far as there is any involvement from the French side, including our collaboration in the liberation of your civil servant. But of course, I ask your government to continue with the discretion followed till now."

The Turkish Ambassador, who had listened with attention to the French President, did not seem to be convinced by the reaction of Perrier. The diplomat still had not abandoned the idea that the President of France could have devised, alone or in combination with others, a strategy to get rid of the lover of his wife by arranging his disappearance till the First Lady would have forgotten or even .... making him disappear forever.

"Excellency, I will transmit to my government what you have said to me," replied the Ambassador, "but please keep in mind that this is for us a very delicate issue, a family is waiting for the reappearance of their beloved, and in this case we are talking about the family of an aide of our President. So, I have to ask you to do the best you can. For both of us, we should try to settle this nasty affair without major damage to any side. As I said before Mister President, there is always the risk of information ending up in wrong hands. I can assure you once more that my government would not like to be put in the position of having to disclose unpleasant information about your wife."

"Dear Ambassador, this will not happen. I would like to add that you could also transmit to your government that the French position concerning Turkey in relation to the EU is becoming softer than before, and if our federation of nine progresses, Turkey will be most welcome to integrate in a common market with us."

After formal words of farewell among the two, the Turkish Ambassador left L'Elisée, and back in his car, the man tried to lean back and relax from the somewhat unpleasant encounter. Hardly a minute had past however when his Blackberry started ringing. With a certain air of disinterests-he really had suffered enough during the unusual conversation with the President of France-he answered and immediately became aware of something that produced him a shock that hit his old heart even harder. He was informed by his head-quarters that the French Ambassador to Ankara has been kidnapped by, possibly, a Kurdish separatist group.

Following the message, the Ambassador had to grasp for air as he considered that this new event could be read by the French President as a change of pieces in an unfortunate chess game unleashed by him just now to force the result Turkey desired: the devolution of Ibrahim by whoever had abducted him.

* * *

However, inside the Palace, Jacques Perrier decided to distract himself from the unpleasant message of the Turkish Ambassador, by concentrating his thoughts on federation issues, in particular on some aspects of the provisional draft of the constitution. He started carefully valuing the representativeness of the Federation Parliament. In his view the Federation would need a parliament with no more than four or five parties. Strict, proportional representation should be excluded along the first, two decades of the life of the Federation. He had to acknowledge that any step given in false could blow up the project, reason why the adopted policies should be supported by important majorities, be these supplied by one single party or by a coalition of two.

The solution was clear from the perspective of Jacques; it would be necessary to create federal parties, these being large parties formed out of the cooperation of national parties with the same ideology (conservatives, labor, Christian-democrats, liberal, green). But contrary to the existing loose groupings already formed in the current European Parliament in Strasbourg, for the European Federation the federal parties should be formal and full-fledged. Translated to the constitutional terminology of the Federation, this would mean that to enter in the federal parliament, the federal political parties should get five-percent of the total issued votes and these should have been gathered in a minimum of fifteen-percent of the federal districts, as this would give more stability to the Federal Parliament.

While Perrier continued the profiling and weighting of representative aspects of the future federation parliament, the French Minister of Foreign Affairs interrupted with a call to bring the bad news to the President that the French Ambassador to Ankara had unfortunately been kidnapped by midday while in the presence of the French Consul, just when the two were visiting the Galatas District at the outskirts of Istanbul, where the Ambassador was to inaugurate a hypermarket of an important French firm.

The French Minister confirmed that attempts of extremists had lately been less frequent in Istanbul than in other parts of the country, but according to the Turkish police-and taking into account available information-one should not exclude extremists involvement in the abduction of the French Ambassador, as the terrorists were constantly trying to attract attention from the international community.

"You have to check this information and report to me as soon as possible!" exclaimed a sweating Jacques while hiding his discomfort for his Minister. Of course he could not say more, but it crossed his mind that this could be a case of retaliation by the secret service of the Turks against him, just to force-in case that this could be possible-an action of the French President to liberate Ibrahim.

* * *

After hanging up the phone, Jacques Perrier instinctively decided to privately call the Vice Security Advisor to the US President. Maybe she would have additional or relevant information to break the cycle.

"Hello Betsy, how are you?"

"I am fine, although commotional, Mr. President" she answered,

"But I suppose you, Mr. President, may be extremely concerned at this very moment. For your information, however, we think that this event is not an issue of extremists. We have some confidents in

Ankara and Istanbul who swear by the eternal paradise of all their ancestors, that this is simply an operation of the Turkish Secret Service against someone in France, not against France. Luckily, only you and I may have a clue to the problem: the unfortunate relation between your wife and the advisor of the Turkish President."

"But you said to me something enigmatic time ago in relation to this business," replied Jacques. "Could you be more explicit this time on the issue, please? I feel deeply discomforted in this case because I cannot say the truth even to my own wife! Please, by our old friendship, I pray you to explain to me all you know on the matter. The abduction of my French Ambassador is probably a next stage in the process of hidden tensions between France and Turkey on a private issue. The last thing I need."

"Do not worry Jacques, you are adopting these days a very supportive and brave position in North Africa and the Middle East and I know that the US President is very willing to support France in any aspect connected with global matters. As a consequence, as far as I know, I can promise you that we will fully participate in solving the problem of your Ambassador without any collateral damage. When I have gathered all the information related to the case and made some calls to the Turkish Foreign Office to make a deal, I will inform you. After a positive outcome, which as far as I know is very likely, you even could go to Turkey in a blitz trip; and perhaps only some thirty minutes after your arrival, you will be able to embrace your Ambassador in Ankara and travel back to France with him in triumph. I'm sure that if things are as we in my office believe- just a proxy-retaliation operation with exchanging purposes-at the end of the day, this nasty experience may result profitable for you. By the way, it would be convenient, when all this is finished, that you explain your ideas about the European Federation to my president", Betsy continued, "He is concerned with the influence of this project on the economy of the US and the defense system of the West.

149

Perhaps the forthcoming G20 meeting in Florence would be a good opportunity to have a tête-a-tête with him."

* * *

After the rather comforting conversation with Betsy, in relation to the "Ambassador kidnapping", the heart of Jacques Perrier started beating somewhat softer than before.

Even more, within an hour-and after several calls realised by Betsy to different Centres for Treatment of Information-she informed Perrier that she could certify not only that Ibrahim had already weeks before secretly been transferred to a US prison in Germany, after having been in a centre in Africa, but also that he had been cleared since he had been taken by mistake from the Hotel Sheraton Creek in Dubai.

What had happened in his case, was that Jacques Perrier had, via his Security Officer, requested information about Ibrahim, but his petition-instead of being handled as an information inquiry requested by French Intelligence to US Intelligence-had by incident been listed by staff in Virginia as a French arrest request concerning a suspect belonging to a listed Islamic organisation.

Consequently, the Vice-Advisor for National Security of the US President, after her consults, could easily order to free Ibrahim and to transfer him back to the place he had been abducted. So Ibrahim's liberation would be in Dubai, provided he agreed on the terms and conditions including no word to anyone on the places in which he had been questioned and how. In exchange, Ibrahim would receive a compensation of half-a-million dollar-over five years-on condition of remaining silent and a business class ticket to return him from Dubai to Ankara; conditions Ibrahim wholeheartedly accepted in order to be able to go home soon.

150

As far as these internal negotiations were successful, Betsy called the President of France two days later and greeted him in an exultant way, saying, "Dear President, I have good news. Tomorrow will be a great day for you and for France. One of your most serious domestic problems has been solved. I have not only localised where this person, Ibrahim, was but also negotiated internally the conditions and terms to set him free in Dubai, by tomorrow. The rest of my job consisted of certifying that your Ambassador in Ankara was more or less in official or semi-official hands-guess you understand me-and not in hands of any terrorist group. This has also taken little time, and finally your Ambassador will simultaneously be liberated and accompanied to the French Embassy in Ankara. In terms of timing the exchange is set for 3:00 pm tomorrow."

"Wonderful Betsy, how can I thank you? I will travel to Ankara by midday to personally welcome and comfort my ambassador. Could you keep me duly informed to be able to solemnize the operation? Between you and me, certainly it would have been politically more rewarding if the exchange had no private base."

"But my dear friend, I guess with your diplomatic skills you will well be capable to push the information on the liberation of your Ambassador away from the Dubai part and place it in a more profitable direction for your polls. Anyway, although the operation is practically closed, we still have one loose end. A loose end-I have to confess-which is out of my and your control. This is something that will need the collaboration of your wife and the Turkish man. Your wife will have to convince Ibrahim that he should collaborate fully in staying away from her and keeping silent on the Dubai encounter. Otherwise your political future, Mister President, could be in danger. Indeed, this short-cut initiative of the Turkish Intelligence has somewhat put us all in a difficult situation, in particular you and your beloved wife."

"I fully agree with what you are saying, Betsy. I will have to convince Alexandra to enter in touch with Ibrahim, by telephone, let us say to a number you will disclose to me at the right moment."

"I am at your service," was Betsy's smiling answer.

* * *

Taking first a deep breath and thereafter reflecting silently for some minutes, Jacques followed by calling Alexandra to update her on the good news concerning Ibrahim, but of course without giving any impression that he had been involved in his abduction or that he could have been hiding any information for her on the unfortunate case.

"Hello, Darling, I have unexpected news about your friend Ibrahim, the Turkish aide who disappeared. He is going to be liberated by his kidnappers by tomorrow. Contrary to what you hinted at to my mother, our friend was mistakenly abducted by American Middle East allies, as my Security Service has discovered. And you may now accept that I had nothing to do with this whole unpleasant business. It has been a case of bad luck caused by an administrative error. As I understood, the US administration will compensate him well for the disturbance he suffered."

As Alexandra only heaved a deep sigh, Jacques continued, "I do not know how this information may play a role in our lives. You have accused me wrongly but understandably and believe me, I'm still deeply in love with you. I hope you feel the same way too. I am aware that I have certainly in the beginning of our marriage committed severe mistakes in our relation, mainly by not paying all the attention you deserved, but I have changed my attitude in the last months as you may have noticed and I'm determined to improve things even more."

As Alexandra kept silent, Jacques persisted, "Alexandra, I can swear to you that I have neither participated directly nor indirectly in any form in the disappearance of Ibrahim in Dubai. I was not aware of anything and as you know, such an activity isn't my style."

Finally an emotional Alexandra replied, "Jacques, I have thought and rethought about the painful developments of the past months, and I have been ashamed of myself but also of you. How could we have got involved in this? I have concluded that, without looking for an excuse, I have perhaps been attracted by Ibrahim as a consequence of your total lack of attention to me. And of course I was wrong, very wrong with my revanchist behaviour. I can assure you that this will never ever happen again. I dislike cheating, for myself and for you and believe me, I love you dearly".

Now it was time for Jacques Perrier to sigh in relief while Alexandra continued, "I will try to explain all this also to Ibrahim and hope he will understand. I think he is a good person, perhaps a little precarious of him to fall in love with the wife of the President of France, but it seemed honest. And Jacques, I would lie if I say that I did not like him, he was cheerful and I needed that so much in those days, but it was selfish of me, very selfish to compromise you and the French Republic. I hope Ibrahim will not feel offended, particularly if I promise to continue being a good friend to him. It will be just a superficial relation, a telephone call once in a while, but I will call him as soon as you order me to do so, my love."

"Okay darling, thank you for your words. Let us put a line under this nasty episode for all involved and move ahead. I feel that things between us will improve necessarily. Nothing more desired by me than that. Thank you Alexandra, my love, a kiss.

153

As planned, Ibrahim was released at three pm at the Sheraton Creek Hotel in Dubai by two men. As the sun was still in zenith and outside temperatures were nearing 45 degrees Celsius, Ibrahim Orzgol rushed into the coffee shop of the hotel where suddenly an old faculty friend from Ankara greeted him and invited him for a coffee. As the two were waiting for the coffee to arrive, a somewhat confused Ibrahim was looking around in the hotel lobby, where he had actually stayed only few minutes some months before.

His friend apologized for having to make an urgent call and the still-dazed Ibrahim could then hear him saying, "Ibrahim has a very good aspect," before he disconnected.

Back to Ibrahim the old faculty friend explained: "My wife, Gulay, was on the line; I just told her that I ran into you. She has gone shopping happily with the rest of the family, our two kids. Tell me Ibrahim, how are you doing? Long time, no see."

In reality, the call was to Turkey and his sentence was the agreed code to start the release of the France Ambassador in Ankara. After twenty minutes of some more familiar talks about his wife and kids whom Ibrahim hardly remembered, the two fellows embraced each other and Ibrahim left the hotel for the airport.

He started looking for a taxi at the sideway parking of the Sheraton Creek Hotel and the yellow taxi was driven by none other than the Pakistani who transported him first and Alexandra later from the airport to the hotel. With a smile, revealing his teeth that entirely lost their colours due to the use of a red, Asian chewing tobacco, the taxi driver cheerfully shouted as if he was updated on the liberation of Ibrahim.

"You, Sir .... going home after all this time? Home is the best place to stay after many bad luck. I always say my wife: the best of life is quietness. And I know: women not wife always create problems. Much problems gave, especially European madam."

This time, Ibrahim decided not to enter into any conversation with the Pakistani. He only shifted a little more comfortable in his seat and ordered to drive to the airport. During the drive at medium speed Ibrahim started reflecting silently on the obscure, useless, and painful time he spent being questioned in secret places by aggressive people. It had been a real nightmare. As he had been doing in the long, dark weeks, he tried to rationalise once again the cause of his abduction and one way or another he felt he had to blame himself.

Although the horrifying questioning-which mainly took place with him being blindfolded-had been very insistent and on issues of which he constantly and truthful had denied being involved with, he finally understood that he could only survive by letting go and not by resisting. He took for granted that he probably had fallen prey to his stupidity of falling in love with the French First Lady.

No one would ever be able to imagine what he had gone through.

The price he paid for his idiocy had been extremely high. He would not easily forget the confusing experience of losing all sense of day and night due to six, huge, halogen light balls shining on him endlessly. Or other times, when all was dark and he could not see but feel cold water creeping up from his feet till his neck or other moments when he could clearly hear the rattling of snakes or the peeping of rats very close to his naked body. With some mental exercise he taught himself to let go by swooning away as soon as the questioning started. So much so that he would remember practically nothing of the rest of the session that day or that night, except for a vague and disturbing suspicion when he regained consciousness that he had been crying.

That he all in all survived without suffering an overnight, psychotic attack or became totally insane was also thanks to the fact that he knew and prayed that his friends in Ankara would not give up on looking for him.

He could on principle have refused the compensation they offered him at the release, especially when they explained that his arrest had been an administrative mistake, but during the negotiations he became aware of the fact that they would not let him go without settling and signing. But as his professor at University in Ankara used to say quoting Einstein, "*The true sign of intelligence is not knowledge but imagination*"; Ibrahim had imagined that a quiet life would be possible only after signing and sealing.

The compensation would perhaps make it easier for him to radically change his life, for instance by starting a quiet family life in a place near the Black Sea coast, or by going somewhere else, but where?

* * *

Meanwhile in Ankara the French Ambassador had been transferred to the back door of the Grand Hyatt Hotel and his Blackberry had been returned to him, which he immediately used to enter in touch with his staff at the French Embassy.
He thereafter took a taxi instead of waiting for his car, as the Embassy was very near and he preferred not to attract any attention from people in and around the hotel before he was back in his office, which would be the case if his black BMW with flag would arrive in front of the hotel to collect him.

Nearing the building, he noticed that there were many police cars in the neighbourhood and even a minibus of the Turkish TV parked in double line. Consequently, the Ambassador requested the cab driver to turn off and approach the private small gate of the Embassy in a narrow side street where he rushed out of the car and slipped in the garden of the building, passing under the arm of the concierge whom he had called to open the normally tightly locked door. So a first escape from the multitude of cameras of Turkish and French media had been successful.

A second escape however was impossible as the concierge had already announced his arrival to the Embassy staff and a music band in the hall of the building had set in for the "Marseillaise", while the entire staff and some relatives had lined up including the wife of the Ambassador and the President of France. Arriving from the back side of the building instead of via the front door, the welcome committee suddenly had to change positions and an emotional, gazing President Perrier turned around and rushed to embrace the liberated Ambassador, both men shedding some tears, be it each for different reasons.

After some moments of expressive greeting of the Ambassador by his wife and the entire staff, the President took the Ambassador with him to the office of the Head of Mission and behind closed doors Perrier remarked, "Dear Francois, sometimes in life we suffer the cruel arrows of destiny, or of adverse fortune, as Hamlet would have said.
Anyway, I am asking you for a very personal favour. You have to forget these days of misfortune and keep your lips sealed. We are flying together this evening to Paris. Your wife has prepared the luggage and all necessary for the two of you to enjoy three weeks of holidays quietly in Normandy, in order for you to recover from the horrible experience. Thereafter you will go back to Ankara, but only to organise your departure and prepare for your provisional posting at L'Elisée as my special advisor. Following, in the next round of appointments of Head of Missions, I can assure you that you will be

honoured to represent the Republic in one of our most prestigious Embassies: Washington, London, Rome, etc."

"Okay, Sir, although I very much appreciated my assignment to Turkey, I understand that I have no choice than to surrender to your orders. You may have your reasons, and I am at your service."

"Yes, you are right. Believe me, Francois, your kidnapping has been the result of a chain of mistakes, bad luck, and political bargaining that no one of us could have imagined. But the world works in many ways out of our control. So do not think too much on it, turn the page, and start a new stage of your life. Of course, you have not been alone in your problem. As you see, the President of the Republic has been busy with all this and is now by your side. So let us return to France, and I have arranged that on arriving, we will discretely abandon the airport, without any comment to the press."

"Okay, Mr. President, I guess and hope that at one stage someone will perhaps disclose the background to me. As for now, my lips are sealed."

* * *

Two days later, in a modest apartment in Ankara, the telephone rang at 11:00 am and a still discomforted Ibrahim answered the phone to found Alexandra speaking on the other end of the line. Following a rather reserved greeting from both sides she maintained, "I have been informed in the last days that you had erroneously been abducted in Dubai. I feel very sorry for you. It must have been a horrible experience. So sorry... of course, at first I supposed that my husband was involved in it, but gladly this thinking of me was also wrong." As Ibrahim remained silent, Alexandra continued, "In the first days after the event in Dubai I suffered very much thinking of you, but thanks God, finally all this is over, so how are you?"

"I'm well now, although the people that kept me and questioned me, did not treat me careful, you understand me, do not you? It was horrifying and humiliating at the same time. On top of that I had strong emotions, thinking that our future had vanished forever and finally I deduced that our relation was driving me to the abyss."

"Oh I am so sad for you. It takes my breath away if I think of what you have gone through because of me," reacted a crazed Alexandra.

"I am the guilty. People like me, all the time exposed to the media, cannot have a complicated, private life. And if they try, as I did, they may be caught by the media, by the circumstances of the world, in this case the battle against terrorism, or whatever. I know that my love for you was beautiful while it lasted, but our circumstances were very different. I went a bridge too far, but believe me, I did not do so on purpose and I did not misuse you. I'm very sorry. I repent. I pray that we may continue being friends at a distance." said Alexandra tearfully.

"Dear Xandra, I have never in my worst moments in isolation in the centres had a single thought of you being using or misusing me. I believe we were both sincere but perhaps naïve in our love. But I have my doubts if your new proposal will be possible. That will not be possible and also we both will be better off without any contact, I believe."

"Okay, we will see. Anyway I am glad to hear that you are well, and I feel finally better since I had been feeling responsible and guilty for what had happened to you. Believe me, during our time together I was fully sincere. I will remember it, all my life. I wish you the best, including starting a new and happy family life. Let us try to be happy over the rainbow."

"Alexandra, I wish you the same. You know that I was also very sincere with you", Ibrahim replied. "Really, in the darkest period of my life, caged as I was, I often cried myself to sleep and dreamt being with you forever", said Ibrahim emotional. "But we have both wakened up to harsh reality. Thank you for those unforgettable moments we have been together. Many people will not have lived something alike in their whole lives. Thank you. Goodbye, Xandra, goodbye."

"Friends forever, my love," replied Alexandra, while hanging the telephone.

Twelve

Florence in chaos with protesting beauties and new friendship to arise

It must have been around midday, when the news spread that access to the Grand Hotel at the Piazza Orginissenti in the heart of Florence, was blocked by thousands of young protestors who arrived in the capital of Tuscany from all different continents across the globe.

That June day started with temperatures well above twenty degrees Celsius and by midday the heat of the sparkling sun was all around, in particular nestling in the cobblestones of the various places of the historical city with its many touristic attractions. Even at the waterfront at Ponte Vecchio, no coolness could be found, no breeze, no snap of wind while hundreds of tourists were merging with the thousands of protestors in jointly hunting for some little shadow.

As claimed by their several, colourful spokesmen, the new generation protestors arriving from the different continents were demanding accountability of the G20 leaders, who were meeting in an extraordinary gathering in Florence, called for by the American President.

While the presidents and premiers of the G-20 countries were to stay in the Grand Hotel-a monumental building at the south bank of the river Arno dating back to the eighteenth Century with its spacious suites decorated fully antique including large frescos, thus celebrating the artistic culture of Florence-the G20 conference itself was to take place in the Palazio Pitti. This choice, made by the Italian government had high symbolic value since, as the reader may know, the gigantic Palazio Pitti was built in 1458, in the early days of the Renaissance as

Residence of Luca Pitti, one of the first bankers of Italy. As both the Grand Hotel and the Palazio Pitti were located on the bank of the river Arno and near Ponte Vecchio, the G20 leaders would be able to walk the short distance between the two buildings and at the same time catch another glimpse of the facades and collections of art of Florence. But to be able to do so, the road for the short promenade had been totally cleared and besieged by a huge army of Caribinieri.

Understandable since, although not invited to the G20 meeting, thousands of youngsters had quickly mobilised and were arriving in Florence, originating from Madrid, Paris, London, Amsterdam, Berlin, Moscow, Washington, New York, Tokyo, Johannesburg, New Delhi, Beijing, Kuala Lumpur, Sidney, Oslo, Ottawa, Brasilia, and even Havana and Cairo.

The G-20 leaders were to look for joint steps to be taken urgently to shorten the financial crisis and the future of next generations was at stake since recent cracks were pointing at a more prolonged recession in Europe, US, and Japan and widespread fears were growing in relation to increased foreign indebtedness, additional losses of jobs, further decline in consumer-spending, and slimming of middle classes, particularly in these parts of the globe. Ever since the existence of wide middle classes is considered as crucial for sustainability of democracy, fears for political instability were genuinely growing all over Europe.

So the building up of the police and security force near Ponte Vecchio was going hand-in-hand with the building up of colourful demonstrations originating from all points of the compass. According to the brochures, they were distributing to passerby, the claims covered a wide spectrum of issues including: urging the implementation of a European Federation; controlling the international finance markets and banks, establishing a democratic global governing body to administrate the production and prices of scarce energy resources, rejecting nuclear energy, democratising the United Nations, and the introduction of a worldwide inheritance tax to globally finance poverty alleviation.

One of the main initiators of this Youth for Inclusive Democratic Global Governance rally in Florence was the Spanish movement May 1st, a collective formed mainly by educated, jobless youngsters counting for around forty-percent of the total volume of unemployed Spaniards. As the group had requested the Italian Premier and President to be admitted with a delegation of ten representatives from the different continents to participate in the G20 Top, at which no answer had been received, the steering group of the protestors had taken the decision that morning, to block all roads leading to the Grand Hotel and between the Grand Hotel and the Palazzio Pitti.

From ten in the morning onwards one could also see colourful banners in the adjacent streets around the two buildings, mainly addressing bankers and political leaders, reading, *If banks do not give more credits, we will go for the bankers*, *You will have to pay for the crisis irrespective of whether you are idiots or thefts*, and *There is no place for private banks in future, payment systems cannot be private.* And directed to the G20 leaders banners read, "*No globalization without finances controlled by the global society*".

* * *

A more in-depth explanation to the public of the underlying background of the protest was presented on RAI-1 in the news at noon via an interview with a certain Agnani, a popular Italian sociologist currently working in Princeton but also keeping his consultancy firm in Napoli on electoral issues for left-wing politicians.

Agnani, dressed in jeans and red chequer jacket, travelled to Florence on request of the M-1 movement in order to present the demands of the movement in the media.

The first televised question posed to Agnani, was simple, "You really believe that in the twenty-first- century, your Movement for Direct Democracy has any future?"
Agnani took off his glasses and shook his curly, grey, medium long hair, arched his brows, and answered, "Frankly speaking, it will have no future because it will not progress towards institutionalisation. But we are confident that some of our proposals will be implemented at short-midterm by governments. And if I may say, what has no future at all are today's behaviour of politicians and the current architecture of democracies in the West. Many politicians are just money-makers and are not serving their populations. In many cases, the information on critical events is hidden if this is convenient for their interest. Many of them reach power by promising a future in which they hardly believe and, for some of them, it is almost irrelevant if they deliver or not. For the majority it is sufficient just to keep their seats. All this represents a clear treason to the taxpayers."

While his words were tumbling over one another, Agnani pierced his eyes in the camera and continued "Talking about the current crisis, I do think that citizens have at least the right to be informed about the gravity of the situation. As you know, no government in the West has informed citizens on the seriousness of the crisis. Consequently misinterpretations coming from multinationals and partisan academicians have flooded media which has favoured their interest."
The interviewer had quickly lifted his hands in the air, "But Mr. Agnani, are you suggesting that the media is corrupted?"
Looking away from the camera while putting a finger in his right ear and shaking it briskly, Agnani sneered, "I am not suggesting, I am just

affirming categorically that corruption is all around including in the media, and politicians mainly turn a blind eye. It is rare to see someone in government resigning before conviction, a conviction that will only occur long after finishing their political term, as the juridical systems take years in finding the juridical truth. Indeed we have arrived to a situation in which many politicians have excluded themselves from their responsibilities. They spent borrowed money counting with the taxes and revenues that will be paid in future by others. This fast growing debt has become the way to escape from the unpopularity of increasing taxation, thus undemocratically halting financial sources for actions of future politicians."

"How, how, how, stop it! I have seen the pamphlets of the protestors. What has the corruption of politicians to do with the current, financial crisis?"

"Everything, politicians and central bankers are mainly captured by multinational, private banks; they have controlled neither the private banks, nor the Central Banks, thus creating a mess all over the West. And what about the financing of the electoral campaigns, in which almost everyone looked for short cuts?"

An agitated Agnani made a short pause before he finished, "All this and many more issues should be subject for reorganising the political life in our part of the world. As the audience will agree with me, one cannot ask sacrifices from citizens, while along a durable crisis, politicians persistently show irresponsible behaviour, even allowing private bankers to increase their retributions. Indeed, with their leniency, these politicians may be excluding an entire generation from the labour market."

"Do you believe that these things can be corrected easily?"

"The problem is global and therefore needs global solutions. But it is clear that national politicians should have behaved more according to what is expectable in democracies. They should have exerted government in the name of the people and for the people and not in their own interest. If they had acted in favour of people, some European countries, today in dramatic situation, would have been spared many problems."

* * *

Amid the building up of the security on the one hand and the demonstrations on the other, the Italian Premier arrived in Florence the night before as did the President of France, who, accompanied by his wife Alexandra, first spent a day in Rome, sharing time with a visit to the Vatican to explain the progress of the European Federation to the Pope.

During the entire morning a strong cacophony of campaigns coming from the nearby streets of the Grand Hotel could be observed by the two political leaders and their staff who were all becoming rather restless in the atmosphere of waiting for a collision.

* * *

So when the American president landed at midday at Firenze Aero Porto, there was a desiccated whiff of something troublesome in the air. The man was to have a lunch at two that afternoon with the French President to be updated on the projected European Federation, but at leaving the airport, his motorcade was surprisingly halted by protestors in the steaming heat of the radiating sun. But more than the tarmac, it was the smoking of old car-tires set afire that blurred the sight. Immediately a panic stroke hit the President's own security staff who, amid the dark black smoke and unpleasant smell of burning rubber, started speaking alarmed to one another via walky-talkies and were looking for alternatives, while gunned Carabinieri were in stand-off with the demonstrators in trying to clear the street. Further escalation was avoided when two helicopters arrived and-after using teargas-a somewhat edgy, American President left for Grand Hotel via air. Meanwhile the Caribinieri were able to dissolve the rally. But the tone was set and the American president was right in fearing that there was more to come.

* * *

The working lunch of the President of France and his US counterpart, took place in a special small meeting and dining room in the mezzanine of the Grand Hotel, but even here one could hear, be it softer, the protest sounds of the demonstrations nearby. As agreed, both Presidents were accompanied by their advisors. They included an American Nobel Laureate in economics, Professor Burman, and their respective Ambassadors in Paris and Washington.

After the usual greetings and exchanges of politeness, the two delegations set on the main sides of an oval, mahogany table with three, crystal chandeliers hanging low from the ceiling.

Perrier, dressed in summer shirt and tie, began the deliberations by articulating mysteriously, "Mon chère collegue, may I first thank you for your uninterrupted support." He cryptically referred to the Turkish case and his mouth stretched wide in a silky smile, while the American President politely bowed his head. "We are really living in uncertain times in which creative leadership is vital," Perrier continued, "In this context the world is looking at us, Europe, and the USA. So before I update you on our selective Federation, I would gladly be updated by you on the situation concerning the US rating, the public deficit and debt."

In reaction the American Head of State blinked: "Dear friend, I do share your concern and can assure you, it is my nightmare. The recent downgrading of the credit rating of US government resulted not from lack of money, but from poor governance caused by the on-going Congress disruption. A number of political arguments have paralyzed policymaking and made it difficult to address pressing problems.

Unless these conditions improve, it will be difficult for elected leaders to manage the budget deficit and external debt of my country. And as everyone in the western world should know, this is for me an inherited problem coming from a former US president. His party wanted to reduce the public sector and started implementation by the sweeter part of it: reducing taxes mainly for the rich. But they have done little in reducing expenditure; on the contrary they have hugely increased military expenditure in GDP terms by getting disproportionally involved into two wars, paid at credit."

At that point, the US President passed his hand over his chin before sustaining, "So currently, the problem is not an economic but a political one. As you know, the US may easily refinance the next debt payments. But, mon ami, we were here to speak over your projected federation-the USA debt problem and its spill-over effects will be clarified in the G20 by my Secretary of Treasury-so Let's move on to the European Federation."

The American president stopped to catch his breath before inquiring,

"Entering in the subject, tell me please, what is the value added of your federation? Will it economically and politically be more than the addition of the current capacities of the nine involved countries? Are you convinced that finally Germany and France will be successful in rowing against the stream of history? Let's be frank, the candidate countries of the projected federation share a history of serious rivalries and violence including wars of a hundred-years duration." Perrier with a determined brave expression on his face, "I will start from your last observation. The German Chancellor and I do believe that if we, the nine, merge for solving "common problems" related with European public goods and services, past problems of economic wealth differences and constant begging, will simply disappear, since the nine, federating states have a very similar per-capita income. On the other hand, we are already in our seventh decade of peace in Europe, and Europe has changed enormously in that period. The people in general, and above all, the university students move in Europe very at ease. We are now not only neighbours-as it happened before the Second World War-but friends. And if we are friends and have the same purchase power, problems will not come from the social perspective."

And with his forehead wrinkled into deep corrugations right up to his hairline he continued, "At the same time, having a Central Bank for the Federation and a consolidated Ministry of Finances, we will ultimately solve our current problems with the Euro-System, while we may save a lot of money coordinating our most important policies and functions, mainly our defensive system which by itself will enable a saving of one-percent of our collective GDP."

"Your economic arguments are convincing," replied the American President, who previously noticed an indication of approval by Professor Burman who was sitting at his left, "but I don't think that building up a constitution in which every country will have to give up some sovereignty may be an easy thing. There have historically been cases of constructed federations that have not worked because at the end of the day the additional profits for the new, federated states, were not as visible as the sovereignty they gave up in exchange. And let us not forget the so-called enemies of federation: a mountain of people-mainly politicians and civil servants of the current EU-27-who clearly will suffer with the change, being this the same case that normally occurs in mergers and acquisitions in the field of private firms. They will be in for sabotage. But let us listen, if you do not mind, to Professor Burman, who apparently has something to say."

"If you allow me," said Burman, "I would remind you that in the private world. There are professional mediating firms whose activity is to facilitate mergers and acquisitions, and for long they have been successful all across the world. In the domain of federating or joining nations we have less experience, but in moments of distress-and this is clearly one of them, let us not forget that we are for the moment in the second most serious crisis since the Industrial Revolution, coinciding with an accelerated, industrial shift towards Asia. I think that movements towards federation among economically similar countries could be successful, particularly if the transferred competencies were just the core ones-army, foreign representation, and finances-that is to say, just those that do not affect culture, language, and things like that."

At this time Perrier interjected, "History may have played negatively in some cases as President Leonard rightly remarked, but if carefully treated, things may evolve satisfactorily. We do believe that the real problems of our project are not coming from the countries that will become federal members, but from those who in principle will remain out, and these nations are the majority of the current EU-27. It is certainly a matter of concern that the rest of countries, eighteen, will have to remain connected to us, but *only at economic level*, while they will be absolutely out of the political decision making process of the Federation. Certainly, in the Federation we will make our own independent political decisions, not at all conditioned by our recent past of having been members of the EU-27. And those whom my American colleague has called "the enemies of federation" are of the same nature as the "enemies of private mergers". Consequently, compensations may be paid to them at licensing. Observe also that our federation will be in essence a public services merger, something easier to manage as we will not have minimum profit limitations, typical for private firms, while we count with a Central Bank."

"But Jacques, if you allow me to talk more familiar to you," said the US President. "I do not see well how you are forming a common parliament, with people of so different origins, cultures, languages, etc."

"To answer you properly, Leonard, may I remind you that today, we already have an experience of meetings and deliberations in the different EU-27 bodies with representatives with different languages and cultures. We have become used to speaking in many languages and we are not unique in that; the same happens also in the Indian parliament, the Lok Sabha. More important in your remark is the question of democratically establishing a federal parliament. In other words, like your Congress in Washington, representing all Americans regardless of in which state they live. This means that we will have to establish a federal parliament representing the population of all nine member states, regardless of where they are living and what language they speak. Look, we are thinking of building up what we call Federal European Political Parties, conservatives, social-democrats, liberals, greens, etc."

Leonard interrupted with a smile. "Why not just two parties as in the US?"

"As you are experiencing now, the US system is not optimal. And taking in consideration that we are starting from another position than the US, we need a careful and inclusive built-up. First of all the federal parties in the European Federation will have to pass the threshold of obtaining minimal five-percent of all issued votes; and second they should have obtained seats in at least fifteen-percent of the 120 electoral districts, every one of them containing at around two million voters. This will guarantee their representativeness at federal level".

"This sounds well, and what about the *economies of scale*, you emphasized so much in your presentation in Nice?

"Dear President, it is the economy! We have done the tally, and we do believe that, due to the fact that our countries spend in defence around two-percent of our collective GDP, we may save by federating our defence systems around one-percent of our GDP. It will be saving and improving at the same time. Let's be frank, defence budgets are not popular in Europe. So why should we replicate by nine our rather imperfect defence systems, knowing that after merging them, we will tremendously increase effectiveness and reduce costs.

The same will count for our foreign representation. We will be able to move from several small embassies in hosting countries-one for every of the nine members-to one, big Federation embassy per hosting country; at the end of the day, much less expensive but far more influential. But perhaps most important to overcome the current Euro zone crisis will be the merging of the nine finance ministries into the Federal Ministry of Finances in order to control the accountancy of all public institutions in the Federation and implement federal fiscal policies connected with one, single monetary policy. At the same time, the national parliaments in the member states-responsible for the non-transferred competencies of the state governments-will be in charge of controlling the accounts and procedures of the Federal Ministry of Finance. So in brief, the more functions or ministries are merged, the more economies of scale we will achieve. But, Leonard, to start with, we will initially only merge vital, common services and administrate the common federal public goods." Prof. Burman started applauding by thumping with the knobs of his fingers on the table, but the US President was still not fully convinced as he inquired, "Okay, but if you do not mind, can you clarify somewhat on the international politics of the European Federation? Is our transatlantic partnership to be continued?"

"Well Leonard, I may ensure you that we will remain in the NATO although, we will ask for a new treatment in accordance with our new economic and political size. On the other hand, looking into the new realities of the twenty-first century, you will agree with me that the international agreements on issues that are affecting us all, referring to global warming, need of global economic regulation, etc, can only be solved by effective global governance.

In the past twenty years, the economic structure in the world has changed and it will be changing even more in the next, three decades. It is not easy to admit, but all signs point to the fact that in GDP, in international exports, industrial production, and even in defence expenditure of the developing world will have overtaken the current industrial world, that is to say what we call the West. These new global economic structure will have to be complemented with new global political institutions in which the "global society", that is to say the 192 countries of the United Nations, will have to play a more balanced role."

"Although I do agree with you, in the current American political context, it is extremely difficult for me to present this global economic perspective and the consequences for the West, not even in my yearly State of the Union address. I guess you and the German Chancellor are in a similar position. Believe it... I have already started giving hints, in particular making clear that we will no longer be able to continue with our role of policemen in the world. Our military expenditure should decrease in merit of maintaining infrastructures and improving human resource development in my country."

"Yep, my observation concerning global problems," responded Perrier, "was to launch the idea of democratic global governance, for instance, to correct the current, deficient administration of the seas, fisheries, and all that to protect rainforests and to control the production and prices of strategic raw materials as petrol and others. A lack of global governing that already for decades has induced severe economic cycles.

We will have to democratize the UN and give it capacity of enforcement, which means the constitution of an UN army that may intervene when necessary under the command of the new democratic UN."

"Jacques, how brave of you, but it sounds to me little realistic. Are you suggesting the introduction of a majority system in the UN Assembly and taking away veto rights in the Security Council? Come on, that would induce giving, for example, China and India with their huge populations a leading role in global governance decisions. Mind you, China, the largest undemocratic country in the world... that would really be a major setback for civilization."

"I do not think so. Observe, dear Leonard, that in the coming twenty to twenty-five years the population in China will see an increase in their average income per head of up to 25.000 US dollars. At that level, the society in China will count with an extended middle class, which, combined with an expectable high level of education of its citizens- already millions are annually graduating at academic level-will doubtlessly produce a national democracy. As proven in the history of Europe, middle class, levelled education and income will inevitably produce democracy."

The American President was probably losing patience and his voice sounded slightly irritated. "Oh come on Jacques, stop dreaming. My political advisors say that the Communist Party of China will never give up power to the people because in that case China would fall apart in several pieces. I fully endorse their insight. Do not forget that China was an empire in other times with a lot of colonial territories."

"Leonard, I beg to differ. Observe that most Chinese citizens are today already very conscious of the fact that their country is on its way to become the most powerful economy on earth. The position of China as superpower is only some years away. In the light of that, the act of splitting away and diverting from the centre, in a world in which progressively only large entities count, would be to abandon a promising future and a very profitable business. And on top of that, why abandon a socialist empire in transformation to a modern social democracy, just when all the efforts have been done and the harvest is at hand? That would be as to give up exactly what you and your parents have for long fought for."

"Even more," added Perrier, "China will be economically powerful, but I do not think that we have to fear their attempt to become a hegemonic power. Those ambitions are something of the past, when the power structure in the world was far simpler. Today already it is becoming clear that to be hegemonic is giving you more responsibilities than the spoils you may obtain. That is why some intellectuals in the US, take Professor Stiglitz, are fighting for America giving up on policing the world and going for a significant reduction of US defence expenditure."

Now going slightly red, Perrier bent forward and with a boyish smile to the American President concluded, "Besides, do what you do, Leonard, your defence expenditures will finally be overtaken by those of China, and without any special effort by its citizens, just the outcome of China"s rapid growth rate for another two decades. So, the better would be that we persuade China to embrace global demo...."

BANG...NG...NG.

A strong explosion followed by repeated gunshots brought the meeting to standstill and paralyzed the participants. The silence in the mezzanine was in contrast to the screaming which could be heard, probably coming from the Piazza Orginissenti in front of the hotel or from the narrow streets between the Grand Hotel and the Pitti Palace. It was the signal for the presidents and their bodyguards as well as the rest of the men around the table to jump up in terror and rush to the reception area of the hotel.

* * *

In the reception hall of the hotel some more delegates for the G20 top anxiously gathered and all eyes were on the hotel manager and the Italian police inspector who were trying to calm things down. As the hotel manager explained, the explosion was caused by huge firecrackers that had been placed in a barrel. He had been informed that the Carabineers were using plastic bullets to dissolve the rallies and clear the area, in order to make it possible for the delegates to replace themselves to the Pitti Palace, as the top was to start in less than two hours.

While the manager was speaking, one could hear continued shooting but also sirens of ambulances, fire-fighters, and people screaming, as well as the lancing of more primitive projectiles as cobblestones.

"The instruction to the police is to avoid escalation," continued the hotel manager. "Taking into consideration that we all have once been young and have once protested, we should try to clear the area without hurting anyone. Several arrests have been made. As the police inspector explained to me just now, all is under control. No reason for the delegates to worry. I suggest we use the Montebello-1 meeting room as information centre to keep you update before leaving for Palazzio Pitti."

"There, good Lord, let them in please." Alexandra, the first lady of France, was pointing at two, young protestors who were trying to enter the hall by pushing at the door, even bobbing on the glass. The two young women were looking rather fragile with their eyes expressing fear while begging to come in.

"I think we should let them in," Alexandra repeated while all eyes moved in the direction of the two timorous-looking youngsters women of around twenty. Jacques Perrier supported his wife in her call to assist and to give refuge to the protestors. So did President Leonard, at which the Italian Premier affirmed while neglecting the rejection of the Indian Prime Minister.

But the latter raised his brushy Indian brows and looking rather disturbed, he made the observation. "Once you join the protest, you should have the courage to fight your way home as the others do. A rally is not a tea party."

176

At which the Italian Premier reacted, "Have you always been so cynical?"

"No, it took me years!" was the smiling reply of the Indian leader.

As soon as the youngsters were inside the hall, the American president took the lead and started making an effort to calm them down.

"Ladies, you may stay here till the roads are cleared for you to go home. All of us here have once rallied when we were young. We went to the protest gatherings even though we were afraid since it was considered a necessary part of the transition from adolescence to grownup. In a more popular version my mother used to say,

"Eighteen and no socialist, you have no heart, thirty and still a socialist, you have no brains." However, for most of us the real challenge in our participation was being heard without letting things run out of hands. It is an art to find effective ways to express different points of views and to be heard. If my colleagues allow me, I will now give the two of you some minutes to speak out your demands in front of us. Consider it your lucky day, historically only you two will have been able to address your concerns directly to G20 leaders. Signorinas, we are all ears."

One of the youngsters, smiling released, started speaking hastily, "Sir, we are not unwilling to adjust to globalisation, but we are observing growing difficulties to find suitable jobs in Europe and America while our friends in Asia are working long hours for little wages and no protection. This is unbalanced and absurd. You, the politicians, may defend globalisation as a matter of principle, and this is probably correct, but what you cannot defend is the total lack of control. The economic situation enjoyed by our parents was very favourable and probably undeserved from the perspective of non-Westerners, but what is bizarre, is that you, the global politicians have unconditionally given way for capital to gain money in developing countries, thereby condemning the current generation of Europeans, regardless of their education, to have less jobs, while the little remaining job opportunities will be more precarious and significantly worse paid. So we, the so-called best educated generation in Western history demand democratic global governance to rebalance things."

The expressions of both the French and the American presidents were ones of surprise and Perrier was the first to react, speaking enthusiastic, "What a speech, I thought that you were not politicians, but you are! Allow me a little correction. France does not fully fit in your picture.
You are right in saying that in the last three decades the world has quickly moved towards liberalism, but France has tried to keep its traditional position in relation to the control of the markets. However, with our participation in the European Union, we had to swim with the mainstream, which resulted in us joining in mistakes such as the weak architecture of the Euro, which have put us all into crisis today.
But with the European Federation which is in the making, we will repair the errors, I promise."

Leonard moved forward to push Perrier aside and with a sarcastic smile added, "And France is putting all its weight to create a new and democratic UN. As you may have understood, we politicians do have the necessary solutions in our heads, but we fail to explain them to you. So, may I thank you on behalf of all the G20 leaders for your explanation and have a save journey home."
The Chinese president, who was silent till now, commented, "As I experienced in my years in the University of Beijing, those who fail in explanation prove that they do not understand what they are talking about."
The Indian Premier nodded but added, "I fully agree with my Chinese colleague, although I hope that his experience dates from the days after the Cultural Revolution."

Thirteen

The tragic end of Bopoulos

Without in any way wanting to admit defeat, Carlos Bopoulos, president of the fast-declining European Commission, had been forced to accept the invitation of the German Ambassador in Brussels to attend the garden party the latter was hosting to celebrate the success of the referendum on the European Federation.

The referendum had been held in all the nine, federating countries at the same day and information and communications leading up to that moment had also been streamlined in all countries. Release and happiness was all over when, above expectations, in most of the countries the Yes vote was around a ninety-five percent. The only meagre results came from Finland and the Netherlands with a Yes percentage of respectively fifty-two and fifty-four, but this could not temper the joy among the populations.

For Carlos Bopoulos and his attempts to put a bar in the wheel of the federating process, the outcome of the referendum had been a blow, although deep in his heart he had expected that the populations in the nine countries would favour the best way out of the Euro crisis.

Sitting at the back seat of the black Mercedes in which he was being driven to the German residence, Carlos was preparing himself for the many awkward questions he might receive from other attending Ambassadors and diplomats over the future of the European Union of twenty-seven, now that the most influential member states were pulling out to join a federation. Admitting defeat was one thing; going to a celebration party to make it public was something else.

That Carlos Bopoulos accepted the invitation was not only to keep all balls in the air, but perhaps also to expose that he was a man who bear setbacks without bitterness. Never know how things might in the end favour him and by that he was not thinking of the gesture of the Spanish Prime Minister who offered him the Spanish nationality.

Come to think of it, the British Prime Minister had kept his distance from the moment Carlos reported that their agreed undermining actions to halt the participation of Spain and Italy in the Federation had not been successful. Albeit, the silence of the British Prime Minister was remarkable as he at least one day had hinted at having a stick: the affair with Clara. On the other hand, it was possible that the Prime Minister had some data over the fact that the whole Clara business had dissolved itself much more easily than expected. Carlos had simply refused to answer any of her phone calls, but at the same time he had twice transferred an amount of Euros to her account, and although she had never reacted he believed that his transfers had been recognized by her as the promised compensation.

Then there was the rest of the EU-27, that is to say, the eighteen mainly small and weak countries, who-with the exception of Britain-even before the referendum, had started in a pragmatic way to look into the consequences of the European Federation for their economies, and how not to be side-lined. Those who were in the Euro zone were mainly looking into the consequences of staying in the Euro zone without having any political control on the currency, more or less in a similar position to countries using the US dollar as their currency in other parts of the world.

Others, those not in the Euro zone, were working out possibilities to join with the Federation in a common market, considering that this would be the best option for continuing the economic advantages of the EU in the past, be it now in a far better structured way.

Of course, the British were hardly participating in any of these future projections of the rest of EU-27. London was back on the island and looking for a far greater alternative. As Carlos had seen on the BBC, a new round of heated debates had started over the British decision to join the EU, about staying out of the euro, about the priority of transatlantic partnership, and about the value of the loss of British influence on mainland Europe as a consequence of the Federation.

But, over and again, the British Prime Minister on the screen tried to calm things down by suggesting waiting and seeing since putting the idea of a federation into practise was not going to be easy, as history had proven. The mere fact that in the past ten years it had been almost impossible to agree among the member states on simple things like one pension age or on the same number of holidays per year in all EU countries was proof that making the federation work would be extremely difficult, not in the least with great, inflexible countries like France.

All these debates and developments were of utter importance for the president of the European Commission, who overnight had passed from being the political boss of EU-27 with quiet a number of globally influential countries, to being the PressCom of seventeen or eighteen mainly periphery countries excluded from the centre. So every time the naked truth of this reality crossed his mind, Carlos Bopoulos experienced problems with breathing. Even more, the dominance of the new European Federation changed the terms of any negotiation on the continent, and with the exception of Britain, the future for the seventeen excluded countries under his guidance would be one of adhesion to the proposals of the Federation and not vice verse.

* * *

When the black Mercedes arrived at the residence of the German Ambassador, a dark blue BMW quickly past and thereafter stopped in front of them. In the manoeuvre with far too much speed, the side mirror of the Mercedes was hit and with a bang fall apart in many pieces. Immediately after the hit, the four men involved: two drivers, Carlos Bopoulos, President of the European Commission, and the German, Joachim Steckman, Commissioner for Competition, approached the place with the broken mirror.

Standing alongside the Mercedes, Steckman instantly started scolding the driver of Bopoulos while totally neglecting the President of the European Commission who actually was his superior. It took Carlos Bopoulos by surprise. Who would have thought that the arrogance would pop up so quickly just hours after the success of the referendum?

"Hey, hey, Steckman, the crash was caused by your driver and you know it. And wouldn't it be better to leave the matter for the two drivers to solve?" a highly irritated Carlos screamed. But instead of answering, Steckman almost demonstratively turned his back on Carlos Bopoulos and instructed his driver in German to make sure that no form was filled with any accusation in it, before he strolled away in the direction of the garden, leaving Bopoulos gasping for air.

"Monsieur le Président de la Commission, soyez le bienvenu". Unclear if the German Ambassador had observed the incident, but he was advancing amicably over the lawn in the direction of Carlos.

Bopoulos tried to put bad memory aside as he rushed towards the German exclaiming, "Toutes mes felicitations for the outcome of the referendum. This was the most successful German-French initiative in modern history!"

As they met, they embraced warmly and during the act the German Ambassador murmured close to the ears of Bopoulos that his secretary had been calling for him already twice; it was urgent.

The first reaction of Carlos was to search for, but not find his Blackberry-he probably left it in his office. Consequently he accepted the invitation of the Ambassador to use the phone in the library, and it was there that Carlos Bopoulos got the information that a police inspector was waiting for him in the office and that things were too important to wait for tomorrow. So he had no other choice than a quick farewell, promising he would eventually return and be driven back to his office. Truth be told, he was happy to be able to prematurely leave the party of the federation triumphs.

* * *

On his way back to the office, he was naturally praying that neither his wife nor his daughters were involved in an accident because this is what people usually think when a police inspector is waiting for them.

Accordingly, back in the Rue de la Loi he rushed to his office on the third floor, to find a large female police inspector in the forties waiting in the corridor. However, with her sleazy blonde hair, red apple cheeks under small watery blue eyes, and her uniform spanning tight over her belly, she looked more like a big mama than a keeper of law and order.

"Inspector Leni Boor, Brussels Police," she said pulling a plump hand in his direction.

"Brussels police," Carlos repeated, "Carlos Boloulos, sorry that I kept you waiting. Can I be of any help?"

Inspector Boor was looking straight in the eyes of Carlos as she suggested that they would close the door first and then sat down on the comfortable sofa across his desk. Carlos automatically obeyed but while he was following her orders he was only trying to read any bad news from her eyes.

"Mr. Bopoulos, I will be frank with you, it is about Clara Polar."

"What about her?" he said, and he first felt relieved that his daughters were okay before his mind started fighting with images of Clara in a car accident.

"So, can I conclude that you admit knowing Clara Polar?"

"I am sorry, is she okay? What is this all about?"

"Clara Polar is okay under the circumstances. Any chance the two of you had a sexual relation Mr. Bopoulos?"

"Inspector, I will give an answer to that, but then you will first have to explain to me what is going on."

"Clara Polar has filled a serious allegation against you at the police station in Brussels North this morning."

At the last words of the inspector, Carlos gasped and his mind was racing in all directions ending with a vile vision of Clara handing a written accusation over his presumed abuse of her, probably with the help of friends.

"Inspector, can you tell me what allegation?" Carlos tried biting back as frowns collected his forehead.

"Of course Mr. Bopoulos, that is why I am here."

Inspector Boor was now taking out some papers from a brown bag on her laps, and with her eyes moving by turn from his face to a paper in her hands she started, "According to Clara Polar, the two of you till recently had a sexual relation and over a period of four months. After you suddenly rejected further contact, she had a routine medical control a week ago and the results, presented to her two days after the check-up, shockingly diagnosed her HIV-positive. As she had no other sexual relation, neither before, nor after the love affair with you, the AIDS infection could only have come from you."

"Utterly nonsense!

"Moreover, Clara Polar is convinced that you knew that you were having AIDS and deliberately infected her. Mr. Bopoulos, this is a very serious allegation for which you could be arrested immediately, as we would have to make sure that you could not make more victims in the time between the investigations and court ruling."

"Inspector Boor, I am shocked. This woman is a criminal. This is her revenge for me breaking up with her. She is crazy. To think that I would deliberately infect her makes me a criminal. And why would the police believe her? We have not had any contact for the last months so she could have been infected by someone else."

"Mr. Bopoulos, there are two things playing against you in this case. First, you seem to have been telling Clara Polar by repetition about an affair you had in Goa, India, about a year ago with a twenty-six-year-old woman who at one stage in her life had been exposed to risky sexual activity."

"No Inspector, Clara is making things up. Yes, I have told her about a relation in Goa, but it was a simple affair of two people attracted to each other, and I swear, the Indian women had no such thing as risky sexual activity. Clara's accusations are based on revenge, lies, and fantasy, perhaps hatred. All I hear you reporting are pathetic lies and utterly nonsense from a dangerous charlatan."

"Perhaps Mr. Bopoulos, for God's sake, you should let me continue with the clarification of the allegations. I have it here on paper. These are words of Clara Polar. You will have to falsify her accusation by proving the opposite. I can assure you, the statement is rather consistent and I have personally been taking a great risk by not summoning you to the police station. But as I am a very humane person I have come to your office to give you the opportunity to give me another perspective on the case before I take any of the steps I am supposed to take as a police officer. I am hired to put the justice machinery and the victim protection procedures into working without getting involved. So are you willing to cooperate?"

An even more bewildered Carlos Bopoulos lifted himself from the sofa, loosened his tie, opened the collar of his shirt to be able to inhale some more air, and walked around the room. In reaction to Inspector Boor's advice that he should cooperate, he was nervously gesturing with his hands that he was willing to do so, as he seemed to have lost his voice.

The inspector continued, "Am I right if I say that you just confirmed, Mr. Bopoulos, that you had a sexual affair with an Indian woman in Goa almost a year ago, right?"

Carlos confirmed by nodding his head. He felt bilious.

Inspector Boor sustained, "It was a simple vendor in a small shop of handicrafts near the hotel in which you were staying with your wife and your two adolescent daughters. You need to know that according to Clara Polar-and she has given a detailed description of things as you seemed to have told her the experience more than once-from the moment you entered the shop, you were attracted by the Indian women with her beautiful, deep, velvet eyes looking mysteriously at you while you started telling her in a humoristic way about the daily life in Brussels. She had never left Goa and as very few people came into her shop, your visits and your entertaining stories were most welcome. While your wife and children were on the beach, believing that you were reading a book in the garden of the hotel, you would pass up to two hours with the vendor in her shop. Already at the first day you noted that the vendor was melting down like butter in the sun for your anecdotes; her dark eyes in laughter were following every movement of your lips, as she was leaning towards you over the counter. Next you became aware that you were almost hypnotizing her with your words as she was slightly opening her lips, and you could see her eyes glazed with a covert desire.

By the second day, it was in the air that you would end up making love with her, but it happened on the third day. It happened just after she had told you her own life history. Starting with her arranged marriage at the age of sixteen and her repudiation at the age of twenty-four as she seemed infertile, she had explained, looking shy, that she had been thrown out of the house by her mother in law after her husband had announced her repudiation to Allah. Thereafter, she wandered in the streets of Goa for many days before an older woman offered her shelter. In exchange, she cleaned the place and cooked, but after three weeks she was invited to accompany her benefactress to a bar, to find out that around six women more or less of her age were all supposed to entertain the guests physically. For three nights she was forced to do so and the fourth night she finally managed to run away and found refuge in a Catholic nunnery in the centre of Goa. The sisters helped her to start her handicraft shop some months later. So, after three days, you passionately made love to her on an old sofa behind the counter and, from then onwards, every day, till you and your family left for Brussels six days later. Ten months later, according to Clara Polar, you must have found out having been infected with AIDS, which made you so enraged that you started looking for a victim. And so you infected her, Clara Polar."

"Inspector Boor, stop it please; these are, at best, half-truths, I can assure you." Carlos recovered his voice, although his eyes were looking thoroughly frightened.

"Mr. Bopoulos, I am almost there, please let me finish. I have seen the test results of Clara Polar. No doubt, she is HIV-positive. So tell me Sir, have you at any time in the past year submitted yourself to a medical check-up and would you be able to show me the results?

187

Often at check-ups doctors also ask for testing on sexually transmitted diseases."

"No, inspector, I have not. I am only controlling my blood pressure."

"Okay, before anything else, Mr. Bopoulos, I want you to go for a check on sexual transmitted diseases. Tomorrow, ultimately the day after tomorrow, and if you are cleared, you are a free man. If not, your misery will start. I probably will have to arrest you. You will have to inform your wife, putting your marriage at risk. You will have to appear in court. And on top of that, with your status, media will hunt you down."

Lamely, Bopoulos returned to the sofa, and speaking now as a broken man he murmured,

"Inspector Boor, don't you see that Clara Polar is trying to break me, my family, and my career?"

"Mr. Bopoulos, first you do the test for eventual falsification of the allegations. If disappointing, you will have to find yourself a good lawyer. And for now, I want you to sign this document for me. It states that I had a first interrogation and granted you forty-eight hours to deliver a medical test report."

After a quick glance at the document, Carlos exclaimed, "I cannot, it states that I made love to the Indian women more than once. False, it was only once."

"Mr. Bopoulos, I am not convinced and it looks like you will have a hard time convincing any judge. It is common knowledge that adultery occurs, but what is still expected from all of us is that we protect those we love or make love to. They must be able to trust us for that, Mr. Bopoulos. You were, be it indirect, told beforehand in Goa that there was a risk, and nevertheless you broke the code towards your wife and Clara Polar alike. It is possible that a verdict will be built on the fact that with your behaviour you proved to be selfish and never more trustable. But I have trusted you coming to your office, so please sign here. This does not imply that you agree with the allegations of Clara Polar, but only that I have informed you on the content."

* * *

To make things worse, Inspector Boor hardly entered the elevator at the third floor on her way out when Carlos who was rushing back to his office after letting her out heard his Blackberry ringing on his desk. It was a call from the British Prime Minister.

"Hello Carlos, I have not heard from you in a while, I hope everything is well."

"Yes, I'm fine, and how can I help you?" was the cold answer of Bopoulos.

"Feel like you are running away, my friend. Is not it time for us to talk about the future of the excluding federation?"

"What is there to say Prime Minister? The referendum has been successful and things will develop independently of you and me."

"I do not believe so. For me the future of the federation is very gloomy. It is practically impossible that these nine countries may change into one single state. In fact many others have made similar attempts in history and as far as I know, no one has succeeded, at times also with a little help from outside. And believe me Bopoulos ... you are in an excellent position to support the failure. Think of Italy and Spain; these two Prime Ministers could easily be persuaded by you. I have no doubts whatsoever on your skills to intrigue. "

"I would not know what to say," Carlos mumbled while his face was turning red. This really was not his day, but he instantly felt that he should bounce back adding, "Sorry my friend, I am not convinced, and I cannot promise you anything. Maybe you should first give things a second thought."

"Do not give me that, Bopoulos. If you fail in your endeavour to positively correct the trajectory of Europe, a tsunami may reach Britain but also Algarve," was the enigmatic answer of the British Prime Minister.

Apparently the conundrum was rapidly understood as Carlos, with a clear warning in his voice replied, "For some time already, I had, by references and history, some idea of how you played politics, but I would never have imagined that you would in the twenty-first century play it on the man. I don't care what information you think you can blackmail me with, but I think you are in a mistake. Do not touch my family as I will pursue you till the end of the world. Hope I have been clear." At his last words, he promptly hung up the telephone in the ears of the Brit, well aware that for the first time he firmly protected his family. It seemed that he was able to freely breathe again.

* * *

That night, Carlos did not sleep. He stayed awake for the full, eight hours even after drinking a sleeping pill. Luckily, when he had arrived home from the office at 8:30 pm, he found his wife and daughters away for the cinema, so he had decided to go to bed as soon as possible, thus avoiding having to look the three women he adored into their eyes. He left a note at the table in the living room, left a copy in the dining room, explaining that he was dog-tired and therefore had decided to sleep in the guest room at the third floor, as to make sure that he would not be disturbed by their home coming.

He wished them a happy goodnight and signed by writing, *Love you all very much, Carlos.* Hereafter, he googled HIV testing places and selected two with results in twenty-four hours, deleted the history of his search, and finally took the stairs up to the guestroom.

190

* * *

Lying awake and constantly turning from one side into the other, he could think of nothing else than the test, its possible results, and the consequences. I know I am not infected, he said to himself, and yet it was possible. He was painfully aware of the fact that many exercises of humiliation might be awaiting him and that he would have to show to his children how sorry and ashamed he was about the very bad things he had been doing. He thought of confession and repentance in the cathedral at Grand Place, but actually being an orthodox, this exercise was far from him. If tested positive, would he inform his wife? And would she inform her parents? What would papers head when he was arrested?

* * *

He managed to hide his identity at the clinic by: 1) paying cash and agreeing that he would personally collect the results at the end of the next day, 2) by twisting the information on the form he had to fill in to clarify where he thought he could have been infected, and 3) by selecting a clinic seventy-eight kilometres south of Brussels in a so-called sleeping suburb.

* * *

The two days he spent waiting for the results became days of constantly distorting information and communications towards his family and in his office, and this exhausted him completely.
Combined with more than thirty-six hours of sleeplessness and growing fears over what was lying ahead of him, he had started losing

concentration, loosing calm, and even loosing memory. The man who in other-not faraway-times had been warm and lively, sympathetic, and highly entertaining with a remarkable capacity to speak and joke in several languages, that man had in little time changed into an extremely nervous, bad tempered, manic depressed, and sometimes rude person. This was in brief the state of mind of Carlos Bopoulos, at the moment when he finally collected the test results.

Positive... He did reread the word three times, but it did not disappear from the paper. Killingly, it stared at him... he had tested HIV-positive. It could have been in Goa or by Clara, who would know? What mattered most was that he thereafter might have infected his wife and that he had definitely blown his career, even if the latter had already reached troubled waters with the Federation.

Things now definitely turned uphill for him and sitting in his car with the test results in his hands and, his hands leaning at the steering wheel, he was confused and he could only think of a trip to nowhere, to an unknown place in Asia or Latin America, thousand miles away from home.

The nurse who gave him the test results had repeatedly explained that HIV infection had long time ago turned into a disease not causing death. Not in Europe, perhaps in Goa. Clara would survive, be it drinking medicine for the rest of her life financed via her health insurance, similarly to persons with diabetics drinking their medicine three times a day, the rest of their lives. He would have to do the same. So would his wife.

Alas, he was caught progressively in a terrible cobweb of shame and fear. He felt deeply depressed and completely deserted. Clearly, no one would believe that he had made love to the sympathetic Goa youngster mainly to help her to restore her self-esteem. Similarly, no-one would believe that not a single hair on his head had ever thought of infecting Clara with such a stigmatizing disease, and even more, he had always been a family man with deep warm feelings for his wife and daughters, and certainly he had never been interested in the life of a womanizer or a bachelor always on the hunt.

Nevertheless he was trapped in a disgraceful and unsolvable problem, in a labyrinth without exit. The wish to disappear forever before having to face any of his victims seemed to be the only way out for him, the only solution.

* * *

At 11:00 pm, in a breaking news flash on TV and radio all over Europe, the public was informed that the President of the European Commission, Carlos Bopoulos, had tragically died in a car accident on the E-19 highway from Brussels to Namur. Showing the wreckage of a black Mercedes, the newsreaders explained in the many languages that, around 10:15, pm the car hit a light mast in full speed at the E-19. The highway police considered it likely that the sixty-two-years-old PresCom fell asleep behind the wheel and confirmed that no alcohol was found at autopsy. Carlos Boloulos left behind a widow and two daughters. A number of Cabinet Ministers and Prime Ministers in the European Union Capitals were expressing grieve on TV and their sympathy for the wife and children of the deceased President of the European Commission.

* * *

The funeral of Carlos Bopoulos was solemn. In the Catholic Cathedral of Brussels, a mourning mass was held. In attendance were his entire family, from Greek and the Portuguese side, and many

Prime Ministers and Chief of States. The British Prime Minister was one of the speakers, as was the German Chancellor. Amid the saddened eulogies, the Brit added that the late Bopoulos was the only person who could have averted the European Union's demolition. Indeed a great loss.

Fourteen

Passionate loss for the makers in the first federal elections

As Aunt Frieda used to say back in Weimar, "*The first astonishment always goes deepest, and any surprise after the first, only adds to the deep impression of the first.*"

So, when at 5:00 pm, advisor Hans Schmidt entered the office of the German Chancellor to bid farewell, Marlein Ditch was still digesting the experience of two hours before at the voting station, which had left her in deep astonishment, and consequently she possessed neither the will nor the energy to show much surprise at this second event.

Hans Schmidt-dressed in a colourful Hawaii shirt, creamy Levy Straus pants, and a new half-long bushy hairstyle-looked having gone through a total makeover. A correct observation since in reality, Schmidt had been making revolution in his personal life, resulting finally in his sudden resignation from his top advisor job. Even more, he was to fly out of the country the next day as he had changed from a conventional bibliophile into an innovative adventurer. More precise, he was on his way to explore his possibilities to contribute to the salvation of the Brazilian Amazon rainforest.

Clearly much of Schmidt's conversion should be attributed to the young woman who accompanied him at his farewell tour in the Chancellor's Headquarters in Berlin. With her jet-black hair with ponytail and her dark, quick and clever sparkling eyes just visible under the Asiatic eyelids, the young lady was unmistakably descending from one of the many Amerindian tribes in South America. While Schmidt was proudly introducing his fiancée, Amaras Gusto a pharmacist who specialised in research on medicinal plants and in the discovery of new

195

healing species, the young beauty was simply smiling alleviating, showing her white teeth while eloquently bowing her head.

On invitation of Marlein Ditch, the young couple took a seat at the sofa in the Chancellor's office and drinks were ordered.

"Nice to meet you," the Chancellor babbled while taking a good look at fiancée Amaras. And without winking an eyelid she continued, "I wish you both all happiness in your new live in Brazil. I will certainly miss my faithful advisor, and I pity not even having been able to get acquainted to his fiancée," she ended looking directly at Hans Schmidt, who as usual had started redirecting the conversation away from his private live by remarking.

"What a day!" he said "I went to the polling station this morning to do my duty as European citizen, but it was rather unpleasant to have to vote for an unknown first candidate on the list of the European Conservative Democratic Party. How things have changed in the past eight months. Who would have thought, Mrs Chancellor, that neither you nor the French

President, the two founding fathers of the European Federation, would be present among the candidates to be leading the European Federation Government in the coming five years? You unquestionably deserved better."

The German Chancellor sighed and shook her head before waiving his grievances away by recalling: "This is democracy my friend. As you know, eight months ago, when fourteen parties, Christian Democratic and centre-right Conservative, in the nine federating countries had agreed to jointly form the Federal Conservative Democratic Party (FCD), we suddenly ended up in a bitter battle for the candidacy.

Between you and me, I am convinced that if Jacques Perrier had supported me instead of throwing his full weight against me at the time of list-formation, one of us would have won the primary. As they say, while two dogs are fighting for a bone, a clever third dog will run away with it. This is what happened in the Federal Conservative Democratic Party, be it behind the screens. In the end, we both failed. Of course I could have accepted a lower ranking on the list, but that would mean opting not to become the head of the federal government, which in itself would have tremendously harmed my position inside German politics with our Chancellor Elections just months away".

"Madam, you did not deserve less than to be the Premier of the Federation," fiancée Amaras remarked.
Hans Schmidt added, "Probably Perrier was forced to make a similar judgement, and as we know, he nevertheless lost the presidential elections in France last month. Tragic that such an advanced politician should be retired at the top of his career. The two of you pushed for the Federation to bring Europe out of crisis, thereby also improving the economic perspective of Germany and France, but paradoxically time was not on Perrier's side. Let us hope that over two months the Germans vote for you with more compassion."
"Ach Hans, after my experience of this afternoon, I would not be surprised if my faith in the upcoming German election would appear analogous to Jacques. The financial crisis was in the making long before I became Chancellor, but with the water up to their lips, voters tend to blame only the incumbents. Sadly at this time of the first Federal Elections almost in all nine federal states Christian Democratic or Conservative and Liberal parties are in power. Could you imagine eleven months ago, when the flag of the European Federation was raised on all-important buildings in the capitals of the nine federating countries, that today I would be visiting a polling station to cast my vote to select a first European Federal government, and that not one single journalist, cameraman, or photographer was around. As if my role in bringing about the European Federation was something of a long grey past, a happening of a hundreds of years ago. What a rare

experience to be erased completely in so little time. It was astonishing and I am still digesting it."

"In the way it is wiping off memories, time is a big traitor. Especially good services are easily forgotten while the blaming game for the bad and the stigma's remains vivid in people's minds," Amaras lyrically spelled out with her deep, sing-song voice.

Marlein Ditch sat silent and was looking away from the two young lovers while she let memory pass over the developments in the past months.

First a provisional government of the Federation, recognised as that by the provisional Constitution, had been formed eleven months ago via consensus by the top executives of the nine federating countries (Prime Ministers or executive Presidents). This provisional federal government, consisting of a provisional Federal Premier and five, provisional Federal Ministers, had as its core business the preparations of the first federal elections to select a parliament and a government for the European Federation of nine.

Already in the first month, the provisional federal government supported by the five commissions had agreed on date, rules, procedures, and infrastructure of the elections, as well as the registration period, conditions and eligibility of federal political parties and candidates. Parties on regional or single issues, as well as parties excluding some citizens of the Federation on the base of ethnicity, gender, or sexual preference, were not eligible. So quite a number of parties would be disqualified such as the Anti-Globalist party, the Non-Smokers party, the European Unemployed party, and all nationalist or religious parties.

Then there was the problem defining the electoral districts-let us remember that according to the constitution each electoral district would have around two-million electors without disenfranchising voters in the five smaller but richer states (Luxembourg, Netherlands, Finland, Austria, and Slovenia). This had been solved by introducing a period of transition of ten years in which electoral districts were defined in such a way that of the 360 elected representative for the Federal Parliament; ninety representatives would be elected in the thirty districts of these five small member states. However, the rules that parties should pass the threshold of obtaining minimal five-percent of all issued votes, and that they should obtain seats in at least fifteen-percent of the 120 electoral districts, remained intact.

Similarly, the creation of frontier voting districts between two or more federating countries, particularly in regions with some special historical connotations was temporarily allowed. All this resulted in a total of 120 voting districts, with election of three representatives per district, which, with all variations included, would provide for 360 elected federal representatives.

Soon after, the various families of parties in the different member states-social-democrats, conservatives, greens, liberals, etc.-started meetings to form federal parties on their specific characteristics, at times with large margins such as Socialists and Labour Parties.

It was logical that when the political parties of Jacques Perrier and Marlein Ditch, both belonging to the family of centrum-right parties, entered into negotiations with another to form the Federal Democratic Conservative Party, Jacques personally contacted Marlein to harmonize expectations.

"Hello Marlein, as things look now, I suppose there will be only two main political forces dominating the scene, our FDC party and the Federal Labour-Socialists. Perhaps the Greens might also enter in the Federal Parliament, but the Premier of the Federal Government will stem from FDC or FLS. In any case I do not believe that the rest of parties will overcome the thresholds of the five and the fifteen-percent, not even the liberals. Even more, bearing in mind the personal contributions of you and me, our FDC certainly has the best expectations."

"Not only, said Marlein, I just finished reading in Le Monde that you explicated in an interview on France-2 that you will probably be First Candidate on the FDC list. Premature, is not it? We have yet to talk about this issue that I understand as essential to win the elections."

"Ach, you know how journalist are. I am sorry. I may have hinted in that direction during the interview, but nothing more. And by the way, I really thought overhearing you saying weeks ago that your preference was to continue heading government in Germany, or am I mistaken?" Jacques quickly replied.

As Marlein kept silent, he continued, "We both know that the power at federation level will be far less important as in the US and this while the responsibilities at global scale will be relevant."

"For me," answered Marlein, "Germany is a business done. It does not represent much more of a challenge for me. But on the contrary, to become the first Premier of the Federation, a first Federal Premier being a woman, would historically be a breakthrough. Come on Jacques, you and I have worked well together in the last year to create the Federation. So, why would you not continue with me, if I take the executive head of the Federation?"

"Frankly speaking Marlein, it is not for us to decide. First our boards are on set, and thereafter the electorate. I will not withdraw my candidacy and suggest you should neither."

"No, you are mistaken," reacted Marlein. "We have to clarify this issue from the very beginning in order to transmit to the electorate of the Federation that we are already very prepared to execute the Federal agenda, but if we continue giving interviews with contradicting information, I mean, I could also inform the public on our dirty battle for the Premiership. This could work out in favour of our adversaries, the FLS (Labour-Socialists) and we could even loose the elections. And my friend, do not forget that most of the Federation citizens expect you and me teaming up, to solve the recent economic problems in our countries. You are now breaking the team."

"I prefer the involved boards to decide democratically on the First Candidate. Let the internal primaries speak. I think that for you as well as for me, to change the level of our activity moving up to the Federation is the best bet we may take and I would not want to exclude myself without giving it a try. Hope you can understand."

"No I cannot. Do I have to remind you Jacques that our main target was that after a transitory period of twenty-five years, just a generation, citizens of the EU Federation would have identical treatment in all aspects of social security? In the next quarter of a century, really a small period in the history of our nations of origin and in the future life of the Federation, all citizens would speak and write in their own home language and in English, besides other languages they want to learn.
Besides, all of them would have the same opportunities for personal development. We would have one federal migration rule and one, unique frontier police. Our economy would be an efficient mix economy of market, in which the risks receive compensation, but not an egoistic economy in which everyone has to look for their own survival. We both know that most traditional market economies have a per-capita income far of those typical of the social economies of market like ours. Do I have to remind you that social economies of market have recently been identified as feminine societies? Tell me, which of us would be better to lead the execution of this policy?"

"Marlein, how disappointing you sound. I cannot but consider your fragmented exposition-although containing much of our common goals-as deliberately twisting facts. It seems to me no more than an attempt to give a blow beyond the belt. Thought we had become friends, but perhaps in the power game there are no friends."

"Jacques, do not play martyr, you seem to forget who first pissed outside the pot. I did not make any statement on TV. Let us wait for the primaries, and for now, please do not call me anymore."
And so their last personal conversation ended before history took a ride with Jacques and Marlein by the nomination of a third candidate, the

Prime Minister of Austria, as First Candidate on the FDC list; a development which soon after proved leaving more chances for the FLS to win.

* * *

To break the silence, Hans Schmidt had started coughing and the German Chancellor slowly turned back to reality. In an attempt to set aside the bitterness of the memories, she now focused on fiancée Amaras.

"Tell me, Fraulein Amaras, what secret prescription have you used to convince my advisor that his future is lying in the Amazon jungle of Brazil with you? I have tried long to convince him to quit his bachelor life, but thereafter I would have preferred keeping him here. Ha ha!"

At this point the Chancellor was smiling unarmed and once again Hans Schmidt made an effort to redirect the conversation, this time away from his fiancée and the relation.

"Madam Chancellor, first prognoses are coming in on my Blackberry. They suggest victory for the Federal Labour Socialist Party, but without a majority. FDC will be second. Surprisingly, favourable results are also foreseen for the Federal Green Party, who will become third. So we will have the first coalition Federal Government. Challenging!"

However, neither Amaras, nor the German Chancellor was willing this time to give in to the diplomat, and the two even started speaking over Hans Schmidt as if he was not in the room.

Fraulein Amaras, smiling contentedly, informed Frau Ditch on her first encounter with Hans and the start of the relation. As she explained, some seven months ago, she met Hans in the canteen of the Academic Hospital in Berlin, where he had visited his ill father and she had presented the outcome of the testing of new herbal medicines to

202

medical students. According to Amaras, Hans had walked over to her and requested her company. As she later understood, he had been advised by the medical doctor of his father to contact Amaras over alternative medicines to slowdown Alzheimer. Anyway, he had been very original in his approach.

Bowing like a knight, he had added, "Madam, we have met before, or more accurate, I have met you on my computer screen in YouTube.

And truth be spoken, reality defeats the screen of my PC. Would you be willing to share some of your precious time with me, a humble diplomat? Can I offer you a coffee? It is about my father, if that does not scare you off, but perhaps also a little about me, if I am lucky."

And while Amaras and Hans were walking towards a table in the canteen, Hans suddenly remarked, "Irresistible of Givengy. I love the smell."

"Correct, how come you recognize women perfume on brand from a distance?"

"Madame, I shall tell you my secret. I have passed many waiting hours –in airports and on boring Saturday afternoons in Berlin-testing perfumes in glamorous stores and whether I like it or not, I have become an expert. And now my nose can identify the precise perfume being used by a lady walking at a distance of up to two meters from where I am." Amaras was still laughing at the memory and in reaction the Chancellor cried out, "How sweet! Not a single hair on my head would have imagined that my bibliophile advisor could be so charming. So, you had coffee with him and he ended up leaving the service to go on adventure with you in the Amazon forest"

"No, we talked a lot over the problems of his father and alternative medicines and over my research. But three days later, his father died. My pharmaceutical suggestions were too little and too late. It was very painful for all of us, but of course mostly for Hans."

"I know, Amaras. It is a sad story. And as far as I was informed, Hans had done all he could to make life more bearable for his father.

Excuse me to insist, but after the failed prescriptions, how come Hans still decided to follow you up into the Amazon tropical forest?"

"The most shocking was the fact that his father had lost all memory. This was already the case when Hans and I met. His father could not recognize his only son and it was not possible to introduce me to him," said Amaras.

Meanwhile Hans Schmidt sat humble and silent on the sofa, Marlein Ditch was stroking the back of one hand with the fingers of the other and Amaras Gusto took a deep breath before she corrected the Chancellor.

"May I take the freedom to precise on one of your question, Madam Chancellor? To be accurate, I am not a Brazilian, I am Peruvian, and the choice to go to Brazil was not mine in the first place. I am just following my partner."

With his eyes on his Blackberry, Hans Schmidt made a new attempt to divert the conversation between the two ladies by observing, "I have no doubt that our children and grandchildren will remember this day as the most important day of the history of modern Europe. The traditional democratic deficit of the EU-27 was buried today in the Federation. Perhaps my children will not understand what we are talking about, if I tell them the stories of the flop of the EU Constitution of 2004, or the frustrations over the Euro crisis starting in 2008".

"Congratulations, dear advisor, but let us stick to the purpose of your visit. Why leave the service, why go to the middle of nowhere, why force this talented young lady to follow you? What education will your children have?" the Chancellor insisted.

As their eyes crossed, Hans Schmidt remembered how irritated he used to feel when the Chancellor kept asking things over his private life.

The last time was during the flight back from Madrid on the day of the parliamentary vote on the draft constitution for the Federation.

"Madam Chancellor, remember that we often spoke about the fact that European citizens would have to adjust to the new circumstances of globalization? I mean, the industrial shift to the East creating structural loss of jobs in the West, global warming and climate change, the end of one superpower policing the world and administrating scant, raw materials, emerging superpowers in Asia influencing international politics for peace and security, etc. We agreed that Europeans would have to change much of their life style to adjust to the new, emerging world. I mean: not only their overconsumption and individualistic materialism in comparison to the rest of the world, but also their values and behaviours including revaluing family life, leisure time, and decompressing social relations. And last but not least we should actively reduce our so-called footprint to save the earth for future generations."

"I remember Hans, but do not tell me that you are going to pioneer on this necessary new lifestyle by going to the Amazon forest. What a waste of talent."

"Mrs. Chancellor, this is exactly what I am going to do. For your knowledge, we will not be living in the jungle; we will be working in Manaus, in the University of the Amazonas. As the Amazon jungle represents over half of the planet's remaining rainforest and it comprises the largest and most species-rich tract of tropical rainforest in the world, Amaras and I are proud that we will be able to contribute, be it humble, in its conservation. Besides, I will be writing as a correspondent for *Berliner Zeitung*, so you may follow our practices. My articles will suggest ways in which Germans can contribute in their daily life to the conservation of the lungs of our planet."

Placing three fingers of a hand under her chin, the Chancellor held,

"Dear advisor, everyone according to his merits. I am proud of you and so would your late father have been. Wish both of you success with your idealism and hope it does not turn out to have been illusionism."

* * *

Back home in his apartment, Hans and Amaras prepared themselves for the final outcome of the federal elections on TV. They made themselves comfortable on an old, green, sit-sleep sofa, one of the few things that had not been packed that morning by the movers. The sofa had been a present of the mother of Hans when he left home for campus. Although Amaras was curious to know why the sofa was not going to Manaus, she learned that speaking of anything related to the mother of Hans was a subject to be avoided in the relation.

The old, analogue television was the other thing that had not been placed in the container for Brazil. For the rest the living room was completely empty, showing only the difference in colour of the wall paint at the places were the many book cupboards had been leaning on.

Sitting close to each other on the sofa with a bottle of red wine, two glasses, and some pretzels in a small plate on a side-table-the third and last thing not packed for Brazil-they were watching the screen with the outcomes of the counting per polling district. One after another the figures came in, and what Amaras and Hans saw made them cling closer in each other's arms as it represented a pleasant surprise.

First of all, the turnout was remarkable large, in particular in the more outsized states of the Federation a majority of eighty-percent of the electorate had cast their votes. Only in Finland and Slovenia, the turnout was more in the range of sixty to sixty-five-percent. The final outcome was outstandingly in line with earlier predictions: Federal Labour-Socialist was leading with 160 seats, Federal Conservative Democrats had won 118 seats, and the Greens had managed to gather an astonishing 82 seats. None of the other participating parties had managed to pass the thresholds.

Moving ever closer to Hans, Amaras inquired, "Darling, forgive me for saying, but I heard you telling the Chancellor today that you had voted for the Conservative Democrats, correct? I thought you favoured the Greens."

While caressing her nose tip with his finger Hans admitted, "Yes, I voted green. My lovely flat nose, this afternoon was perhaps my last diplomatic meeting. From now on, it will be the truth and nothing else than the truth."

"Why lie to the Chancellor when she was not even running? I was taken by surprise as I clearly noticed some warmth between the two of you. I think she really likes you and, concerning her being out of the federal power play, I feel that you should have played fair."

"You may be right Amaras, but it was difficult, even at my farewell. Perhaps because people consider her distanced and cold, perhaps because of her plain Jane look, perhaps because I never have been open to her, even though my real experience in her neighbourhood had often been the opposite of her image. I think she is far more sensitive than she shows, but one cannot be at ease in her neighbourhood. And when she met her ex in Moscow-by the way she never even hinted at it to me, but the man himself told me the history the same evening-I sensed tangible sadness for the rest of our stay in Russia."

"I had the feeling that she was also quite sad today. And it is probably not because you leave, but because of her being side lined in the federal elections. I can imagine that, after all the energy she has put in the federation."

"Amaras, you are a good observer. It must have hurt her that she also lost the friendship with Perrier. Even I felt down at her explanation this afternoon."

"Look Hans, the future Premier of the European Federation will speak to the European citizens," Amaras said.

Both were now staring at the television on which professor Jan-Hein Escalleno, First Candidate of the Federal Labour-Socialist (FLS) party, appeared.

Jan-Hein Escalleno, an old member of the Italian socialists, counting sixty-nine years, was swaying gently from side to side as he approached the table at the podium. He was selected in primaries in the FLS as a compromise since no-one in the centre-left family of parties forming the FLS truly believed that victory in the first federal elections would move from the brave initiators in the FDC to the back benchers and even slackers in the FLS.

Don Escalleno was a remarkable person as he was born in Madrid out of the marriage between a Dutch opera singer and an Italian bank clerk, and he had past his youth in three, different European countries before he studied ethics in Florence.

The emeritus professor of ethics, looking overwhelmed, received a warm applause. He was a respected old man who had accumulated experience in Strasbourg since the birth of the first Parliament in 1979. And for a short period in between, Jan-Hein Escalleno had also been minister of education and culture in Rome. Would his multicultural experience be enough to guide the Federal ship to calmer waters?

"Darling, do you see what I see? Marlein Ditch, German Chancellor, will react to Premier Escalleno's speech via a video-conference."

"Yes, and also the French President, I mean ex-President Perrier."

The TV presenter announced that the initiators of the Federation were going to be interviewed on the historical event of today, but first the citizens of the Federation were invited to listen to the words of the first elected Premier of the European Federation.

When the emotions of Professor Escalleno and many leaders of the centre-left parties in the member-states-who either joined the podium or were reacting via video-conference-ebbed away, there was silence as the official federation anthem, taken from Mozart, was played.

Thereafter the campaign song of the Federal Labour Socialists was played, not in the least, because the script was written by Escalleno himself. In combination with a dynamic video clip, it had become a hit on YouTube, TV and radio across all nine federal states as it was sung in ten languages.

The song read: *Every state where government intervene to correct market failures; every land where justice is done to the fortunate and the less fortunate alike; every place where government considers solidarity part of daily life; any state where caring for the earth and its environment is common practise, there is my fatherland, there is where I want to live, and that is the EF.*

And the refrain: *There is my fatherland, there is where I want to live, and that is the EF lead by the FLS.*

After thanking the European citizens for the trust in him and his party, and after promising to solve the economic problems of the young Federation, the envisaged Premier of the European Federation, launched a call to the two other parties to consider coalition, as he "thought that a first federal government should have the broadest support possible of the European citizens". A big applause erupted as the camera moved away and now Jacques Perrier in a dark suit appeared on the screen.

The TV presenter requested, "Mister Perrier, the future Premier of the first federal government has invited your party to join in a coalition government. What is your reaction? And maybe you could reflect on the outcomes of the first federal elections, as your party has lost."

"Concerning FDC joining a FLS federal government, I think that for the first parliament of the Federation, the FDC should be in the opposition. The Federation is in a process of building up and we will collaborate from our points of view. I think that the Federation is not in crisis and so it does not need a concentration government. On the other hand, the provisional constitution clarifies the agenda of the Federation, to which every government should adjust. My heartfelt congratulations to Professor Escalleno and I wish him success for the

209

good of the Federation. As to the second question, I dare to say that FDC has lost because we had a bad campaign, almost defensive instead of continuing the good start the German Chancellor and I made. In general the public is short of memory, but we should have reminded them of the pioneers work done. And of course there was the so-called incumbent factor, which also caused me now being under resignation."

As the cameras in Paris gave way to cameras in Berlin, Marlein Ditch appeared on the screen, dressed in a light blue, two-piece looking rather at ease.

The presenter requested, "Madame Chancellor, how do you feel at the results of this first federal election? Contrary to what seemed logic, the party of the makers of the Federation has lost. Do you have any explanation for this?"

"I have a slightly different understanding of reality than my French colleague. Perhaps the loss of our party has been a punishment of the electorate. A punishment we deserve. We have spent valuable energy and resources on infighting to prepare the candidate list. As we have not been able to offer an image of stability in our federal party, it has clearly been impossible to convince enough voters that we would stabilize the federation, and voters are free in their choice. Regrets, I may have a few but, then again, I wish Jan-Hein Escalleno great acumen to create the prosperous future the citizens of the federation are dreaming of."

At the last words of the Chancellor, an emotional Amaras screamed,

"Oh Hans please, it is so unfair! She sounded very near to tears."

"Come on Amaras, pull yourself together; there is nothing we can do about it. Nothing else than to accept the outcome; and Marlein Ditch was not even a candidate."

As tears were now freely running over Amaras cheeks, Hans Schmidt was trying to comfort her, putting one hand in her neck and the other on her chin while closing in to her face and whispering.

"Please I cannot see you crying, Fraulein Ditch has lost, it is sad but nothing can change that. You have no idea of how much I had wished my mother had not told my father ever that he was suffering from Alzheimer, but she did instantaneously. That day I felt most pain because the truth was a one-way situation, no return and no escape. And then, as my father was in the first stage of the illness, he could fully understand the meaning and the consequences of what my mother had just told him and he knew, or better, all three of us knew that there was no way back. I feel the same now, Amaras. The pioneers have lost and that is it. No way back. Sad, very sad, so Amaras, I beg you; please don't cry!"

Fifteen

Celebrating the fifth anniversary of the Federation

It was the year 2018, and 10:30 in the morning of an ordinary Thursday in Hotel Negresco in Nice, Cote d'Azur. The people moving up and down in the English pub, furnished in old brown and olive green, were waiters and waitresses busy setting tables and refilling the bar and the glass vitrines of the counter with drinks and snacks. Indeed all employees were focused on the arrival of VIP guests from all over Europe to celebrate the fifth anniversary of the European Federation.

An early arrived was sitting at the extreme of the bar of the pub, reading at the same time *Le Figaro* and *Nice-Matin* at the lights of a Victorian-style, green lamp. He was the sole customer, a man in progressive glasses, in black frame original from Hermenegildo Zegna, which elegantly contrasted with his white hair and beard. He was dressed in a deep green checker jacket on which one could recognize the shield of the Golf Club of Calcutta, and his olive green shirt not only contrasted with a black butterfly, but also with Levy Strauss jeans and sporty Clark shoes.

After five years of practically having abandoned public life and after having aged at a speed twice as fast as normal, and due to the effect of hiding behind thick glasses, only the person who was surveying him discretely from the entrance, his uniformed bodyguard, was able to recognize him. But as the readers may imagine, the early arrived was no one less than the ex-President de la Republique, Monsieur Perrier Jr. and son of the late coffee-retailer of Bayonne.

Wrapped in a soft, musical background with a band playing the theme of the film, *Gone with the Wind*, Perrier was calmly reading when suddenly two, oriental girls of four and six, rushed in, pursuing a small, brown dog. The laughter and races of the girls was complemented with that of the two waitresses who were also trying to capture the dog in order to attach the lace and collier to his neck.

Finally, when the dog was under control, a sweaty and breathless lady entered the English Pub. She had her dark blonde hair carelessly tied up with a pin and was dressed in a flowered, pink and blue blouse, hanging baggy over tight black trousers. Notwithstanding her youthful dressing style and the young age of the two girls calling her mom, her wrinkled forehead and fallen neck witnessed that she apparently was in her second fifties.

With all the noise produced by the small event, Perrier had diverted his eyes from the newspapers and was amusingly observing the development of the capture of the dog. Looking at the lady, Perrier had a strong feeling of having met her before. So, while listening to the conversation between the woman and her girls, he had a closer look at her and could not believe what he was seeing. Here she was, an old friend of him, Frau Ditch, the "German Spinster", best known as the ex-German Chancellor.

Consequently, when the group of three, accompanied by a German bodyguard were near to leave the Pub, he screamed, "Excuse me, you are Marlein Ditch, are you not?"

"Yes" she said turning around. At that very moment the bodyguard of Marlein rushed to Perrier and showing his identification as a German police officer requested him to identify himself.

While showing his ID to the German police, Perrier exclaimed in loud voice to Marlein, "I am Perrier, the former president of France." And he added while walking over to her, "Haven't seen you for a hundred years."

"Jacques, how pleasant is the surprise! Although, I had somewhat expected to see you tonight, as we should all be here celebrating the Federation, meeting you just now is nice. How are you doing?"

"I am okay, but clearly less than you. You look happy, mommy Marlein! Would you be able to join me for a cup of coffee, to catch up?"

"I would love to, Jacques, but first let me introduce you to my two daughters before they leave to the garden with the nanny. Girls…this is Jacques Perrier, mommy's best friend."

"Daddy, daddy," shouted the smallest of the two dark-skinned children while she immediately grasped the leg of Jacques, who was still rather amused over the total, changed outlook of Marlein.

"I guess your daddy would look far more Indian than me," replied Jacques looking at Marlein with smiling eyes.

"You may be right, Jacques, I really do not know their parents, but I'm happy to introduce my two girls, Laksmi and Shanti, six and three. As they were without parents in Penang, in Malaysia, and the orphanage accepted me to take care of them, we are happy the three of us, building a nice family. Frankly, I myself am disproportionately satisfied," Marlein replied.

Perrier had now grasped the hand of Marlein. "Dear friend, I guess you are also in the broadcasting of tonight, I mean the Euro-News special, in celebration of five-year anniversary of the European Federation? It is live broadcasting and I think that we will perform together. Just minutes ago, I was thinking of the press conference we had here seven years ago. You remember the proxy-ETA attack coming from the ceiling? What a day. Ha-ha. We sweat blood for some minutes."

"Yes," exclaimed Marlein. "I remember you sweating, not me. I remained calm but you did not, do you recall? As to the Euro-News special of tonight, I have also been invited. I agree that we should speak with one voice Jacques. And we can speak from our hearts, since both of us have left the political arena. I am now living in Dresden with my two kids."

"You have left Berlin for Dresden?"

"Oh, yes, after we lost the general elections to the Federation and in six months time I also lost the Bundestag elections in Germany-you may recall-I resigned from all my political compromises and decided to go back to my beloved Dresden. You know, that is where I did my university studies and lost my innocence. Perhaps you are not aware...but I married young in Dresden, although sadly my husband prematurely died."

"You Marlein, married?" Jacques interjected.

"I had no children with him, and after the, let us say, lukewarm experience in marriage in Dresden I have never felt the urge to repeat it. But surprisingly, the kid part came back after I left politics, so I went for them and really they are a godsend for me. Of course I knew that you had also lost your elections in France. I should have written to you, but finally I did not. Sorry. But Jacques..., how is your life now?"

"These days, my life is horribly quiet. To the extent that I think that so much inaction may kill me in little time. I think that I have aged fast in the last years for the lack of using my adrenaline. It makes me nervous during the day and at night produces me nightmares."

"To tell the truth, Jacques, I would not have been able to recognize you. You look very elegant, but you look like another person, someone of the world of intellectuals, with your glasses, your new look...frankly, it suits you extremely well."

"Marlein, as you said before, we will be free to speak from our hearts tonight. So what will we speak about? I think that whatever questions are put before us, we should be absolutely truthful and the European citizens should know the background of the economic decisions we have made to solve the Euro crisis and to construct the federation."

"How time may change our perspectives?" exclaimed Marlein rising the cup of coffee.

After a meditative sip she continued, "Although I am extremely proud of having promoted the European Federation with you Jacques, I am no longer convinced of the correctness of the economic policies of my government in the pre-federation days in Germany.

We blindly followed the ideas of some neo-liberal economists of those days, who today, six years later, are under strong criticism.

Certainly, some of them are now in full discredit while others are considered pure malefactors. In particular top executives of Central Banks and even some Nobel Prizes of those days should today hide in shame. They made us to believe during three decades that what they preached, the goodness of the total freedom of markets, was the utter truth. And finally we have become aware that the whole bunch had been captured by Wall Street."

"But Marlein, may I deduce from your words that you have now become a Keynesian?"

"Not exactly, but today I am more flexible than in those days. Even more, I have stopped worshipping the central idea in Germany of the utter relevance of price stability, overseeing any other economic target, for instance job-creation."

"So Marlein, you are now finally on my field."

"Could be, but for me the importance of our cooperation in those days, was first and foremost the establishment of a selective European Federation. Something, which as we can see today, has been far more relevant than interested disputes over monetary stability, financed by private banks, and backed by polluted academicians."

"Marlein, although I would not say this ever in public, you and I perfectly knew that most of our fellows of those days were mainstreamers and followers. As it is said, those who move do not

217

appear in the photo regardless of if they are from the political right or left. As far as you and I were not elected in the Federation, nor in our own national polls, this is for me a proof that with our initiative for Federation, we moved out of the box; we abandoned mainstream."

"Yes Jacques, I have continued moving out of the box, to the extent that I am now actively promoting a multicultural Europe. Would you believe that? But ever since I went to Penang to collect my girls and I was confronted with the relaxed multicultural and multi-religious character of the Penang society, I have converted in promoting far more openness towards other cultures and religions in Europe. In Penang I have walked in streets with mosques, Christian churches, a synagogue, and a number of Hindu temples, and I felt embarrassed over my remarks on the subject years before, even though my remarks were actually provoked by the then rising populist parties."

The conversation between Marlein and Jacques continued for another half an hour till Marlein remembered that she had promised her children to take them to the attractions park at Biot before lunch. As the friendship had been restored, the two amiably said goodbye.

They would meet again at six that evening in the studio of France2 in Nice, where a live debate between the two initiators of the European Federation, and with participation of the federal Premier and two Nobel Laureates in economics, would be broadcasted.

* * *

At five to six, Marlein arrived at the TV building where she was received by the officials and taken to the broadcasting studio to be introduced to the other guests: Escalleno, Perrier, and the two economists Ackerman and Burman.

The guests were sitting around an oval glass table, microphones attached to their collars, and a glass of orange juice or water in front of them. The bottle of champagne in the silver bucket was to be opened for the toast just at the end of the program.

As a starter, the audience at home was watching a compilation of images of the past seventy years of the European unification project, arranged mainly around issues and not so much in sequence of time. From the "Congress of Europe" meeting in The Hague in May 1948, reporters quickly mentioned the 1951 European Community for Coal and Steel, to jump to the Treaty of Rome in 1957, followed by the Maastricht agreement in 1992 which resulted in the introduction of the Euro coins and notes in 2002. Thereafter the focus was on the celebrations of the 2004-2007 omnibus enlargements, turning into the desperate Euro crisis, but leading up to the successful establishment of the European Federation in 2013. Subsequent the arrangement of positive union developments were contrasted with images of setbacks such as the no-vote in 2005 of the French and Dutch populations on the Referendum on the Constitution, and images of the bleak days of the Balkan War in the 1990s combined with images of pathetic discussions, over the need and legitimacy of an invasion in Iraq in 2003, to destroy non-existing weapons of mass destruction.

At the end of the compilation, the studio debate started with first remarks of the reporter directed to Jan-Hein Escalleno.

"Premier Escalleno, congratulations! How does it feel to have headed the European Federation in its first, successful, five years?"

"Would you allow me to transfer your congratulations for the success of the Federation to Marlein Ditch and Jacques Perrier? Without their brave and consistent efforts, we would perhaps today have remained on a ship of twenty-seven captains, totally out of

219

course. That situation was putting at risk not only economies in Europe but also in the rest of the world. At the end of the first decade of the 21st Century, the Euro crisis and the huge externalities on a world scale had put us on a steep wounding route to deep recession and we should thank Marlein and Jacques for having turned the boat. Madame ... Frau Ditch, Monsieur Perrier,...chapeau!"

At his last words, the audience in the studio, including the cameramen and the TV presenter, started applauding exhaustively.

Consequently, the program presenter lost reserve as he minutes later addressed Perrier.

"My admired and respected former president of France, Mr. Perrier, could you explain when and why you felt the inspiration to propose the creation of a European federation?

"Although there had been arguments for the formation of a federation already in the early 1970s, it was the financial crisis of 2008-mainly hitting the West, I mean Europe, US, and Japan-which gave us the opportunity to breakthrough. All of a sudden, we were confronted not only with high youth unemployment, but also with an economic decadence and a political stalemate. The EU-27 was incapable to take any decision and a number of Euro zone countries were putting the monetary union at risk. And this while we were losing the train of economic progress, and the economic gravity centre of the world was moving to Asia. Not to mention the fact that even before the Balkan war, the then EU-15 had little role in international politics except backing-or-not of the Americans in their foreign policies. It is against this background that Marlein and I launched the proposal for a selective Federation. It had to be selective since some EU members were not interested while others in the Euro zone simply did not pass the test of economic homogeneity."

A new round of applause followed the rationalization of Perrier, while cameras were turning towards the Nobel Laureate Burman, and the presenter requested, "Mister Burman, although the idea of federating could in principle be acceptable, did it not contain a great risk of creating a multicultural-multilingual monster-state, more inefficient than the old EU-27?"

Burman, a man already far in his fifties, first took a sip from his glass, then placed his fingertips of both hands against each other, and looked around as if he was trying to gain time before finally answering, "As it has been remarked at many occasions by the promoters, the federation would surely achieve huge economies of scale, mainly in relation with the external and international functions of the federation. I mean defence, international cooperation, economic and commerce policy and external representation. And as an external observer, I have to say that these assumed economies of scale have today become real even ahead of schedule."

"And what about the improvement of economic governance" inquired the reporter now watching Ackerman, the other economist, and a man more-or-less of the same age as Burman.

"Certainly," said Ackerman, specialist in dynamic economics, while looking at Perrier and Ditch, "when the two of you initiated the process, the situation of the Euro zone was really pathetic, as a consequence of the very deficient architecture of the Euro-system in the Maastricht Treaty. But you had the courage to initiate a correction, which had to be selective because many Euro zone members were totally paralyzed by the financial crisis, others could not fulfil healthy debt criteria, and some others did not want to transfer more sovereignty to Brussels. So, the two of you took the right decision: to move forward with a group of pioneers, while promising the rest that they would not be abandoned to their own survival."

Moving microphone and cameras in the direction of Marlein Ditch, the program presenter requested, " But Madame, don't you believe it highly unfair that many countries that had come a long way with the rest by belonging to the Euro-system, finally remained excluded from the federation? I am referring to Ireland, Portugal, and Greece."

At this point, Marlein Ditch arched her brows as if she was going to say something very original, before she remarked "In those days, the exclusion of these countries was motivated by the heavy load of their public debts and the difficulties of some of their banks. We believed that the inclusion of these three countries would have been very negative for the federation as we already counted with the burdens of Spain and Italy, countries with a joint population of more than 100-million people. Indeed, we felt that it was an unaffordable burden for the young federation to take responsibility for such a big debt for so scant population in these three small countries. On the other hand, the audience should remember that it was also a matter of the governments of these three countries themselves who acted in such a way that their countries had to be excluded. Come to think of it, with the experience we have now, perhaps the problem could have been solved in those days by including the three of them in the federation and paying their debts, if necessary with new printed Euros. Such an alternative approach, although additionally increasing the rate of inflation in the first two or three years, would have solved two problems: first, the rescue of these countries and second, the rebalancing of the Euro. Let me remind you all that at the moment of its birth, the Euro quoted at a rate of Euro-Dollar 1:1.17 and progressed to quotations of 1: 1.50 at the beginning of the financial crisis in 2008. Of course, the overvaluation of the Euro in those days was not good for the European exports as it was wrong to keep the interest rates in the Euro zone so low for so long. I dare to say now that our Euro policy then resulted in an inefficient allocation of our investments in those years.

Similarly, I dare to say that we, the Germans, exaggerated a lot with our anti-inflationary paranoia. I feel even now that I have to apologise for this. Probably it was a matter of weighing between two bad things, the unemployment and the inflation, and not so much as we did, to stick at all costs to an inflation of maximal two-percent. I think that this was a real mistake since modern monetary controls of Central Banks are much better than those in times of the Republic of Weimar. On the other hand, to force populations to fully pay for the mistakes of their politicians, as we did with Greece, Ireland, and Portugal, was neither fair nor intelligent. As I have learned from history-I am referring to the decisions back then in Versailles, forcing huge transfers against Germany-creditors should not strangle the economies of debtors because this finally works against the creditors own interest."

The outspoken remarks of Marlein Ditch were welcomed with another exhaustive applause, while the TV presenter approached Burman by asking, "Monsieur le Professeur, and what about the countries that were left out of the Federation but kept the Euro as their currency... do they have a better economic perspective now than let us say the new comers of 2004 who did not accede to the Euro?"

"Certainly, according to the theory of economic policy, to have more instruments to correct a negative economic situation is better than to have less. Their decision to keep the Euro without being able to participate in monetary policy decisions was the best they could do under the circumstances."

For now the audience was presented with a new compilation, and this time the snapshots were about the past 5 years of the European Federation and its positive achievements for its citizens. The camera was also portraying successful foreign policy of the European Federation, starting with the Federal Embassy in Beijing, were viewers could see a variety of promotional materials and actions directed to the Chinese middle classes to encourage not only their touristic participation in cultural highlights in the nine states of the

Federation, but also to raise awareness in China concerning advanced high-tech engineering, sophisticated water management and renewable energy capabilities in the European Federation.

"Last question to all of you," exclaimed the TV presenter. "Taking into account the phenomenon of long-lasting, high, youth unemployment in many countries in Europe and recalling the rioting in many capitals at the start of the Federation, have anyone of you any idea of what could be done to offer a better future to our youth?" The guests were looking slightly hesitant at each other when Burman dared to give his view.

"I know for sure that high rates of youth unemployment, wherever they occur, will coincide with the existence of discrimination in the labor markets. The context will be one in which you will find a submarket of indefinite contracts for senior workers while the young workers will have access only to temporal and part-time jobs.
Logically, when in such a context a deep economic crisis arrives, the first to be expelled from jobs will be the young workers.
Consequently, governments should first and foremost eliminate the current dualism in the labor market to improve efficiency and the expectations of the youth."

While Burman was talking three of the four remaining guests-Escalleno, Ditch, and Perrier-were shaking their heads showing profound disapproval. Consequently, the TV presenter turned to them and invited Escalleno for explanation.

"I fully disagree with Professor Burman. If we were to unify labor contracting by making all contracts only time-bound and giving employers the right to easily hire and fire, something typically requested by private employers, we would be moving backwards in history from social democracy towards traditional unfair capitalism", Escalleno clarified.

"Wrong!" interrupted Ackerman, "I think that preventing injustice by distorting markets is not the best solution. Indeed, the dualistic employment contracting in the labor market over past decades in Europe, has resulted in high unemployment rates of young workers and that is precisely a derivative of the partial dismantling of the protection of workers, by putting the stress of the adjustment only on the youth. Protecting just one segment of workers, the senior workers, is perhaps the worst of solutions. Or you protect all workers, which would be absurd from the perspective of an economy of market, or you do not protect any one, which would leave workers to their own survival in front of abusive entrepreneurs. As far as these two situations are undesirable, there must be a point of a balanced protection for all, to be defined by democratic government and without internal discriminations in markets."

"Gentlemen please, what are we talking about?" was the reaction of a slightly irritated Marlein. "We are here reflecting on the European Federation at its fifth birthday, and any of us will have to agree that in the Federation youth unemployment rates have gone down and are well under control. We have moved from figures of up to forty-percent of unemployment under youngsters-I am thinking of the case of Spain-to current maximum levels of just ten percent. And if this process has implied higher rates of unemployment in the segment of workers over fifty-five, we should also not overlook the fact that these workers are far less productive than the younger. Thanks to creative solutions initiated by Premier Escalleno, such as for instance copying good labor practices from Holland – I mean their job sharing, more flexible working hours, and more part-time jobs for older workers-Federal member states have been able to save the future of our youth. This is what we mark today!" At the last words of Marlein Ditch the TV presenter requested his guests to raise their glasses for a toast on the economic and socio-political success of the European Federation. It was time to celebrate.

* * *

It is not enough to say that the festivity decorations along the Promenade des Anglais in Nice were abundant. It seemed as if for the celebrations of the fifth anniversary of the European Federation, which was to start at 9:00 pm in the ballroom of hotel Negresco, all decorative imagination in all member states had been tapped and no costs had been spared. The long road along the beautiful bay was meandering down to Villefranche-sur-Mer in glittering stars caused by the thousands of white and bright, little party lights at two levels, including directly at the waterfront, while in the bay itself hundreds of boats and yachts were illuminated with colorful beams. All was to bring back memories of the first announcement of the federation initiative by Germany and France in a more buoyant way, so this time the ballroom itself had been overtly decorated with artifacts and images of almost seventy years of the EU project, leading up to its centre peace, the European Federation. The exclusive invitations for the optimistic party had this time been distributed not only in wider Europe, but also in Asia, Australia, Africa and South and North America. Royalty of federal member states, ministers of the federal cabinet, ministers of member states, chiefs of the European parties, private sector representatives, top executives of the main mass media, and representatives of societal organizations and of academic institutions, had all been invited to give *acte de presence* at the commemoration.

By 9:30 pm the ballroom was, as they say, packed to almost overflowing; at the farthest end there was not a corner empty and elegantly dressed women of all ages were mingling with dark suited man in black tie, all looking rather optimistic. Among the guests, one could also find former premiers and presidents, even old presidents of the European Commission or their widow's such as the Duchess of Algarve, the widow of Bopoulos, who mingled accompanied by her father, an old man who had kept the brisk manners of his time as a Swiss banker during the Second World War. Contrary to her husband, Alexandra, the wife of former French President Perrier, had reserved her beauty as if her aging had stopped one decade before, and even old mother Perrier, now nearly ninety, had dared to dress in sparkling red and yellow silk to be seen. Today, to be European was very worthwhile: they had become first-class citizens governed by a first-class government, although convoyed by the long shadow of increasing China-already the largest economy of the world in GDP-PPP terms-and by rapidly emerging India, a country with no problems of ageing population, contrary to the reality in other leading countries of the globe.

* * *

Everyone began to applaud when, in the company of some Royalty, the Premier and the President of the European Federation entered the small podium at the upper end of the ball room, where also the orchestra cornered. But before any brief toasting speech could take off, the orchestra suddenly started the Turkish March of Mozart and an impressive entrée was made by a man dressed in a white and orange gala-uniform with a white turban on his dark hair and a golden sword and dagger with brilliant stones crossing his chest. All eyes now quickly shifted to observe the extravagant appearance of the man who was announced by the pianist as the Turkish Ambassador to the European Federation... but no one except Alexandra

227

recognized him. Staring at his face with the curled moustache, she murmured "Ibrahim" and at that very moment their eyes crossed.

However, there was one other person in the ballroom who noticed the intensity of the surprising encounter of the two former lovers: the old Mrs. Perrier, who had been standing close to Alexandra. While Alexandra was recovering from the surprise, Ibrahim immediately walked over to her and elegantly kissed her hand.

"Madam Perrier…looking beautiful as ever. What a cheer to see you again and please accept me saying that time has fully respected your magnificence."

"Uh …uh " was the reaction of the old Mrs. Perrier as Ambassador Ibrahim had been speaking loud enough to be heard also by the surrounding ladies. This was the sign for some of them to move forward to introduce themselves to the charming man, who in many ways reminded them either of a younger and modern version of Rudolf Valentino or a slightly older copy of the Australian film star, George Clooney.

Although known for being shy, Mrs. Bopoulos rushed forward and with her high-pitched voice announced, "Sir, may I take the liberty to introduce myself. Benita Bopoulos. My friend, Alexandra is the wife of an ex-president, and so am I." With a broad smile all over her face she continued, "I am the widow of the former president of the European Commission. As you may recall, my husband, Carlos, was in office when negotiations with Turkey to enter into the EU started."

Ibrahim, without giving much attention to Mrs. Bopoulos, slightly bowed before directing his attention to the old man who was accompanying her. Looking at the old man in surprise Ibrahim approached his ears and murmured, "Didn't we meet in Tel Aviv some years ago? I have the recollection of our encounter at the ministry of Foreign Affairs when a delegation of the Turkish

President was presenting Turkish protest in the case of the Flotilla, the Israeli attack on boats carrying humanitarian aid to Gaza."

To which the old "Duke" quickly replied, "No, I am sorry. It must have been someone else! My sole relation with the Israeli government was on banking issues. Let us say, that it was on attempts of the Israelis to recover an imagined huge amount of gold deposited by German Jews long ago in a Swiss bank where I worked."

At the last words of the old man, Ibrahim started showing his teeth and while touching the shoulder of the old man he exclaimed, "So you are the Duke of Algarve, known also in Istanbul. What a pleasant surprise. Turkey should have had a banker like you in times of the Ottoman Empire."

Jacques Perrier, who had joined the gathering of women around the Turkish ambassador, frowned at the last remark of Ibrahim. Putting his arm around Alexandra's shoulder, he started pulling her away from the group.

When they were out of hearing he inquired at low voice, "Do you know this man? What a disgusting show-off. I was surprised seeing him kissing your hand. Who is he?"

Without interrupting the waterfall of queries of Jacques, Alexandra first shook off his hand from her shoulders before answering,

"Darling, you have never met him, but you know him. Let us say, he is the man who disappeared in Dubai in the days when I was visiting the city with old classmates, some years ago. He was kidnapped from Sheraton Creek Hotel in Dubai. And as we later learned, he was kidnapped because of an administrative mistake following a request of a friendly nation."

"My love, do not confuse the things. I do not know him as I do not know anything about his kidnapping. And after having listened to him just now, I am not even interested to meet him. Please accompany me to the toast."

At that point, Marlein Ditch approached the couple. The former Chancellor looked rather buoyant, a state of mind she explained to Jacques, which was directly related to an extremely interesting discussion she had just now with the Turkish ambassador. Surely an attractive man, but even more appealing was his insight on the future of multicultural Europe.

"Jacques, you remember me telling you this morning about my new goal in life since I have received my two girls. Well, I found the thoughts of the Turkish ambassador on the topic really refreshing. I have made an appointment with him to search opportunities for our joint cooperation."

"Marlein, if I may be frank, be careful with this man. He has a history of being an unbeatable womanizer."

"Oh, but Jacques," said Marlein, "Mrs. Bopoulos, who had a quick scan on the man at the spot, be it with help of her father, informed us just now that the ambassador is not only unmarried but also he has not been spotted with any woman in the past five years. So I wonder if he . . ."

Alexandra interrupted, "Really Jacques, I thought you just said that you did not know him. You are confused. Anyway, it is time for our toast on the success of five years European Federation. Let us go for a refill of our glasses."

About The Authors

Rita Dulci Rahman is Dutch born in Aruba, Dutch Antilles. In 1970, she won a literacy prize Van der Rijn - prize in the Netherlands - for her debut collection of short stories. Between 1973 and 1979, she published a number of children books and in 1983 she wrote a column for a newspaper in the Netherlands before publishing her first novel in 2001, *Love's Perfumes*. The novel has been published in Dutch (In de Knipscheer) and English (Penguin).

Besides fiction, Rita Dulci Rahman is co-author (together with Jose Miguel Andreu) of a number of non-fiction books on global, socio-economic issues (2001: *Financing Development for Human Security;* 2004: *Responsible Global Governance;* 2005: *Overcoming the EU crisis;* 2006: *China and India, towards global supremacy?* and 2009: *Global Democracy for sustaining Global Capitalism*). Rita Dulci Rahman is a career diplomat, currently posted as Ambassador of the Kingdom of the Netherlands in the Dominican Republic and for Haiti.

Jose Miguel Andreu is a Spaniard born in Bilbao, and professor of macroeconomic at the University of Sevilla. *Love and Death in Saving Europe* is his first fiction book, but his non-fiction writing dates back to 1970. Between 1980 and 1999, he published a number of books on macroeconomic issues for University students in Spain, of which his book on banking is most famous. From 2001 onward, he has been writing on global, socio-economic issues (together with Rita Dulci Rahman) projecting possible solutions for contemporary global, socio-economic problems (2001: *Financing Development for Human Security;* 2002:*A federation with Enlargement for European Prosperity;* 2004: *Responsible Global Governance;* 2005: *Over-coming the EU crisis;* 2006: *China and India, towards global supremacy?* and 2009: *Global Democracy for sustaining Global Capitalism*).